SEARCHING FOR JULIETTE

There one minute
Gone the next

A. K. Adams

First published in Great Britain

All paper used in the printing of this book has been made from wood grown in managed, sustainable forests.

ISBN: 978-1-78003-808-7

Printed and bound in the UK

Pen Press is an imprint of
Author Essentials
4 The Courtyard
South Street
Falmer
East Sussex
BN1 9PQ

A catalogue record of this book is available from the British Library

Cover design by Jacqueline Abromeit
Cover photo: A.K. Adams

"We must, however, acknowledge...that man with all his noble qualities...still bears in his bodily frame the indelible stamp of his lowly origin."

Charles Darwin. *The Descent of Man*

Thanks go to my wife, Nora, for her support and contribution to this novel and my writing.

I am also grateful to my grandson, Christopher Wheeler, fellow writer Daphne Clarke, my well-read dental surgeon Teresa Robinson, and my good friends Ken & Lorrie Honisett.

I wish to particularly thank Chris Wayman for his contribution on police matters.

...and to all those who helped along the way.

Prologue

There was nobody about. The moon was hidden behind light clouds that gently crossed the slate grey Mediterranean sky. It was a warm, humid evening as they strolled along, the railing of the top deck on their left hand side. The sea could be heard a long way below making a relaxing slapping and gushing sound.

He knew the time had come to do something. It was going to be such a shame for her to take a dip so late at night. He wasn't even sure if she could swim. But it didn't matter - he didn't care.

Looking around, he was certain there was no one else about. They were alone, enjoying the fresh night air. He stopped, both hands resting on the edge of the railing as he looked at her and smiled, not knowing whether he should give her one last kiss. Standing close to him, she wanted to feel his body touching hers.

But she'd lost that attractiveness she once had. The shine had gone from her eyes, her skin had lost its tone, crow's feet had got wider. In less time than it takes to say 'goodbye', he wrapped his arm around her waist and over she went. Despite a struggle, there were no screams. In fact he heard nothing. Even her body hitting the green-blue water couldn't be heard above the waves thudding into the sides of the cruise liner . . .

Soon she'd be food for the fishes. Even the lobsters would get a good feed.

'Oh, dear, what a shame', he thought to himself. 'It's time for a drink.' He ran his fingers through his hair,

straightened his tie, adjusted his cuff-links and wiped his hands on the back of his trousers. Heading for the bar it was time to complete his plan . . .

But wait, did he hear someone hiding in the shadows on the deck, or was it the gentle breeze ruffling the folded parasols? Looking along the side of the deck, there was nobody there . . .

Chapter 1

"What are you going to do? Why would somebody do that?" asked Anthea standing in the kitchen of the caravan. She was making a pot of tea for breakfast and popped two slices of bread into the toaster. After a take-away from their favourite Chinese restaurant in Berwick-upon-Tweed the night before, neither of them was very hungry. The empty polystyrene containers had been thrown down carelessly. Sauce had been slowly seeping out onto the dark blue mat inside the door. The air smelt of prawns and chop suey; fresh air needed to be let in. Anthea pushed the kitchen window open a few inches. Two flattened beer cans lay on the floor. Harry lit up his first of the day as he stood on the outside step.

"I'm not sure. It seems odd, doesn't it? A note on the window." Cigarettes were still his crutch to keep him going. His lungs were probably carbon coated, but so what? At 56 years of age he didn't plan to live forever. He'd left school without any formal qualifications, but enjoyed metalwork. At sixteen Harry had started working for a sheet metalworkers in Saltburn on the North Yorkshire coast and got involved with fabrication and welding in steel and aluminium. After ten years there he went to work for a bespoke metal products company in Stockton-on-Tees in Cleveland. More 'upmarket' he used to say. His speciality was the wrought iron gate. He often thought that if he had a pound for every gate he'd made, he would be rich!

Harry had a philosophic outlook on life. 'If your names on the bullet ...' he used to think to himself. He didn't really care, though. His dad had died of an asbestos related lung disease. Something to do with knocking down those prefabs in Stockton that were built just after the war. The doctor had told him it was a long medical term beginning with 'm' and ending in 'oma' He had made his mind up that if his time was up, then so be it.

"You could always phone the number and ask some questions." Anthea was a good foil for Harry. She was bright with a good taste in house furnishings and clothes and had managed three GCSE's when she left school and started out working for an aunt who owned a health food shop in Middlesbrough. She'd learnt all about vitamins and minerals as well as nutrition and 'well-being'.

They didn't have any children between them, although Anthea had been married to an alcoholic accountant called Peter Watkinson and she had given birth to a daughter. He'd worked for ICI in Billingham and they'd lived in Yarm for sixteen years, just near the river. Being good at his job, and with a first class degree in mathematics from Teesside University, he was smart with figures. The trouble was that he began drinking more heavily soon after they had tied the knot. Anthea and Peter had actually lived together for three years before getting married. There had never been any problems with alcohol and they both enjoyed a glass of wine with a meal, or during the evening. But things began to change, and not for the better.

Two months after placing a ring on Anthea's finger, he started going to the pub more often. 'The Bluebell' served several ales on draught as well as some fine wines. Some were locally brewed, and the landlord would often have a 'guest beer'. After a bad day at the office, calculating how much profit or loss the company had made, Peter liked to stop off at 'The Bluebell'. The landlord, Les, was an amiable fellow. He'd been a stand up comedian and had appeared on several TV shows. Apart from a few beers, Peter also enjoyed the jokes that Les would tell.

Looking at figures all day was depressing, but Les always managed to bring a smile to Peter's face. Once a decent pint had been pulled, Les would kick in with "Have you heard the one about . . .?" As time went by, Peter got home later and later. Anthea was less impressed as she had to re-heat his evening meal two or three times a week. Week-ends with friends could be embarrassing when Peter had 'one over the eight'. He'd raise his voice more than normal, and Anthea became concerned at his behaviour.

Anthea and Peter's daughter, Juliette, had attended the local junior school and then had won a scholarship to nearby Polkam Hall School where she did very well. Juliette was fifteen years old when her parents divorced. Anthea had had enough of her husband and the last straw came when he didn't return home one night. Never being absolutely certain where he'd been, she couldn't trust him anymore. Peter told her he'd had too many at 'The Bluebell' one night and stayed with a colleague; losing his mobile phone and collapsing on his settee – or so he claimed. That was the finish.

When Anthea broached the subject with Peter's colleague, Jim, he'd said he himself was blind drunk and couldn't recall anything. So that was it, and the divorce went through easily. He moved out but saw Juliette when he could, which wasn't often. They grew apart. Having qualified as a beautician, and earning a good wage, Anthea knew she'd cope. She'd have to.

And it was good riddance to Peter Watkinson. He moved in with a friend for a while before finding a small flat in Billingham. His drinking got worse – sorrows were drowned – and he missed 'The Bluebell' and the jokes of Les, the landlord.

Chapter 2

"I'll make a call in ten minutes or so." Six years of marriage, and they'd been going out for a while before that, Anthea and Harry had a good relationship. They understood each other, read minds, and knew when not to ask one extra question. He took a gulp of tea from his mug with 'MY HERO' written on the side, a present from Anthea, and chomped on a piece of toast. Ironically, changing their caravan had been on their minds for a while, but a trade-in price with their local caravan dealer was below their expectation. Harry was no sucker when it came to salesmen, in fact he hated them. A published guide book full of listed values. Huh! No account taken of condition or extras! Huh! What did they know? He'd been put off going for another model when he'd have to find another £5,000 to upgrade to something bigger. 'No, we'll leave it,' he'd tell Anthea and she agreed.

Although they both enjoyed the caravan, there were times when Harry doubted the benefits of the outdoor life. In cold weather it was hell. Setting up the 'van, corner steadies down, electricity connected up, re-tune the TV . . . Fingers numb when filling the water container, and emptying the toilet was smelly. The best part was being inside the caravan with the heating on and the television tuned in to a favourite programme. With feet up, slippers on, and an old pair of jogging bottoms hugging his hips, a can of beer to hand, it was near bliss. Only a front row seat at a boxing ring watching a world heavyweight fight came nearer.

Breakfast was eventually finished, and although Harry usually liked a cooked breakfast, after the Chinese take-away he still felt full. Anthea didn't eat much as she wanted to keep her figure, one slice of toast being sufficient. Her job as the owner of a beauty centre meant that she needed to look the part. Slim, lithe, trim, her nails perfect and her make-up was faultless; hair was always smartly kept and almost fit for a photo on the front page of a model magazine. Looking a million times better than when she lived with Peter Watkinson, she felt good about herself.

Local station Radio Newcastle told them that it was going to be a little cloudy with sunny spells, so they planned a trip to Bamburgh Castle. They hadn't been before but the free brochure they'd picked up in a cafe looked interesting. Perhaps they'd have fish and chips for lunch? The north east coast of England was the best place in the world for cod and chips, but Blackpool restaurants would tell you otherwise. Cod, haddock, and other white fish landed at local ports were second to none, and thick chips fried in beef dripping made from the best local grown potatoes left nothing to be desired, unless it was a portion of mushy peas.

"Where's that piece of paper?" asked Harry.

"Over there, near the kettle," replied Anthea. Picking it up, Harry looked at the phone number on the note. He dialled the number.

"Ello. Me not here now. You leave message and number. I call you back velly soon." What! A message with a Chinese accent. Was it a joke? Maybe it was the Chinese take-away in Berwick. Harry was perplexed.

"What did they say?" asked Anthea.

"A bloomin' Chink's message!" said Harry, telling Anthea the gist of it. "I'll leave it until later," he suggested. As they got ready to go out, Harry couldn't help but think about the phone message. Why would a Chinese guy want to make an offer on their caravan and where had he come from? In any case the caravan park had its own security barrier so 'Joe Public' couldn't just drive in and wander around the place.

"I'll get rid of last night's rubbish," said Anthea putting on some old casual shoes and stepping out of the caravan. Harry hadn't shaved but he'd do it later. With tousled hair, its 'salt and pepper' look gave him a handsome, rugged appearance and he kept himself fit by weight lifting and doing press ups. Three years in the army had given him a taste of physical fitness and he could even do one handed press ups despite his forty a day habit.

A second hand car business kept Harry busy. Well, he called it that, but no vehicles were handled, he was the go-between. Car adverts were placed on the internet for vehicles that didn't exist and he never gave registration numbers, just a brief description of the car. When there was any interest he'd trawl the second hand car web sites and find a vehicle that fitted the description, and buy it, and drive the car to the prospective purchaser and get a bus home. It seemed to work, most of the time anyway, but sometimes he'd end up with something he couldn't sell.

Around a thousand pounds profit on a car deal was normal and two or three a week meant a decent income for them both. Anthea never really knew the ins and outs of what he did, but then she had her own business to run and her expertise was in nails, although she was good at hair and facials, and had excellent skills in eye make-up. A marble statue could be made to look like Cleopatra. The beauty salon was called 'Angel Face' and located in

Marton on the outskirts of Middlesbrough. Her friend, Jackie, helped run the place and Anthea could take a few days off knowing it was in good hands. They had about ninety regular customers so they were kept busy. Two other girls called Jane and Rebecca also worked at 'Angel Face', both had a certificate from Redcar and Cleveland College and were keen, enthusiastic and full of fun. Jane wore a discrete nose-ring but Anthea didn't mind – it helped to bring in the younger generation. It was small and 18 carat gold - almost like Jane's own personality.

Rebecca reminded Anthea of her daughter and she often wondered what had happened to Juliette on that school trip to Denmark all those years ago. The trip that resulted in Juliette's disappearance.

There one minute sipping a chocolate milk shake, gone the next.

Chapter 3

"What a wonderful castle!" exclaimed Anthea, the morning sun catching the reddened stone. The sheer walls of the south west side of the castle seemed to make this fortress invincible. There had been a fortification of some sort on this hill since the sixth century, and the Normans had built a new castle on this site to form the core of the present one. It was now the oldest inhabited castle in England.

"Yes, it's great," Harry replied as he locked the blue Toyota RAV4 parked in the castle car park, his eyes scanning the terracotta coloured masonry. "Let's go and have a look around." They walked around to the large, arched doorway, paid their entrance money to a man who had the look of someone wishing he was elsewhere. They went in, past hundreds of years of history, guns on the walls. Photography was allowed in parts of the castle and Anthea was going to make sure she had enough digital images of their visit to download, and reminisce over at some time in the future. Outside a tarmac footpath took them to a line of cannon majestically overlooking the sea, looking like the fingers of a black giant. The day was getting warmer but the Northumberland air still had a slight chill to it. A breeze blew in from the east, whipping up small white horses on the top edges of the little waves like feathers on a swan's wings. Within five minutes they decided to go back inside and tour the castle rooms, large printed arrows perched on stands - 'This Way' - showing them of which way to go.

The lower rooms were cool, but upstairs it was warmer with small heaters helping dispel that 'my finger tips still feel cold' effect. After half an hour of admiring oil paintings and swords on the walls Anthea decided that she wanted a cup of coffee and she and Harry headed for the small cafe in the castle grounds. The coffee shop was cosy and the two waitresses were polite. *Cafe latte* and two small blueberry muffins sounded a good idea, a slice of toast hadn't been much breakfast after all. When they'd finished Harry headed outside to light up a cigarette while Anthea went to the ladies to check her make-up and 'powder her nose.'

"It's getting warmer out here and it's brightening up," he said as she came out. Harry was just finishing his fourth of the day. Flicking the stub with his thumb and forefinger over a high wall hoping that there was no dry grass on the other side.

"Yes, about time, too. We should plan a trip to Madeira or somewhere like that if it stays this cool." Since they'd been together Harry and Anthea had enjoyed a number of holidays. Often flying from Newcastle airport, they'd been to Malta & Gozo, the Costa Blanca, Tenerife and Cyprus. Although they both enjoyed looking around the local areas on holiday, most days were spent blissfully soaking up the sun with a good book. Harry pulled the collar up on his heavy outdoor jacket. They went back to the upper floor and browsed around a bit longer, chatting to the volunteer guides as they ambled through the castle. They weren't sure where they'd head for lunch but Anthea spotted an elderly gent wearing an old brown coat and a flat cap gazing up at an old oil painting. 'A relative of Andy Capp from Hartlepool' she thought to herself.

"Excuse me," she whispered to him. "Can you recommend anywhere for a bite to eat around here?"

"Way aye, canny lass," he replied in a local brogue, "I allas like to have fish and chips in Seahouses. If you gan doon to the harbour, there's the Bamburgh Castle Inn. Reet on the harbour side. Try a table in the window – smashing views, like." He grinned at her affectionately as he finished speaking, revealing several tobacco stained teeth. A few other visitors glanced round and smiled as it seemed as though the old man fancied her. He probably did! Harry and Anthea headed for the exit, still following the arrows on the direction signs as Anthea took a few more photos from the main entrance looking southwards, making sure she got the correct proportion of sky and land. Three seagulls flew overhead and she clicked the camera shutter at exactly the right instant and reviewed the image, showing it to Harry. Feeling proud of her composed photo, she turned the camera screen towards him and asked for a comment, resulting in Harry grunting as though to say 'yes, it's OK.' The camera was put away for the time being but Anthea would use it later.

They drove south from Bamburgh to Seahouses along the barren coastal road, the sky turning a shade of baby blue as scudding clouds crossed the horizon. Walkers, a few of them wearing shorts, could be seen ambling along dune tops, partly hidden by tufts of sea grass. The weather was improving as seagulls battled the easterly winds and strong breezes along this stretch had blown golden sand across the road in places through gaps in the dunes. As they approached the small town, passing a large static caravan site on the right hand side, they pulled into a car park. The Toyota just managed to get under the overhead barrier at the car park entrance, designed to keep out motor-homes and other larger vehicles. Having paid for two hours parking they wandered down to the quay side where several boats were waiting to take visitors to the Farne Islands. 'Shiel Bros. Trust us. We'll safely get you there and back' was one such sales pitch. 'You'd expect that, wouldn't you!' thought Harry to himself as they walked back up the gentle incline to look around the town.

The *National Heritage* shop was situated on the roundabout in the town centre and Anthea decided that she would like to buy a tea-towel with Bamburgh Castle on it as a souvenir, but when she saw the price tag, she changed her mind. The tea-towel could stay on the shelf, and anyway she had several in a kitchen drawer at home. 'Odd isn't it?' she mused, 'ordinary folk like us who don't live a million miles away seem to buy items like a fridge magnet or a tea towel to take home. Why?' As they left the shop, Anthea noticed the broken nails of the girl at the counter but then she would, thinking it wasn't a good indicator of the image that the shop wanted to portray. For £30 Anthea could have helped her at 'Angel Face'. They walked to a newsagent's and Harry went in to buy *The Daily Mail*. It was his favourite read – lots of easy-to-read news and competitions.

A five minute stroll then took them down to the restaurant recommended by the elderly gent. They walked in, noticing how pleasant it was, and were ushered to a table overlooking the harbour. It was very beginning to get busy – always a good sign – and the menu was scanned. The waitress, called Peggy, suggested a few minutes to browse the menu and she'd be back to take their order. Three small fishing boats, two blue and one red, were gently bobbing in the water while two old 'salts' were mending fishing nets on the

18

quayside. The sun was shining brightly now as Peggy returned with her dog-eared pad and licked her pencil, smiling at Harry. Anthea immediately ordered two beer battered haddock, chips and peas. The tartar sauce was in a small polythene sachet, of which there were several, squeezed into a round pot in the middle of the table, accompanied by the regular brown and tomato sauce sachets, too. Vinegar, dark brown and already exuding its aroma, stood like a sentinel next to the upright fingers of sauces. A pot of tea and two slices of bread and butter were also requested, just to complete the meal. It was served within five minutes and was piping hot.

Harry and Anthea took their time, savouring each mouthful as they looked out on the North Sea and the quaint harbour. Talking about nothing very important, they were just finishing lunch, the bread useful to mop up the last of the tartar sauce, when Harry heard someone behind them talking rather loudly.

"Velly good fish and chips. Me come back velly soon." A Chinese guy was just leaving the restaurant. That voice seemed familiar to Harry and he thought he'd heard it before. Turning around, Harry saw the man, wearing a dark anorak leave the cafe quickly, striding away towards the town centre. When Harry got up to pay the bill he casually asked Peggy if the Chinese man was a regular customer, she was slightly surprised at his question, but as she gave him his change she replied.

"Oh, yes. Hokun Tu Ying comes in regularly – usually near the start of the month. I'm not sure what he does, but he's OK. We call him Hokey for short. He seems harmless enough." Harry slipped a pound coin into the saucer near the till, already filling up with silver and copper, before he and Anthea left the Inn. Harry did not realise then that he and Hokun Tu Ying were going to meet again.

It was time for another cigarette, another nicotine fix. He needed it, but was surprised to notice his right hand was shaking slightly as he joined the lighter flame to the cigarette tip. Inhaling deeply, he looked around, his eyes searching for this man called Hokey, his brain ticking over quicker than usual.

"Are you OK?" Asked Anthea, as darker clouds began to roll in from the east.

Chapter 4

Anthea had always blamed her first husband, Peter, for the disappearance of Juliette. He said she should go on the school visit and he'd offered to pay all of her expenses. 'It will broaden her mind' he used to say, 'spending two weeks with a Danish family will do her good', but Anthea had her doubts. The school hadn't clarified details that Anthea had asked for regarding the Danish family, and all that she was given was an address in a place called Kokkedal, north of Copenhagen. The family's name was Jorgsholm, and they had two children, Agnatha and Louisa, who were about the same age as Juliette. She would spend two weeks with the family, getting to know the Danish way of life, attending school with the daughters, and generally gaining a better understanding of the country. The head of school had assured Anthea and Peter that the Jorgsholm family had cared for other girls previously and there had never been any issues.

"I can't see what you're concerned about," Peter had said to Anthea over dinner one evening. "We've got the names and address of the family, they have two daughters about Juliette's age, and it'll do her a world of good. She'll be picked up at Copenhagen airport on arrival and the Jorgsholm's will look after her."

"I'm just not sure about this. I've got a gut feeling that tells me all is not well with the arrangement. I can't put my finger on it, but, oh well, if you think it will be all right." Anthea gave in. Peter poured another glass of white wine while they ate their evening meal but Anthea was unsettled and hardly touched hers. Peter ignored her body language, taking a sip of his wine. He could be like that sometimes.

"We don't know what Mr. And Mrs. Jorgsholm do, do we?" asked Anthea after a few more minutes of silence.

"Does it really matter?" Peter replied. "He's called Carl, and her name is Anna. I'm sure they'll be fine upstanding Danish citizens, live in a nice house and they'll take good care of our precious girl. Don't worry." Peter poured himself another glass of wine.

Juliette was seen off at Durham Tees Valley airport by her parents in mid June. She was flying to London Heathrow for a connection to Copenhagen and the flight times were good, with little waiting time once Juliette arrived at Heathrow. She just needed to get across to the terminal to catch the Boeing 737 for the one hour and forty minute trip and her suitcase was checked in all the way. Needing only to carry her hand luggage on board, she hoped she had enough clothes for her stay. A light outdoor jacket in case it was cool was carried on her arm. Denmark could be chilly, even in summer, but she'd packed a swimming costume, too. Juliette was forever the optimist.

A 'Rough Guide' book on Denmark, borrowed from their neighbour Daphne, had given Juliette an idea of the country. Although she didn't need to know about places to stay and eat, it was useful to get a feel about food and drink, and the area around Kokkedal. Pickled herring, however, with cold meats, cheeses and crisp-bread for breakfast hadn't filled her with much enthusiasm. And they used butter - the Danes love butter! However, she was willing to give it a go. It seemed the Scandinavians weren't big on vegetables, and Juliette had read that a main meal was mostly meat and potatoes. 'Oh, well, when in Rome...' she said to herself. Juliette was mature for her age. She was fourteen going on twenty five. With a little make up on she could pass for nineteen or twenty and was wearing clothes that Anthea would never have dreamed of putting on at her age. Juliette had shoulder length blonde hair and she would often let it hang down, but for school she had to wear it tied up to look tidy and smart.

The Boeing 737 touched down at Copenhagen right on schedule with a wisp of blue-black smoke and the faintest of squeals as the big tyres caressed the tarmac. The aircraft came to a halt in front of the wide terminal building, sun reflecting off the big plate glass windows. Juliette collected her suitcase off the carousel and made her way to the exit, following the yellow and black signs for 'Bus' and 'Taxi'. Her letter from the school had indicated that the Jorgsholm's would be waiting for her and holding a large card with her full name on it. Juliette walked out into the arrivals area and after a few anxious moments eventually spotted her name in large black letters on a card held aloft by a man dressed in a dark suit. She walked over.

"Hello. Welcome to Denmark!" exclaimed Carl Jorgsholm. "You must be Juliette!"

"Yes, I am, and you are Mr. Jorgsholm, I presume?" She thought of Stanley and Livingstone meeting in Africa.

"Call me Carl, please," he replied, smiling broadly and showing his perfectly white teeth. "This way. Here let me take your suitcase." Jorgsholm pulled the telescopic handle on Juliette's case and wheeled it behind him as they made their way to the car park.

"Did you have a good flight?" asked the Dane.

"Yes, it was OK, thanks. Where's Mrs. Jorgsholm?"

"She wanted to make sure the house was in order, and your bedroom was tidy. She's also getting the evening meal ready. Pork meatballs and dumplings. Our favourite!" Juliette groaned inwardly. The 'Rough Guide' was correct so far! Jorgsholm told Juliette that his daughters would be home from school soon and that they were really looking forward to meeting their new guest.

Carl Jorgsholm lifted the suitcase into the boot of the VW Passat. She was about to walk around to the left side of the car when she realised it was left hand drive! Correcting her movements, and feeling slightly embarrassed, she rapidly went around the front of the car to the other side. Jorgsholm held the door open for her and Juliette got in. Swinging her long legs in together like a model, Jorgsholm looked her in the eye after glancing at her thighs. She couldn't help but notice his enigmatic smile. The kind of smile that a niece may get from an uncle that she doesn't quite trust.

Little was said on the journey to the Jorgsholm's home although Carl made light polite conversation. He had his mind on other things, and Juliette wondered how her visit would turn out. She toyed with her mobile phone, wondering when to let her mum know she had arrived safely.

Chapter 5

Harry and Anthea had almost finished looking around Seahouses, but not before they'd gone down to the harbour to take a look at the boats. They were sturdy craft, quite capable of heading out into the North Sea in all weathers. Anthea took half a dozen pictures and included two shots of an old weather-beaten man who was mending nets. His face seemed as though it had been carved from an old pine log. He looked up and smiled at Anthea as they ambled along the quayside. He had a toothless grin, save for one stump in the middle of his lower jaw. A pipe hung in his mouth – smokeless.

"Afternoon!" he said. "You'se two on holiday, then?" Anthea nodded. Harry smiled at the old man.

"Yes, in our caravan near Berwick. We're going home tomorrow."

"Way, man, Berwick's a canny toon, though but. I met me first love near the bridge ower the Tweed. I loved her to bits, 'til she left me for a soldier from Carlisle. Bloomin' sergeant, too!"

"Are you married now?" asked Anthea.

"Nay, widowed. The old lass passed away three years ago. Cancer. I keep busy down here, though. I'm happy enough. Been in fishing all me life – it's in me blood." Harry imagined salt water ran through his veins and arteries. His unlit pipe waggled around as he spoke, seemingly attached to his lips.

They walked back towards the car park after they'd bade the old man farewell. The Toyota had about ten minutes left on the parking ticket but Harry made time to

25

pop into a newsagents to buy another pack of Rothmans cigarettes and he also grabbed a Mars bar. Sometimes his blood sugar got low, especially after a bit of weightlifting. He wasn't planning to pump iron that day, but he would be lifting the water container and unhitching the caravan in the morning. And anyway he loved chocolate. Having paid for the goods he walked out to find Anthea was window shopping, looking in a dress shop further down the street. A long black dress with a low back, silver sequins down the front in a wide sweeping arc had gained her attention.

"You don't want that," Harry said. She turned and gave him a look that said 'I agree - just browsing - leave me alone.' Anthea had more clothes than she needed and charity bags were often filled and collected from their house. "The 'Angel Face' dinner dance is coming up soon. I'll need something for that." Harry looked skyward and grunted. He knew she had sufficient dresses and frocks to clothe a small African country.

The beauty business was doing well and she'd put her charges up from the beginning of April as usual, as well as changing some of the treatments, but that had not deterred her regular customers. One of them, called Joan Bobbins, was an awkward customer who had spent time in Durham Gaol for manslaughter, at least that's what had been stated in *The Northern Echo*. She had made her own breakfast cereal for her husband, a type of muesli, a recipe out of her head, but she never ate any of it. Joan Bobbins preferred toast and marmalade. The local health food shop, 'We're Going Nuts', sold a wide range of different seeds and cereals and Joan mixed these in equal proportions and then added her own dried apple pips. Joan Bobbins later claimed that she did not know that these contained a glycoside called amygdalin that could cause cyanide poisoning but others thought differently. It was the slow, debilitating effect of these that had allegedly killed her husband, George.

The defence claimed that he wasn't in good health anyway, with diabetes and emphysema affecting his body. However, George had won over four million pounds on the national lottery and his wife was going to benefit from that. Joan Bobbins spent some of the winnings in 'Angel Face', so Anthea benefited from her lavish expenditure whilst having to put up with her complaints and attitude. She called a spade a spade, and gossiped about folk of whom she knew little.

When Harry and Anthea got back to the Berwick caravan site they began to do some packing, but Anthea wanted a quick look at her photos first and she went through the pictures. The castle shots were excellent, with fine sky and cloud effects, as well as good perspective on the cannon, lined up on parade. Some pictures taken in Seahouses near the quay were almost worthy of a competition entry – the colours of the fishing boats were nice and bright, nets hung over wooden frames and the odd seagull was perched on a lobster pot. She was about to close the review function on her digital camera when she noticed one of the boats - somehow, the single red one didn't look quite right. There was no lifting gear on the back to haul the nets in and the cabin had darkened windows. Looking closely at the name on the side of the boat, she slowly breathed out.

"Harry," she paused, "don't you think that 'Kwangsi Chuang' seems a strange sounding name for a fishing boat in Seahouses?"

"Does it come with fried rice?" replied Harry, grinning at what he thought was a clever response.

Chapter 6

The Jorgsholm's lived in a smart up-market area of
Kokkedal, and their four bedroomed detached house
with a large garden and double garage was lovely. It was
in a long curved avenue with different designs of houses
complimented by mature trees and shrubs. Juliette, with
slight trepidation, was delighted to meet Agnatha and
Louisa when they came home from school. In fact, when
the three girls stood together, they almost looked like
triplets - the same height, blonde hair, and similar
features. Mrs. Jorgsholm had made Juliette most
welcome, and Carl Jorgsholm couldn't do enough for
her. He'd carried her suitcase upstairs, opened the
window slightly, and put the luggage on a low side unit.
The wide, single bed along one side of the room had a
light duvet on with a bright red and blue pattern. Being
Friday, the two daughters had the week-end to spend
with Juliette, however Louisa had a slight problem in
pronouncing the name of their English guest, so Juliette
suggested they all call her 'Jules' – and she spelt it out.
J-U-L-E-S she said slowly, and they all laughed.

Agnatha and Louisa helped Juliette to unpack. The
furniture looked as though it probably didn't come from
IKEA, and within no time her clothes were hanging up
in the wardrobe, shoes placed under the bed, and other
items – underwear, cosmetics, toiletries and so forth,
neatly put into drawers. An ironing board and iron were
in the corner – she thought she might use them later.
Jules changed into more comfortable clothes, brushed
her long hair, and put on a dab of *Miss Dior* perfume.

She slowly went downstairs and found the family sitting in the lounge, the two girls reading magazines whilst Mrs. Jorgsholm was doing some knitting. Carl Jorgsholm was scanning a laptop screen perched on his knees but he quickly lowered the top as Jules walked past him.

Mrs. Jorgsholm stood up. "Let me get you a drink, Jules, what would you like? Milk, tea, coffee, fruit juice?"

"Milk would be fine," replied Jules. Real Danish milk! Would it taste different from the milk on Teesside? She looked forward to that. Juliette had decided that she wanted to immerse herself into the Danish way of life and this was the start. She might even learn some of the language. Tomorrow the Jorgsholm girls had promised to take Jules into Kokkedal to look around, and visit the local park in the afternoon. Agnatha and Louise took Jules up to Louise's bedroom for a 'girlie chat' before dinner. They talked first about their school, favourite subjects, and the worst teachers. Then they moved on to more interesting subjects – boys, film stars, pop singers and the like. All giggled when they looked at a poster of Brad Pitt on the wall. He was dressed, or undressed, in a small pair of faded denim shorts. They chatted for a bit longer, and then Mrs. Jorgsholm called them down for their evening meal. Two white candles on the table had been lit, and the cutlery and glassware were laid out perfectly.

"We enjoy our meat and potatoes," said Carl as Jules remembered the 'Rough Guide' comments. Mrs. Jorgsholm poured fruit juice out into their glasses. The meal was delicious, and a side salad accompanied the meal. 'So, some vitamin C, then!' thought Juliette, but overall it was quite healthy. They chatted about the differences in culture between England and Denmark,

29

joked about football and avoided politics. Jules noticed the curtains were left open when the evening lights were switched on. Apparently it dated back to the period after the second world war when the Danes were so relieved that they no longer had to have a black-out that the open curtain policy became a sign of 'freedom and openness'.

Carl Jorgsholm seemed a bit guarded when it came to occupation. His wife, Anna, was a full time mother and housewife, but she had been trained as a nurse at Copenhagen Hospital, specialising in paediatrics. Carl said he worked for a government department involved with human affairs but nothing more. Juliette did not think it was her place to push the matter and smiled politely, telling the family about her life on Teesside. The two daughters had plans to go to university, and then to possibly read law or medicine. All in all, the meal was a pleasant experience, with lots of idle banter on a wide variety of subjects.

"If you don't mind, I'm feeling quite tired," said Juliette. "Would you mind if I went up to bed?" She rubbed her eyes.

"Not at all, Jules." Mrs. Jorgsholm understood. "Our girls will see you upstairs to ensure all is well. Breakfast will be ready at eight o'clock, if that's OK." Juliette thanked the family for their hospitality and went upstairs but as she left the room she sensed that Carl was watching her carefully. Just an intuition . . . Agnatha and Louisa saw to it that Jules got herself sorted out and after brushing her teeth, she was ready for bed. As she lay on her soft mattress under the duvet, Juliette thought that she really should have telephoned her parents. Her mum and dad would be wondering how she was.

A phone call would be made in the morning, but tomorrow was to bring something that nobody could have predicted.

Chapter 7

The caravan departure plans were under way - the toilet was emptied, water container drained, electricity unhooked and things put away. Harry hitched the 'van up to the Toyota and they slowly drove out of the park and began to make their way down the A1 towards Yarm. Harry had moved in with Anthea soon after she and Peter had divorced. Peter had met another woman from Stockton-on-Tees at a party and went to live with her. She was allegedly a high flier and ran her own consulting business from an office in Eaglescliffe. It was unlikely to last very long, Andrea had thought to herself, and she was right. His 'girlfriend' kicked him out after six months.

The caravan was easily and effortlessly towed along the dual carriageway, mostly old Roman road, and they stopped off once at a services near the turn off for Lindisfarne. Harry was bursting for a pee, and Anthea was ready for coffee. After he'd been to the gents, Harry and Anthea went into the cafe and she ordered two Americanos at the counter.

"When are you going to phone the Chinese guy again?" she asked as they sat near the window.

"I can do it now," replied Harry, getting his phone from its leather holder on his belt. The place wasn't busy so Harry felt comfortable to make the call. He'd sugared his coffee and stirred it several times. Anthea held his hand for a few seconds, almost as a supportive gesture. Looking at her, he told her he loved her, and then remembered that he didn't do that often enough; he'd try to do it more often in future. Harry dialled the number.

"Ero? Who is that?" Harry thought he'd come in part way through a Karate Kid film.

"You left a message on our caravan window in Berwick. Are you interested in buying our caravan?"

"Ah, so. Yes, me interested. Me give you good price. How much you want for it?" Harry had to think.

"We're not sure we want to sell. We've just insured it again and were told the current market price is £12,000." It was really a thousand less.

"I give you £14,000, but you need to deliver it for me. I can give you address now?"

Harry was taken aback. The Chinaman was offering three thousand pounds over the current value! Hesitating for a few seconds Harry quickly said,

"I'll call you back." He ended the call.

"What was all that about?" asked Anthea, sipping her coffee. Harry explained the offer.

"What do you want to do?" Anthea's brow furrowed.

"Well, we were thinking about selling it a while ago weren't we, maybe upgrading? Fourteen thousand sounds a good offer. I'll phone him back and tell him it's a deal. But, we take everything out. He just gets the bare shell. Agreed?" Anthea nodded. He glanced around as though he was in a James Bond film, seeking the villains who might be earwigging or someone with a white Persian cat on their lap? After three rings the call was answered.

"Ero again. What you think of offer?" The Chinaman recognised the mobile number.

Harry drew in a deep breath. The deal was made with the Chinaman within thirty seconds. Harry asked him his name, and how they would arrange the deal.

33

"Me Hokun Tu Ying. You must deliver caravan to address in Middlesbrough. If you have email address I give you details." Harry's blood ran cold. Hokun Tu Ying! Without really thinking, he gave Tu Ying his email details but he immediately regretted doing it. This 'stranger' now had both Harry's mobile number as well as his email address. Harry was about to say 'thanks' when the line went dead. Tu Ying had ended the call.

"I guess we now just wait until we get an email with the delivery address?" Harry was a tough nut, but a shudder went through him as though finger nails had scraped down an old school blackboard. This was the guy the waitress called 'Hokey'. Harry's mind began searching for some reason why Hokey wanted their caravan? Why didn't he go to some dealer? Anthea reached for his hand. He clung onto her fingers for a few seconds, glancing at her before looking out at the rain turning the A1 tarmac from dark grey to jet black. A visit to the ladies was made before they scurried back to their vehicle as the rain got heavier, charcoal clouds coming from the west. Anthea pulled her collar up and walked to avoid the puddles that began to form on the parking area.

They pulled back onto the A1 and turned on the car radio. Sometimes their mood was improved when they listened to Classic FM, not that noisy music by some unknown rapper that made you want to be sick. The volume was turned down to a low level and the car soon reached a comfortable towing speed of about 60 mph as Harry switched to cruise control. There wasn't much traffic going south and they made good time, taking the A689 turn off for Hartlepool, hit the A19 and got onto the A66 for Darlington. The Yarm signpost indicated that they were less than ten minutes from home and as they approached their house Harry slowed down and came to

34

a halt. Anthea got out to open the wide front gates and then Harry drove in, taking a large sweeping turn. He parked the caravan next to a tall hedge on the left side of the property. Within fifteen minutes they had unpacked the car and the caravan, empty used food containers were placed into a washing up bowl, and the kettle switched on to make tea. Harry made sure the 'van was secured – gas taps off, hitch lock on, wheel clamp fitted. The double garage door was opened and the car was reversed in. Harry closed the front door of the house as he went inside.

"I'll go and check the emails," he said to Anthea. "There'll be quite a few to look at. People wanting cars and things – maybe even one from Tu Ying?" He went upstairs to the study. Anthea checked the home phone, and then she'd call the beauty parlour to ask Jackie how things were going. Had Mrs. Bobbins been in? She hoped that if she had, she'd spent lots of money and not upset any customers. . .

The emails were scanned, revealing a small number of regular customers who were possibly interested in buying another car. There were several trash emails from various companies who had got his address as well as two or three from friends who asked how the caravan trip had gone. And then one from a new email address. It was from Tu Ying, the sent address was Htuying@hotmail.dk.

The email came from Denmark. dk was a Danish domain. He looked at it several times. It read 'You take caravan to post code near Middlesbrough. Next Tuesday 3.00 pm. Man in dark suit in car will be waiting for you with agreed cash deal in £50 notes in brown envelope. No ask questions. Give him all keys – both sets please –

and caravan paperwork. You not tell anyone about this deal. H.T.Y.' There was a TS2 post code shown.

It seemed very odd to Harry that Tu Ying had a Danish email address. Did he live there, and what was Harry to make of "you not tell anyone about this deal?" He hoped it would all become clear eventually but he was beginning to feel more uneasy.

How clear it would become was going to be difficult to predict, very difficult. Harry was in for a surprise.

Chapter 8

After a typical Danish breakfast of ham and cheese, bread rolls and strong black coffee, the two girls took Juliette into town. They were dressed casually for the week-end, as young girls tend to do - light trousers, blouse and sweater over the shoulders, each carrying a small handbag and wearing shoes with a low heel. Anna Jorgsholm had told them to be careful when they were out, and to keep an eye on their possessions. They caught the bus at the end of the avenue, and it would take all three of them to the centre in Kokkedal. Juliette had brought sufficient euros to last her for the duration of her stay as long as she didn't spend too much on clothes and shoes! The journey would take about twenty minutes and Juliette was impressed with how clean the countryside looked as the bus trundled towards town. She recalled that Denmark was famous for its bacon but she hadn't seen a single pig anywhere, perhaps they were kept inside? The girls giggled and chatted and eventually the vehicle slowed down as it pulled into a bus lane opposite the main shopping area. Eighteen passengers got off the bus and the three girls went into a *Costa* coffee bar. None of them needed a caffeine burst, but it was a good way of getting your bearings, to see who was about, do some people watching. As they entered, Agnatha offered to buy the drinks, and they all chose milk shakes, two strawberry and one chocolate, the last one for Jules.

The girls continued to talk about life in Denmark, the latest chart hits, TV talent shows and pop groups that were popular. On Monday, Juliette would be going to

37

school with her new friends. How would that be? Would the lessons be in Danish? Probably, but that didn't matter, she would experience life in a secondary school in Denmark. The headmaster had been briefed by Miss Barton-Needwood from Polkam Hall School and Juliette was to experience life in a Danish school as part of a broader schools exchange programme. Her school near Yarm had already received four girls from Denmark that had spent a number of weeks there and the exchange strategy had worked well according to the school governors. Feedback had clearly shown that the other pupils at Polkham Hall had become much more aware of Anglo-Danish relations, all part of an educational socio-economic policy suggested by the deputy head, Miss Thrislington.

It was time to do some shopping, but Juliette needed the toilet. The Jorgsholm girls waited at the table while their guest went to the ladies and Agnatha checked her watch. It was 10.35 am. She glanced across the coffee shop, taking in who was there. A trait she'd got from her dad who was always like that when they went out as a family. A few individuals looked a little unusual or suspicious, but she wasn't sure. Eyeball contact was rare, but one man in the corner of the *Costa* coffee shop seemed odd? Louise thought he looked like an actor from a TV programme called 'Hawaii Five O' that was currently running on Danish television. He seemed to be looking at the girls more than was warranted, almost staring at them.

Louise had been looking at the front page of 'Hello' magazine that she had bought as they entered the shopping mall, while Agnatha checked her mobile phone for messages and sent a text to a friend. When they looked up, 'Hawaii Five O' had gone. Five minutes passed and Juliette had still not come back from the toilet.

"I wonder where Jules has got to?" asked Agnatha, looking anxiously at her sister. "She's been in there a long time."

"I'll go and take a look," offered Louise. She walked to the ladies toilet and went inside, passing a woman coming out.

"Jules?" There wasn't a sound. Louise slowly opened all of the toilet doors. Nothing. Where was Jules? Only the gentle drip of a water tap interrupted the silence. Louise stood still for a few seconds . . .listening intently. Two small windows were open, but not wide enough to squeeze a baby through. Jules had disappeared. But where and how? Louise went back into the cafe and sat down next to her sister.

"Well, where's Jules?" Louise looked at her for what seemed ages.

"She's gone!"

"Gone?"

Jules had simply vanished into thin air.

Chapter 9

The email from Hokey was read and re-read. Fourteen thousand in cash! The caravan was in good condition, a Bailey Senator fitted with a motor mover and it had been kept it in good order; Harry never smoked in the caravan itself. The fridge, cooker and other parts were always cleaned after each trip away so they knew Hokey would get a decent 'van. Harry looked at a map of Teesside, but he wondered where the place was where Hokey wanted the 'van delivering? It was a TS2 postcode so Harry picked up his Garmin sat-nav and switched it on. He entered the whole post code and the sat-nav gave the distance as 16 miles and a travelling time of 25 minutes. It wasn't too far, but Harry still wasn't sure where this place was. The 'van would be emptied, with Anthea's help, and he'd get it ready for delivery on Tuesday. Leaving home at about 2.30 pm with the 'van documents and two sets of keys should allow sufficient time to get there and do the deal. Going on his own would be best, and Anthea respected his proposal. She didn't see any danger in this, but she did suggest he might take a guy called Dave Wilks who had been a soldier and Harry had known him for several years. Dave was still fit, capable to look after himself if the going got tough, but Harry declined saying he'd be all right on his own. Harry and Wilks had their differences, and there was something that had happened that had left a hatred between them that Anthea didn't know about.

Tuesday came and the Bailey was hitched up to the Toyota on the front drive. Harry made a quick sandwich for lunch and had a glass of orange juice. Anthea was at 'Angel Face' dealing with the customers who wanted their nails perfect, or hair coiffeured. Joan Bobbins was due in at 3.00 pm. but Anthea wasn't looking forward to that. Maybe she'd get Jackie to look after her. Rebecca and Jane were working well – talking to customers about all the usual things - holidays, men, shoes, and so on. Nails were filed, faces toned, hair curled and coloured, and the magazines on the coffee table showed models on their front pages that had been 'computer enhanced'. Models advertising anti-wrinkle cream who were twenty years of age and who wouldn't know a wrinkle if they stood on one. Some of Anthea's clients expected to look like Joan Collins or Helen Mirren or Meryl Streep when they left the salon and Anthea tried her best not to let them down.

It was approaching half past two when Harry drove along a narrow track towards a desolate piece of ground. He'd gone past the docks and made several turns as his sat-nav took him near to the River Tees. It was an area of reclamation and redevelopment. Dilapidated buildings were in need of pulling down and weeds grew everywhere. Harry was looking for his contact - a man wearing a dark suit - and he noticed somebody sitting in a Ford Mondeo parked over to the side of the waste ground. He slowed down, the caravan rumbling across rutted and pot-holed ground, and came to a halt. Getting out of his car, he walked slowly across to the parked Mondeo where the driver was looking straight ahead, towards the Transporter Bridge. As Harry got closer, the man's head slumped forward, hitting the top of the steering wheel. Harry stopped, feeling very uneasy. One option was for him to walk across to the Mondeo and see if the guy was all right. Wasn't this why he was here? To meet Hokey's man with the cash. Looking around him, he could not see anybody else about.

Harry looked into the car, and put his hand on the handle. As the door was opened, the man fell sideways onto Harry, splashing blood onto Harry's trousers. There was a deep slash across his throat, transecting the carotid artery and laying open the laryngeal cartilage. Deep crimson blood was pooling on the man's lap, his white shirt was soaked. Harry pushed the dead man back into an upright position, getting more blood on his hands and clothes as he did so. A brown paper packet lay on the passenger seat. Harry reached across for it, more blood smearing the sleeves of his light jacket. The packet was bulky, it contained the cash. Harry was just about to open it but when he heard a police car siren in the distance he ran back towards the caravan clutching the package, throwing it through the open car window. He unhitched the 'van in under twenty five seconds, screwed the jockey wheel down, and drove off as quickly as he could, placing the thick brown envelope under his front seat. The caravan was left within thirty yards of the Mondeo, and as Harry got back onto the main road a police car passed him, speeding in the opposite direction towards the spare ground. He drove home as quickly as the traffic allowed him, looking out for any more police cars as he continually glanced in his rear-view and door mirrors.

Pulling onto his drive, Harry switched off the engine. Gripping the steering wheel, he rested his forehead on top of his hands. He was sweating and his pulse rate was high. Looking up he couldn't help but wonder what the hell had happened? Was he dreaming? Some crazy scheme to buy his 'van! Harry looked down at the drying blood on his trousers. If there was one saving grace of what had just occurred, he was glad he'd taken the number plate off the Bailey caravan at the last second and removed the factory fitted plate from inside the door frame before he'd left home. The window-etched vehicle identification number's had been removed so he felt it could not be traced. Easing himself out of the car, he went inside but not before looking around to see if he was being watched by any of his neighbours. Anthea wouldn't be home for another couple of hours or so. Going upstairs he took his clothes off in the bedroom and went into the bathroom. The hot shower felt good as the gushing water hit him hard and washed every pore of his body. Getting out of the cubicle Harry dried himself and got dressed, putting on a clean casual shirt and a pair of jeans. Harry wrapped his bloodied shirt, light jacket and trousers in a black bin liner – double wrapped. These needed to be disposed of, that was quite clear. By now he was beginning to calm down as he sipped a cup of coffee in the kitchen and looking at the brown package in front of him. £14,000 felt good, it was quite heavy. There'd be 280 separate notes in there. Going into the lounge he sat down and opened the packet and tipped it upside down.

Pieces of plain white paper, the size of £50 notes, fell out onto the thick pile carpet.

There wasn't a sterling note to be seen. No Queen's head, no watermarks, just paper.

Chapter 10

"She couldn't simply have vanished!" Anna Jorgsholm was very annoyed to say the least. "How well did you look for her. I mean, how thoroughly did you search the cafe and the shopping mall?" Anna had a nasty feeling in the pit of her stomach.

"Mum, we spent an hour wandering around that part of town, asking people, giving them a description," replied Louise in desperation, and feeling guilty.

"What on earth are we going to tell her parents? Did she phone home last night?"

"I don't think so," said Louise. Agnatha was concerned, too, staring out of the lounge window, trying to piece together in her mind the events in the cafe. Going in, ordering the drinks, sitting down . . .

"Where's the letter from her school? It was here yesterday. I'll need to look for it," said Anna Jorgsholm. She searched for the letter, it was nowhere to be found. Meanwhile, Carl Jorgsholm was at work. Despite being a Saturday he had some important matters to attend to. How long could they wait before they called the police? One hour, two hours? It was almost one o'clock. Anna Jorgsholm had to find the school letter that they had received two months before the arrival of Juliette. It contained contact details, both school and home. Juliette's' mobile phone number had been written down by the two girls just after she arrived in Kokkedal and Louise tried to find it. Going into the study, Anna searched the bureau for the school letter. Feeling a sense of panic, she clawed at the contents of each drawer and the carpet was soon strewn with pieces of note paper.

"I've found it!" Mrs. Jorgsholm shouted walking from the study to the lounge. 'Thank God!' Louise and Agnatha looked at each other and jointly breathed a sigh of relief. Louise ran into to the lounge, joined immediately by Agnatha. Anna read the letter out loud.

'Dear Mr. and Mrs. Jorgsholm,

We are so pleased that you are able to take Juliette Watkinson as your guest for two weeks. This will be valuable experience for her now that she is preparing to enter the sixth form at our school. She is a mature girl, very intelligent, and gets on well with her school friends. Your two daughters will no doubt be excellent company for Juliette, especially at their school in Kokkedal. Juliette's parents, Anthea and Peter have the full support of the school in this exchange programme. You may be aware that Polkam Hall School has had visits from four Danish girls during the past 12 months. They have provided feed-back that indicates it was very favourable in gaining a better understanding of British life.

Mr. and Mrs. Watkinson's address is shown on the attached sheet. Their home telephone number is 01642 989011. Juliette's mobile number is 07977 450912.

We look forward to hearing all about Juliette's experience when she returns.

Yours sincerely,

Miss Cynthia Barton-Needwood M.A. (Oxon)
Headmistress'

"Here's her mobile number!" Anna wrote it down on a post-it note.

"Agnatha – phone Juliette's mobile. Do it now!"

Agnatha responded. She dialled the number. After four rings it picked up.

"Hello, Juliette?" There was no reply, but there was the sound of breathing. Agnatha hesitated.

"Juliette. Is that you?" Nothing. Then the familiar sound of a hang up. Brrrrrrrrrrrrr. The three looked at each other in silence.

"Come on, we're going into town!" said Anna Jorgsholm. Her two daughters exchanged glances, but they knew their mother was in 'go' mode. Maternal instincts were kicking in and she was doing what she would do for her two daughters under the same circumstances. Within minutes they'd gathered their things together, including mobile phones, Louise grabbed a digital camera, and they went out of the front door. Getting into Anna's car, they reversed off the drive and headed into town.

Anna parked in the multi-story car park near the shopping mall. The three of them got out of the car and headed to the lift. Descending to the ground floor, the doors opened onto the wide concourse. Every type of shop surrounded them – clothes, shoes, music, phones, computer, cards, outdoor equipment – they seemed endless. By now it was nearly mid afternoon as shoppers milled about, bumping into each other as they jostled to reach the entrances to the multitude of boutiques.

Anna asked the girls to take her to exactly where they'd had their milkshakes and when they got inside the cafe, Agnatha showed her mum the table at which they sat. There were numerous tables spread across a dark wooden floor half the size of a tennis court. Large pictures of European cities were on the walls, Paris, Madrid, London, and slogans about drinking coffee. The lighting was discrete rather than bright. Looking across at the ladies toilet, and then around the cafe, Anna tried to understand what might have happened. Louise pointed to the table where 'Hawaii Five-O' had been sitting. The place was fairly busy, shopping bags placed as to provide an obstacle course for other users of the cafe. They stayed long enough to get a feel for the possible situation as it might have happened. Anna summed up the situation in her mind, quietly asking the girls if they'd seen anybody else at all who looked suspicious at the time. The girls shook their heads as Anna asked a few more questions before she led the way outside. She suggested sitting down on a wooden slatted bench near a burger bar.

"Do you have *any* explanation at all as to how Juliette could have disappeared," Anna asked, "anything at all?" After several seconds that seemed like an age, Louise replied.

"We were waiting for her. Reading and texting, but waiting for her to come back. After a few minutes I went into the toilet to find her but she wasn't there. She'd taken her handbag with her phone in it. I came out and we looked around for a while, but she wasn't anywhere to be seen. Some customers even asked us if we had lost something. The odd looking guy that we saw in the corner had also gone but we didn't see him leave."

The trip home seemed to take longer than the journey to town as Anna and her daughters returned to their Kokkedal suburb. Anna was going over the details in her mind and her nurse training helped her to sift through the facts and attempt to come to a logical conclusion, almost in the way in which she'd decide on how a patient was to be treated and cared for. Check the symptoms, eliminate irrelevant details, plan the treatment, and then implement it. The trouble was, she couldn't come up with one.

But Anna Jorgsholm knew someone who could help. Someone very close to her.

Her husband, Carl, was a Superintendent in the Danish Police. He was due home in twenty minutes.

Chapter 11

"Tell me again what happened, but more slowly." Anthea had listened to Harry's account of the trip to the waste land in Middlesbrough. She poured herself a gin and tonic, Harry already had a can of beer in his hand. He recounted the drive - towing the caravan to the given post code, pulling up near the Mondeo, opening the car door, the blood spilling onto him . . .

Anthea listened. How and why had the guy with the 'brown package' been murdered? Assuming Hokey was genuine, had somebody known that the plan was in place? If so, had the fourteen grand in cash been replaced with another brown package? Or was Hokey conning Harry, was he untrustworthy?

Harry took another gulp of his beer. The pieces of paper were still on the carpet, he was more concerned about getting rid of his blood stained clothes. It was best to burn the items rather than put them in the bin where they could be found. Going into the back garden with a bottle of white spirit and a box of matches, he used an old galvanised dustbin, crumpled two pages of newspaper, and threw them in. A good splash of white spirit was poured over the clothes – the jacket, trousers, shirt, socks and a Giorgio Armani leather belt. Vapour from the spirit-soaked mass met a lit match and whooosh. Flames rose from the bin as the contents burned, blue-grey smoke rising into the Yarm air. In a few minutes the conflagration began to die down as the black charred mass became unrecognisable as clothes. He hoped and prayed that none of the neighbours were watching as he lit a cigarette and inhaled deeply, sitting down on an old white plastic garden chair to rest. He was feeling guilty, but he could have been burning any household waste, couldn't he?

Neither he nor Anthea felt very hungry, but she prepared a salad with a jacket potato. Sitting at the kitchen table they tried to eat while they contemplated the situation. Harry stared down at the food on his plate.

"Bloody hell, what have we got into?" Harry raised his voice above normal. He'd asked himself the question several times over.

"Why did that Chinese guy, what's his name, Hokun something, want to buy the caravan? What was he doing in Seahouses, and does he really own a boat?" Anthea replied as she looked at her husband. "We don't know for sure if the boat we saw at Seahouses belongs to him. It might be a coincidence that one of those boats had a Chinese name. We do know that he's a regular customer in the cafe that we ate in – the waitress said so. At least we can go back there and find him. Remember, we'd know him if we saw him, but he doesn't know what we look like. So, we have that advantage!"

Harry reflected on her words. Anthea was right. The only contact so far was mobile phone and email. From the conversation and email with Hokun Tu Ying, Harry couldn't help but feel that the Chinaman was genuine, even although he still didn't know why he wanted to buy the 'van'. Harry admitted to himself that the delivery to the waste ground was odd, but maybe it was convenient for Hokey? Thinking about the moment he opened the Mondeo door, why did he grab the package and run? 'I'm innocent' he thought to himself, 'and I didn't have to do what I did.' Harry's army training had taught him to 'hit and run' - throw the hand grenade, rush the enemy, bayonet the soldier, look after number one.

After picking at his meal and leaving half untouched, Harry got up and went back out into the garden and looked into the charred bin. A burnt, black mass lay spread out in the bottom. Carefully tipping the bin up, he emptied the contents into a large heavy gauge black plastic bag, twisted the neck, and tied the bag with garden twine. The local civic amenity tip was only a mile away, and he knew he had to get rid of it. No trace left behind, nothing to connect him with the dead man on the waste ground.

"Harry, you know what this means, don't you?" Anthea looked at him as he put his shoes on and got ready to drive to the tip.

"What's that?" Harry looked at her and waited for her reply. She stared him in the eye.

"You could be a murder suspect!" Harry felt a chill run down his spine as if somebody had dropped an ice cube down the back of his shirt collar.

Chapter 12

"Tell me exactly what the guy looked like." Carl Jorgsholm looked at both of his daughters. He was referring to the 'Hawaii Five-O' character who was sitting in the cafe that morning. Carl Jorgsholm stood six feet four inches in his bare feet. He had blue eyes and blond hair, cut short but not a crew-cut. He was muscular, but didn't look like a night-club bouncer – just fit and trim. Jorgsholm had represented the Danish police in the discus and javelin events at an inter-services athletics competition several years previously.

Both Agnatha and Louise gave their account. However, there was some conflict. Agnatha said he had his hair parted on the left, but Louise disagreed. Louise thought he had a moustache, but Agnatha wasn't sure. Their father looked at them; he seemed disappointed. However, he wasn't surprised. Police work had taught him that when people were asked to describe an individual there usually were differences between accounts – facial features, clothing, height, and so forth. Hence the difficulty of picking out 'Mr. Dunnit' from a line up at the police station.

"What was he wearing?" Carl eyed Agnatha.

"A light coloured shirt and a black jacket, possibly leather. He had a badge on the lapel. I couldn't see what it was, but it looked like a cross of some type. I think it was red." Louise nodded in agreement.

"Did you see him stand up and leave?" The girls shook their heads.

"One minute he was there, then the next he was gone. We were reading and things so we didn't pay much attention. It was only after a few minutes when Jules didn't return that we noticed he'd disappeared," Louise added.

"If I get a photo-fit picture done, you might get a better idea of the guy's features?" Jorgsholm was in full police mode. His daughters gave him some more to go on and Carl made notes. He realised that 'Hawaii Five O', or HFO for short, may have absolutely nothing to do with the disappearance of Juliette Watkinson. He wasn't one to jump to conclusions, never made assumptions – he was too experienced for that, but neither did he leave any stone unturned.

"*When* are going to tell her parents?" asked Anna. It was now approaching 4.00 pm. "And *what* are we going to say?"

"Not yet." Carl Jorgsholm was adamant that it was too soon to cause an alarm. "And anyway, we don't have all the facts." Looking out of the lounge window he was thinking as he chewed on his black ball-point pen cap. After all, Jules may be wandering around Kokkedal? She could be lost, asking people for directions? She had her handbag, her mobile phone and some money with her. Maybe she was confused when she came out of the ladies toilet and turned right instead of left. Was there more than one exit from the toilet? Although they'd tried to contact her on her mobile, someone should try again, and soon.

Anna went up to Jules' bedroom and checked through her drawers. Her passport was still there, along with some euro notes, nothing to suggest that Jules was planning to go anywhere. 'This is silly', Anna thought to herself, 'are we are getting worked up over nothing

53

She'll be back any time now'. Her fingers were crossed behind her back. 'She's going to ring the front door bell soon...'

Carl Jorgsholm went into the study and phoned his office. He asked one of his colleagues to check whether the cafe had any CCTV cameras. He knew the shopping mall had installed three cameras a year ago and he gave sufficient details to another police officer to enable him to begin to compile a photo-fit picture. If they could piece together CCTV images along with the photo-fit they might get somewhere. Meanwhile, Carl gave a description of Juliette to his Detective Sergeant, Merete Glym, who was on duty over the week-end, briefing her on the situation. He asked Glym to circulate it to officers in Kokkedal – both traffic and those on foot patrol in the town centre. He also wanted to involve the Politiets Efterretningstjeneste, or PE for short, the national security intelligence department of Denmark.

All this started in under ten minutes, the action had begun. This was Danish efficiency at its best. Precise, concise, factual, explicit. Carl was still in his study at home when he took a phone call 20 minutes later.

"Hi Carl, Merete here."

"What news?" Carl Jorgsholm was quickly on the edge of his seat.

"Yes, the cafe has CCTV, as well as the shopping mall. I've got someone going there now. All police officers on duty in the area have been briefed on the situation. Juliette's description has been circulated. A photo-fit will be faxed to you in the next few minutes and I'll be in touch again very soon." Precise and concise. Factual and explicit.

Carl knew that the photo-fit was necessary. He hoped that the memory of his young daughters might be jolted by seeing an accurate picture of HFO that could be circulated and later on might help the police or the public to spot him. 'No stone is going to be left unturned' thought Carl to himself as he picked the picture from his fax machine. Agnatha and Louise came downstairs and looked at the photo-fit. After several minutes studying the face they both agreed that it was very like 'HFO' as they had remembered him earlier that day. Suddenly, Louise shouted.

"He had a scar! A small scar on his left cheek!" Agnatha closed her eyes. She was trying to imagine 'HFO' sitting in the corner of the cafe.

"Yes," said Agnatha loudly as she stood next to her sister. "Only two or three centimetres long, but I remember it now!" Their father smiled, but only a little. That was enough to go on for the time being. 'HFO' was beginning to feel familiar to him. He wasn't certain, but maybe – just maybe, Superintendent Jorgsholm and 'HFO' had met before.

Anna called from the kitchen to let them know that a cup of coffee was ready for them. She'd made a pot of coffee and poured some single cream into a small white jug, biscuits were put onto a plate. Carl switched off his computer. As they wandered into the lounge where Anna had placed the tray on the small circular table, his mobile rang. Carl glanced at his watch. It was exactly 5.00 pm. His sergeant, Merete Glym, had been working on the case.

"Hi, Carl, are you sitting down? I've got some news for you. You're not going to believe this."

Chapter 13

The burnt remains of Harry's clothes were dumped at the tip. Nothing special, nothing different, he acted casually as he threw the heavy gauge bin liner into the large skip labelled 'General Household Refuse'. He'd left the car engine ticking over. Getting back in he started to slowly drive away but as he left the parking area he noticed one of his neighbours who was dumping some old rotten wooden poles into the next skip. The neighbour gave Harry an odd look as though to say 'I know what you've be up to!' Harry smiled weakly at him and nodded, but tried to dismiss the thought that he'd been seen burning something. Did he have a guilty conscience? He tried not to think of what he'd just done, but he couldn't put it totally out of his mind. He knew he shouldn't worry about the neighbour, but if he'd been seen, he needed a story. A plausible one for anyone who might ask.

When he got home he found that Anthea had gone back to the salon. There were always things to attend to - staff issues, tax returns, PAYE matters. She did some of the beauty care, but the other girls at 'Angel Face' were very capable. Harry went into the lounge where he'd emptied the brown package. The paper was still on the carpet and he knew he ought to pick them up, get rid of them. Most of the remnants were plain paper but Harry noticed a few sheets had some printing on them, spotting the words 'Catterick Garrison' on a few. He looked more closely and saw that some of the pieces also had the words 'report' and 'update'. The British army crest was noticeable on others and Harry quickly realised that these related to military matters – paper from an army source!

Sitting down on the leather sofa, Harry slowed down – his mind had been working overtime. He breathed in, filling his chest with air, then exhaled slowly. A cigarette would be lit soon, a 'nicotine snack' was needed. Dave Wilks came to mind. Wilks! Harry had seen him in 'The Bluebell' only a few nights previously. It wasn't planned, but Harry had fancied a pint, and Dave Wilks was propping up the bar. Harry recalled that Wilks had bought him a drink. Wilks called it a 'special', saying he was celebrating his birthday. Harry drunk it, but it had smelt strange – almost like *Domestos* and blackcurrant it seemed. They chatted for a while, but Harry wasn't really in the mood for talking. Wilks placed another 'special' in front of Harry and insisted he drink it – for old times' sake. Harry had downed it, but his throat burned as the liquid went down.

What Anthea didn't know was that Harry Richards and Dave Wilks had once 'crossed swords'. Some years ago they were on a training week in Aldershot learning how to handle a new advanced rifle that had been developed by the US Army – longer range, laser sight, semi-automatic, but Harry had made a mess of reloading the rifle. They had to be blindfolded to simulate night-time and 'difficult to see' conditions but Wilks had moved the ammunition box away from Harry and also dropped a small nut and bolt into the breech of the gun before putting on his own blindfold. When Harry came to the time trial, fifteen seconds was allowed and obviously he failed. As he took his blindfold off, he saw Wilks looking at him as though to say 'hard cheese, you bastard.' Harry knew it was Wilks and he never forgave him. The sergeant had given Harry a good rollicking, telling him that he'd let himself and the army down. Harry had felt three feet tall at the time.

Now here Harry was, in his own lounge, looking at pieces of army paper. Not many, but enough to make Harry wonder if Dave Wilks had anything to do with the brown package? Wilks had been stationed at the Garrison once. He could have taken, or rather stolen, a quantity of A4 sheets. Nobody would have missed them. He could have cut 70 sheets into quarters and placed these in a brown packet to make it look and feel as if it contained the fourteen thousand pounds in £50 notes.

'But hang on, why would Wilks do that?' Harry stopped his thoughts right there. He'd been through a traumatic few days and his mind was overdoing it. Thinking back to that time in Aldershot, remembering a few other things that had happened, for example his wallet had gone missing from his bedside locker, but it turned up again, minus some cash. His uniform had been daubed with black boot polish and he'd got a rollicking form his sergeant. Was that Wilks, too?

In 'The Bluebell' pub that night, with Dave Wilks celebrating his birthday, Harry never realised that Wilks was adding something to his drink. After Harry had poured his third one down his neck, maybe his tongue had loosened and his brain had turned to blancmange? He simply did not know whether he'd told Wilks about the caravan deal - the arrangement, the waste ground, the cash exchange, even the date and time. Luckily a friend of Harry's had taken him home that night and Anthea was not best pleased when he staggered through the door and stumbled into the lounge, falling onto the sofa where he spent the night.

No, Harry never realised that his loose tongue had wagged too much, but Wilks wasn't the only one listening. There were one or two more in the bar that night.

Chapter 14

"Are you going to contact Hokun?" asked Anthea over toast and marmalade as she poured the coffee. "After all, we think he has our caravan but we don't have his money!"

"I'm not rushing into anything just yet. We don't actually know if he has got the Bailey. The cops may have it?" Harry sipped the strong black coffee as he buttered another piece of toast. *The Northern Echo* had reported on the killing in Middlesbrough – a full front page. It gave a factual account of the situation, but nothing on any vehicle being spotted near the scene. The caravan description was given, but it was also reported that the 'van had been 'cleaned' so that its ID was unknown. No window VIN, no makers plate, no registration number left on the rear. The Mondeo was a silver coloured estate car with a tow bar fitted. The registration was NW 03 BBX, and it had been stolen a few days previously. The identity of the murdered driver was still a mystery. There was no identification on him – no credit cards, driving licence, nothing. He had a wad of twenty pound notes, about £400, in the back pocket of his trousers. Of mixed race, the driver had a tattoo of two crossed samurai swords on his right forearm. Anyone with any information was asked to contact Inspector Robin Carey at Cleveland police headquarters, and a telephone number was given. Police were suggesting that the caravan may have been towed to the waste ground by the Mondeo and then unhitched for some reason. However, they'd asked the question as to why there wasn't a number plate on the 'van.

What the *Echo* newspaper didn't report, owing to the police not revealing all the facts, was that the autopsy showed that death was caused by a firm, single cut to the throat using a very sharp instrument. The angle of the cut, from near the right ear, across the front of the neck towards the left shoulder in a slightly downward direction, strongly indicated that the murderer was left handed. That narrowed it down to one in eight of the population, at least. The depth of the incision also was indicative of a strong person committing the crime, therefore probably male.

"If the neighbours or any friends ask about the caravan we'll tell them we've put it into storage," Harry suggested, looking at Anthea. "Nobody needs to know anything else. It was taking up room on the drive, so we've moved it – simple as that." Harry finished his breakfast and drank the last of his coffee.

"We know Hokun uses the Seahouses cafe. The trouble is we don't know when. Maybe we can go back there and see if that red boat, the 'Kwangsi Chuang', is in the harbour? We can ask a few questions on the quayside – even see the old net mender? Remember he doesn't know what we look like, but he'd stick out like a blind cobbler's thumb. I can take a day off work, and leave the beauty parlour with Jackie. What do you think?" Anthea had done her detective bit as she smiled reassuringly at her husband, but Harry seemed miles away.

"I'm wondering if we should get rid of the Toyota? I got back into it with blood on me. Who knows, a scene of crime officer could pick up traces of blood from the seat, floor mat, anything."

61

"Did you hear what I was saying?" Anthea asked adamantly.

"I heard every word." Harry was staring out of the window at the garden. A thrush had landed on the bird table and was pecking at bird seed. His mind was speeding.

"Let's sell the Toyota, put it in part exchange against another car, and then head out to the coast in a few days. The Halshort-Evens dealer is good. I know one of the salesman quite well. We'll do it now! I'll get the car documents and I want you to come with me. Phone Jackie and say you're taking some time off." Harry jumped up. Anthea knew that when he made his mind up on something like this he'd do it. They drove the short distance into Middlesbrough and pulled up in the customer's parking area at Halshort-Evens.

"Hi, Harry," said Roy. "Long time no see." Roy Jones was a Senior Car Sales Executive. He made the coffee, changed loo rolls in the toilets, and delivered cars despite his grand title. "What can I do for you?" Roy gave Anthea a quick look and the kind of wink that only car salesmen can give to a female customer.

"We fancy a change. The Toyota over there is in good condition, but we want something a bit smaller." Roy walked over to the Toyota, had a good look at it and made a few notes on a scrap of paper. The two prospective customers looked at a number of cars and eventually decided on a Suzuki with four wheel drive, cruise control and other features that they liked. It was compact and had better fuel consumption than their current car. Roy checked details on his computer, the things car salesmen do so adeptly, and made Harry a good offer on the Toyota. The deal was made in under ten minutes and Harry arranged with Roy to collect the Suzuki the day after tomorrow. That would give him time to amend his car insurance and to empty the Toyota. 'Empty it as much as I can', he thought. 'I can't guarantee getting rid of the blood stains!'

Driving back home, Anthea and Harry stopped off for a bit of lunch at a newly opened Thai bistro in Yarm High Street. They avoided chatting about their 'current situation' since Harry and Anthea certainly did not want anybody overhearing their conversation. In any case, it seemed they hadn't talked about anything else for ages. So it was weather, friends, and football. After a tasty meal of green curry, rice and a glass of Thai beer they headed home. Parking on the drive they went in, Harry switching the house alarm off as they entered the hall. Anthea immediately checked the telephone for messages and Harry was about to go upstairs when the front door bell rang.

"I'll get it," shouted Harry. He opened the door wide, unable to see who was there through the frosted glass.

"Mr. Richards?" Two police constables were standing looking at Harry.

"Yes." Harry swallowed hard.

"Do you have a minute?" asked one of the officers, smiling politely.

Chapter 15

The annual dinner dance for employees and partners of 'Angel Face' took place at the Marton Hotel and Country Club. Anthea managed to find a suitable dress - black, low cut, with just a hint of sequins so that it didn't look too flirty. She enjoyed dressing up, it made her feel feminine – almost powerful. And Harry liked her to look good. He enjoyed being by her side when she was in this mood since she was the dominant matriarchal figurehead at the event. As well as Anthea and Harry, there were three full time staff, two cleaners, one supplier of hair and nail products, and someone from the marketing agency she used for advertising and promotional activities. In total, there were sixteen people around the long rectangular table with Harry and Anthea sitting at each end.

The table had been reserved in the main restaurant, but set aside from the others to make it semi-private. Two groups of coloured balloons waved in the air, securely tied to heavy silver plated weights. Bottles of red and white wine were uncorked and already placed on the table. Place cards were set out. Anthea planned to mix the group as a way of getting those around the table to talk with those they probably didn't know and maybe even didn't want to know! Everybody was introduced to each other and then asked to take their seats. Some had ordered a drink or two at the bar, whilst others poured themselves a glass of wine after sitting down. It was an informal gathering and as the starters were served the conversational buzz increased - one bee had turned into a small swarm.

Harry had Jackie on his left and Rebecca on his right. They'd met him before when he called into the beauty salon on one or two occasions and had had several telephone conversations. Normally Harry was easy to get on with, but tonight he felt on edge, pretending that all was well. He knew it wasn't. Jackie chatted amiably about her holiday to Cuba whilst Rebecca couldn't say enough about her new boyfriend while Harry listened, but a lot went over his head. He smiled as best he could, asking a few questions about Cuba and the new boyfriend, but it was a struggle. Making his way through his first course of tomato soup and then he poked the food about on his plate when the main dish was served. The steak was a little too well done for his taste, but he couldn't be bothered to complain. The large hand cut chips were nice and he ate a few, one at a time. He fancied some tomato sauce to dip them into, but couldn't be bothered to ask for any.

Harry glanced at Anthea from time to time. She was talking non-stop to those within hearing distance and the life and soul of the party, so to speak. She looked at Harry as if to say 'are you OK?' He smiled at her to say 'yes thanks'. An hour and a half after they'd sat down the desserts were served, and then a glass of sweet Muscatel wine. Everybody around the table was locked in conversation and Anthea was pleased that the evening seemed to be going so well. The partners appeared to get on fine with each other as soon as common ground had been identified - golf, fishing, cars, the Harrogate Spring Flower Show, recent flooding after heavy rains. On it went.

Jackie didn't seem to be getting on too well with her husband. He meandered to the bar for a drink as if drawn by a magnet once they'd all left the table. Jackie took the opportunity to talk more with Harry. Anthea seemed to be doing her 'let's mingle with everybody' role. The small band was playing a number of different tunes and melodies – mostly middle of the road stuff. Rebecca and her boyfriend were first on the dance floor but the music was a little too slow for them. She whispered a few words to the band leader and soon the tempo increased. People got up, including other diners, and the previously empty dance floor became a mass of waving human beings with heads that didn't seem to belong to them.

Sitting down at a small table in the far corner of the bar, Jackie and Harry got some drinks, a gin and tonic for her while Harry sipped on a large diet coke. Jackie pulled her chair closer to Harry which made him feel a little uncomfortable, but he could handle her.

"There's something you need to know. I've spoken to Anthea about it so I'm not talking out of school here. However, she doesn't seem too concerned."

"What's the problem?" Harry leant forward a little.

"It's Joan Bobbins. Her behaviour in the beauty parlour is causing the staff some concern. We know she spends a lot of money – she can afford it of course, but it's the things she talks about."

"What sort of things?" Harry eyed Jackie.

"She's telling customers about her time in Durham Gaol, and how she was innocent of the murder of her husband. She has a strange circle of friends and visits odd places in and around Middlesbrough. She said last week that she has joined a white witches circle, or something like that. And as for her new friend, well she's met a man called Adam Tennant. There's nothing wrong with that, but she doesn't half go on about him."

"Is she a good customer? I mean how much does she spend a month, would you say?"

"It must be around one thousand pounds." Harry raised his eyebrows and took a sip of diet coke. "What does she get for that?"

"Hair colouring, shampoo and set, nails manicured and polished, facial massage, eyebrows plucked, legs waxed . . ."

"OK, OK." Harry interrupted Jackie. They both fell silent for a few minutes. She continued.

"I think it's because she spends so much with us that Anthea doesn't want to lose her as a customer." Harry nodded and obviously understood the Jackie's remark. He stood up.

"I need the loo," he said and started to walk around the polished parquet dance floor to the gents. "Back in a minute," he glanced back at Jackie. Rick, Jackie's husband, left the bar where he'd been talking to Jane and her partner, Oliver, and wandered over to where Jackie was sitting.

"You two seem to be getting cosy? Can I join you or is it a private meeting?"

Smiling slightly sarcastically, Jackie didn't bother to reply but pointed to a chair and Rick sat down. Harry returned from the loo, wringing his hands.

"Those new vacuum hand dryers aren't very good. I had to use some toilet paper!"

"I hope I'm not gate crashing but I couldn't stand talking to that Oliver guy any longer! Him and his damned Honda motorbike." Rick seemed to want to justify his arrival.

"No, not at all," offered Harry. "Jackie and I were just chatting about how this evening is going – everybody seems to be mingling well together. The food was good and the red wine was excellent." Harry lied, he didn't really like his steak. At around midnight the revellers began to leave the Country Club. Taxis pulled up regularly outside and filled up, whisking their passengers off to various parts of Cleveland. Those sober enough, or who imagined they were sober, wandered out into the cool night air and started their car engines. 'Good-nights' were called from voices across the car park and an enjoyable evening had been had by all those at the 'Angel Face' annual dinner dance. That was, though, all but one.

Harry hadn't enjoyed the evening very much, putting on his 'actors' face for the sake of Anthea. He was feeling a little more worried than when he'd started his tomato soup over four hours ago.

He had things to think about - in fact, a lot of things to think about.

Chapter 16

The two police constables, Colin Wayman and Melvin Brass, had entered the house and Harry was feeling uncomfortable. He could have refused them entry, but he wanted to be seen to be cooperative. A few beads of sweat appeared on his brow in seconds, and he didn't know what to say. He decided to let them do the talking. Anthea came up to Harry's side and diffused the slight tension in the air by asking them if they had time for a cup of tea or coffee. One of the policeman smiled and nodded, indicating that coffee would be fine. Anthea went into the kitchen and put the kettle on.

"While your wife, I assume she is your wife, is doing that we'd like to have a look in your back garden if that's all right?" said the taller of the two policemen.

"Yes, she is my wife, and Anthea's her name. Is there any reason for wanting to search the garden?" Harry wiped his damp palms on the back of his trousers as slowly and calmly as possible.

"We didn't say 'search', it's just a routine check, sir. We've had a few reports of suspect burglars in the area." The other policeman answered.

Harry remembered the nosey neighbour at the civic amenity tip. Had he phoned the local police station and told them what he'd seen? Perhaps someone else had told the police that they'd seen him drive away with a caravan and return without one, then read the murder article in the newspaper? He'd changed his car very recently, but that's not a crime, is it?

Harry's mind was racing. He hadn't discussed all this with his wife, so he prayed that they wouldn't ask a question to which they got two different answers.

'We should have sat down and talked this over. But we didn't expect the police to be here.' Harry was talking silently to himself.

"Well, sir?" one of the two constables enquired.

"Oh, yes, sorry. This way." Harry walked to the double doors leading from the lounge into the back garden. "Mind the step." He pointed to a 10 cm raised edge at the bottom of the double glazed door.

The three of them went out onto the patio of Yorkshire stone paving slabs. The two officers stopped and looked around, one of them taking out a pad and making some notes. The taller policeman walked further across the garden, over some gravel, and stood near the shed. Harry moved uneasily as he tried to keep an eye on both of them. He had another quick wipe of his damp hands on the backside of his trousers without them noticing.

"Come and look at this Col," the taller policeman said as he looked up at a tree next to the wall. The other officer went over, spending a few minutes eyeing up the trees around the perimeter of the garden and then asked to look in the garden shed.

'What do they want to look in there for?' Harry asked himself as he opened the door that wasn't locked.

"Do you normally keep this shed locked, sir?" Harry shook his head. "You should do. Thefts from garden sheds are all too common these days – tools, machinery, other equipment." The police officer hesitated for a second. "Excuse me, but do you think I can I use your toilet for a minute?" Brass wanted a pee.

"Of course." Harry took the policeman into the house and pointed to the cloakroom door. Anthea glanced at him as the aroma of fresh ground coffee wafted from the kitchen, her look asking a lot of questions but Harry shrugged his shoulders. He went back out into the garden and stood near a large zebra grass shrub. The police officer was still looking around the garden, his eyes scanning the whole garden like searchlights on a pitch black night.

"Anything I can help you with, officer?"

"Not really, sir. I'll just wait until my colleague gets back."

Waiting uncomfortably, he kept thinking 'why are they looking in our garden, what do they want, is it the dustbin where I burnt the clothes?' After several minutes, the other officer came back out.

"Fred, I think we need to go," one officer said as they finished looking around.

"We'll leave the coffee, thanks," said the taller policeman. "By the way, do you have a caravan, sir? I noticed some caravan parts in the shed."

"Er, yes, we store it locally." Harry lied.

"Oh, it's just that my father-in-law is looking for one. What make do you have?"

"It was a Bailey."

"Was?" asked Wayman.

"I mean 'is'," Harry corrected himself instantly.

"Thank you for your time, Mr. Richards. We can see ourselves out." Wayman and Brass walked to the front door, then Brass turned round and spoke.

"By the way, if you get any reports of people climbing over your back walls or up the trees, do let us know. And keep that shed locked. We're following up on some reports from some of your neighbours who think

71

they may have possibly heard the occasional intruder, with outside lights sensors being triggered. Just routine, you understand. Thanks. Goodbye."

The front door closed with a clunk. Harry sat down and let out his biggest sigh of relief ever.

"Coffee, Harry?" Anthea's dulcet tones came from the kitchen as she poured a cup for both of them.

Harry's face was as white as freshly fallen snow. And almost as cold. He thought about the *routine* visit from Cleveland Constabulary. Was there more to it than checking for back garden thieves? And the comment on the caravan parts in the shed . . .

He couldn't help but feel worried.

His stomach felt like an overcrowded budgie cage, the birds fighting for the cuttlefish shell.

Chapter 17

"We've got Juliette and the man in the cafe on CCTV," said Merete Glym, talking to Jorgsholm who was in his study. "It seems he and Juliette left the cafe together."

"Together? You mean as if they knew each other?"

"Not necessarily. They were walking out of the shopping mall from the exit nearest to the rear of the ladies toilet. There are two exits from the toilets. Maybe Juliette was confused about the way out of there, and he was waiting for her?" Glym emphasised the point.

"Any further CCTV follow up after they had left the mall?" Jorgsholm's tone became more intense.

"Not much. Some film shows they went towards a McDonalds restaurant within 150 metres of the mall, but after that it goes blank."

"Did they seem to be compatible as they walked along? Was there any indication from the CCTV that there was any sign of her being drugged, or coercion?"

"No, none." Glym was adamant that they seemed at ease walking along together.

Jorgsholm was thinking. He could not believe that the man in the cafe knew Juliette, but it could be that he was waiting for her. As if he knew she would be there. Or if he was primed by a pimp to be on the lookout for young women. As a Superintendent in the Danish police force, Jorgsholm had specialised in human trafficking and he knew it had been on the increase. Countries such as Sweden and Norway had seen growing numbers in the past decade. Jorgsholm wondered if Juliette Watkinson was one of these defined females? Young, beautiful, blond. Hopefully not. She was only in Denmark on a school exchange visit after all. He hoped it wasn't a case of 'wrong place, wrong time.'

"So what do you propose that we do next?" asked Jorgsholm. He had formed his own ideas but was testing Glym.

"We need to check all the CCTV we have and try to identify the man. We can check our own files to get a match, that shouldn't be difficult. We believe that he was on his own. Your daughters have described him well enough to give us a photo-fit picture that is already being circulated. The badge on his lapel may help, a red cross of sorts. I'll get the technical guys to get a close up of that. Also, they described him as possibly being of oriental origin."

"Start a search for this man, Merete. Put the photo-fit picture of him on television news as well as communicating with local radio stations and newspapers. We need to find him, and quick! Inform the whole of the police force in Denmark. Keep the PE informed, and don't forget the airports and ports."

"I've already got someone talking with the national newspapers, and two of our detectives are already on the case." Glym sounded calm and in control.

"Excellent! Keep me informed, and use my mobile number, it will be with me all the time." Jorgsholm put the phone down.

Anna Jorgsholm walked into her husband's study. It was late Saturday evening and they hadn't eaten. She asked him if he wanted a steak, or maybe gammon – two of his favourites. There was little enthusiasm in her voice and sadness in her eyes. She sat down next to him putting her arm around his shoulder.

"No, I don't feel like eating right now. Maybe a snack later." He looked at his wife, who appeared tired, her eyes were dull and her face had no expression. Anna Jorgsholm was thinking like Juliette's mother. What would Anthea be thinking when she got the news about her daughter's disappearance? How do you pass the time when a young girl who was entrusted to your care just fades away in a busy town on a Saturday morning? Carl stood up and placed his hand on Anna's shoulder. He kissed the top of her head as he so often did when the situation was strained. She looked up at her husband and spoke.

"We need to let Juliette's parents know." She looked straight at her husband, and he knew she had to do it. It was maternal instinct.

"All right, but let's wait until morning. We will have more news then, possibly something positive. There's no point disturbing them on a Saturday evening with this information." He gave her a reassuring hug and a 'I love you' look. She saw it in his blue eyes.

Agnatha and Louise hadn't eaten either, and the rest of the evening passed slowly. They watched some TV but didn't really see what was on the screen. The sounds were fuzzy, time passed slowly. It always seems to when you're waiting – just waiting.

The waiting game was the worst game of all.

Chapter 18

"We need to contact Hokun. This is ridiculous. I've taken our caravan to his suggested meeting point and I've ended up with pieces of paper! I wonder if he knows that? Does he read *The Northern Echo*? He might be thinking that I've got the money. Equally important, I suppose is, has he got the caravan?" Harry spoke his thoughts aloud.

"Thinking about it, he probably hasn't. If the police were arriving at the waste ground as you left, wouldn't they have impounded the caravan? So, Hokun may be thinking you didn't deliver the 'van at all? He must know by now that the driver in the waiting car is dead but he can't be certain where the money is, and it's impasse?" Anthea was playing her 'Sherlock Holmes' card, trying to look at the situation as an outsider - someone who wasn't directly involved with the whole deal.

The caravan had been delivered, a brown package had been collected, Hokun may or may not have the 'van, and he might know that his 'middle man' had his throat slit by a left handed person. If Hokun hadn't got the 'van he'd be wondering about the deal with Harry Richards. It was so confusing. Harry really didn't know where he was with all of this. There was a simple solution . . . email Hokun. Find out what he knew.

Ten minutes after sending a short, concise email, Harry got a reply.

'Why you no deliver caravan? I give you fourteen grand as agreed. We have contract. I no see your van.

My driver he get killed. What happened? You no mess me about. I have people who can hurt you." Harry had to respond, needing to tell Hokun what he'd been through. He sent the Chinaman a comprehensive account of what had actually happened on the day he took the caravan to the waste ground as previously agreed, but also weighed up the fact that he was putting all this in writing! Finding the murdered man, the package of pieces of paper, his escape before the police sirens got to the place. Harry prayed that Hokun would take his account as genuine. Maybe Hokun was a really wicked individual? A killer, perhaps? Harry was a tough nut – he'd been through his army training, but the psyche of the Chinese was something else. Life was cheap, and he knew that they had torture methods that made the worst dentist look like a children's nanny.

Thinking things through, Harry had to decide on the way forward. He would return to Seahouses and pop into the Bamburgh Castle Inn for a sandwich and cup of tea and then take a look at the boats down at the quay side. There were questions that could be asked where the net mender would be busy knotting his nylon threads. Harry felt he would get some answers. Going on his own would be best and he'd tell Anthea that she needn't accompany him - it would be easier if he was alone. Not because she was a liability, but it really would be better ... just in case.

Harry returned to Seahouses and parked the Suzuki in the same car park as he'd used before. Recalling how Hokun Tu Ying looked, he was certain that Hokun did not know him by sight. Harry would go into the cafe, see if Hokun was there, and check out the quayside for the red boat. On a grey day, with rain in the air, Harry wandered into the town centre and then down to the harbour, looking around casually as though he were a visitor. Remembering that the net mender had offered information about the things that were happening in Seahouses, Harry sauntered along the quayside to find him. Seeing an old woman standing near some lobster pots, he asked about the old man whose skill was mending the old, worn fishing nets thrown off the boats every week.

"Old Bill passed away last week," the elderly woman replied in a broad Northumbrian accent. "Aye, his funeral was a grand affair, lots there. He was a canny lad. Spent most of his time doing the nets when he retired, but also helping Hokey to get across the North Sea with his business doings."

"Business doings?" asked Harry.

"Way aye man. Hokey is always gannin' across the watter to some foreign country. His boat is often left here with something in the back. Way, I'd even seen a small caravan in there, sort of hidden, like."

"A caravan. Hidden?" Harry's eyes lit up, but he kept calm and lowered his voice.

"Aye. His boat is big enough to carry things like that. I'm not sure what he was up to, mind. Folks around here said he was often bringing or takkin' something somewhere." Harry finished talking to the old woman, thanked her, and waited in the cafe for twenty minutes over a cheese sandwich and cup of tea before a Chinese man came in. Certain that it was Hokun, Harry knew it was time to a make his move. He stood up and moved towards him, sitting down on a chair at the table

"Hokun Tu Ying?" asked Harry, fixing him with a firm but friendly stare.

"Who's asking?"

"Harry Richards."

"No, me his brother. I know your name. You must be Arry."

Harry thought that all Chinese people looked the same but now Hokun has a brother!

He wasn't sure where he went from here . . .

Chapter 19

"My name Mao." He ordered a cup of green tea while Harry grabbed his half drunk cup of lukewarm tea from the other table.

"Hokun not a happy man. He no get his calavan. You had deal. He give you good money for your 'van. He send man with pack of cash. Man get murdered – I read in Echo paper." Mao stared into Harry's eyes. A deep, penetrating stare often seen in fortune tellers.

"I didn't get the money." Harry looked straight back into Mao's dark eyes.

"What you say? What you mean? No cash?"

Harry decided to tell Mao about the episode on the waste ground, virtually repeating the contents of his email to Hokey. He had to trust him. This was an opportunity to clarify the situation, and better done face to face even though it wasn't Hokun himself. Harry told Mao how he'd towed the caravan to the post code that Hokun had provided. When he arrived he saw a Mondeo parked up and went over to it. Mao listened to Harry's account. At first Mao looked sceptical, but as he heard the story he relaxed a little. Harry made certain he reinforced the point about the bits of paper in the brown package. Mao's almond shaped eyes brightened up.

"So you no money in package? Who do that? Who know about deal?" Harry shook his head. Mao believed him.

"No idea. But somebody must have known." Harry finished his tea and ordered another. He had more questions for Mao.

"Does your brother own a red boat?"

Mao nodded.

"But he's not a fisherman?"

Mao shook his head.

"So what does he use the boat for?"

"He has business interests. He transports things from north east to other places."

"What sort of things?" Harry focused on Mao and sipped his coffee, never taking his eyes off him. Mao moved a little uncomfortably on his chair.

"He sell calavans to people across water in Denmark. He make profit most of time." Mao had finished his green tea.

"And what else does he deal in, apart from caravans?"

"Only few other bit and piece, nothing serious." Mao stood up. He had a look on his face that indicated 'I've said too much.'

"Me go now." Mao left the cafe after tossing a two pound coin on the counter that slipped over the smooth surface like a puck on an ice hockey rink, and rolled under a cupboard.

Reflecting on what he'd heard from Hokun's brother, Harry went through what he now knew. A boat that looked like it was used for fishing but capable of carrying small vehicles, even caravans. Business abroad. Selling caravans in places like Denmark to make a profit. Why should Harry even care about what Hokun was involved in? He'd lost his caravan, but then Hokun had lost his money – all £14,000 of it. Where was the money now? Harry tried to work out the logistics of the past weeks events. The visit of the two policemen, whether changing the car was a good decision, going out to the pub and seeing Dave Wilks on his birthday.

Something in Harry's mind clicked, very suddenly, like switching on a light bulb. His mind somehow cleared, like an early morning mist, and he focused on that evening in 'The Bluebell'.

He and Wilks had their differences. Harry had gone out for a beer or two and met Wilks who had been over-friendly. Why? He recalled that he'd become quite drunk very quickly, unusual for Harry as he could normally hold his alcohol. He remembered that his head had seemed detached from his body, as though he was in a dream, drifting in and out of some reverie where he'd wake up at any instant. Some basic innate power enabled Harry to bring back the details of that evening and he reversed his mind, like rewinding an old videotape.

Slowly at first, it all started to become apparent. Had Wilks plied him with drinks and had he begun talking? If so, what had he said? Something in his drinks had loosened Harry's tongue, he now knew that. What had he said? A basic psychology course he'd done when he joined the army had taught him that the deep conscience could be brought to the surface when the brain was stimulated in certain ways. Subjects uppermost in the brain were most likely to come out. He'd heard of truth drugs – used in detention camps, with political prisoners, those who wouldn't give up their secrets. Had Wilks used a drug? Harry remembered that his drinks had an unpleasant taste, but the real question for Harry now was 'had he told Wilks, or indeed anybody else, about the caravan deal with Hokun?' If someone in the pub that evening had overheard the information he could have gone to the waste ground and arrived before Harry got there, walked up to the parked Mondeo and committed the murder. But who would have done that? There had to be a way to discover more. Harry was just about to leave the Seahouses cafe when his brain moved up a gear...

Chapter 20

"We've trawled the CCTV pictures," said Merete Glym, talking to Carl Jorgsholm on his mobile, keeping him updated. "After Juliette left the cafe with the man we could see that they turned left into the next road. Another camera picked them up within 50 metres, but as they made the next turn it looked as though a car slowed down. The images are blurred, but my guess is that they both got into the car."

"Any details on the vehicle?" asked Jorgsholm.

"A red Volvo 240 saloon. The number plate is difficult to see, but if we could digitally enhance the image we could probably identify it."

"Good. Go ahead and get the plate number. It's crucial. Anything else?"

"It seems so strange that Juliette walked along with this man," Glym continued. "No struggle, nothing. I wonder if she could she have been sedated. We're interviewing the staff in the cafe – see if they can give us anything else?" Glym sounded positive. "Just a moment, one of the detectives on this case has just passed me a poor image of the rear of the Volvo. We can just see the plate - number is HTY 274."

"OK, good. Get the plate out to all those police involved on this case. As I said before, let's keep an eyes on airports and ports. He may try to get her out of the country, although we know her passport is still in our house."

"Carl, I've just had a report from another of the detectives regarding the cafe staff. One of the girls working there had been in prison and she was involved in drug dealing about a year ago. Another member of staff stated that she knew the man who had been sitting in the cafe on Saturday morning and said that he and the girl who'd served time were very friendly. I wonder how long he'd been sitting there? I do wonder if there was anything going on in terms of what customers were being served?" Jorgsholm interrupted.

"Is there an update on the CCTV pictures from the cafe – something clearer on our suspect?" Jorgsholm was anxious to see progress.

"You can see Agnatha going to the counter to buy the milk shakes. She makes it obvious that the chocolate one is for Juliette as she points to her across the cafe. As the girl behind the counter is about to serve the 'shakes it seems that she puts some white powder into the chocolate milkshake as though it was part of the preparation. Obviously that isn't normal, but you wouldn't notice it in a busy place like that!"

"Are you suggesting that Juliette was drugged?"

"It looks that way." Glym spoke slowly and positively.

"What about a positive ID on the man?" Jorgsholm pressed home the question.

"I think you know him," answered Glym. "We've been through our data bank. You arrested him five years ago on a charge of sexual harassment with under age girls in a night club in Copenhagen. His name is Sven Longe, and he belongs to a Chinese cult. We've enhanced the CCTV and it is possible to see a 'Chinese Liberation Brigade' badge on his jacket lapel."

"Sven Longe!" Jorgsholm fumed. "That swine! I want him caught. He must be found!" Jorgsholm pressed the red phone button on his mobile and ended the call.

He was angry and annoyed. Jorgsholm recalled Longe as being a brutal and savage man with no conscience. He'd been given twelve months for his crime, but he showed no remorse on being taken down. After being released he'd gone to ground. Jorgsholm had heard on the grapevine that Longe had spent some time in England but he wasn't sure where.

Carl Jorgsholm went downstairs. It was late. Pouring himself a double vodka with a splash of lime juice he sat in an old leather armchair and considered the situation. He and his wife had been hosts to a girl from north east England for less than 24 hours before she disappeared. And him a Superintendent in the Danish police force! How would that look? Although he was making it a priority, he had to be careful that he didn't become obsessive about the case. Nevertheless, he felt that if it was Sven Longe, Juliette may be in real trouble.

In the morning they would have to make a telephone call to Yarm. They would tell the parents of Juliette Watkinson that their daughter had been reported missing. They would have to offer hope. Carl Jorgsholm prayed for a miracle as he downed his vodka and lime. He wasn't a religious man, and wasn't sure if he believed in miracles. He'd read about sufferers who'd prayed to God and been cured. Would they have got better anyway? Was it coincidence if you prayed and improved? And what about those who prayed and died?

But miracles do happen, someone once told him. He was about to go upstairs when his mobile phone rang. Glym's number showed up on the small screen.

Chapter 21

"Can we come in?" Detective Chief Inspector Derek Whitehouse asked, showing his ID card. He was stood at the front door of Harry Richards' house with his sergeant, John Smith. Harry nodded as he opened the door wider. Again, being helpful with the police seemed better than refusing entry. Whitehouse was of the old school – gaberdine raincoat, striped suit. A small black moustache, spectacles and slicked back hair completed his outward appearance. He was straight out of a 1950's advertisement for Brylcreem hair cream. Smith was stocky, about five foot six, and looked capable of playing rugby union for Newcastle Falcons as a prop forward. A mop of red hair suggested that both of his parents, or at least one of them, were Scots.

Harry's mind worked at fifty to the dozen as he took the two police detectives into the lounge. 'What the hell do they want?' he thought to himself. Anthea had come down the stairs and entered the room.

"Hello, is there a problem?" asked Anthea. "Please sit down."

Whitehouse and Smith sat together on the wide settee and Smith took out a small notebook.

"You may know that there was a murder that took place on the outskirts of Middlesbrough recently." Whitehouse opened the discussion. "It was reported in some of the newspapers. We're following up a few lines of enquiry. A mid blue Toyota RAV4 was seen on CCTV camera a short time before police arrived at the scene but we didn't get the complete registration number. The letters NX can be made out, and the digits 59. We've narrowed the owners of such blue RAV4's down to seven addresses on Teesside. You're one of them. Also, two police constables visited you and were asking a few questions about burglaries. They went into your back garden and one of the policemen looked into a bin that looked as though something had been burnt there. Perhaps it was garden rubbish? You were in the house at the time the constable checked the bin, Mr. Richards. In addition, a caravan was found at the scene of the murder, all the ID had been erased. One of the constables reported seeing caravan spares in your garden shed." Harry was stunned. "Can you tell us where you were on the afternoon in question?" He just did not know what to say and blurted out very quickly,

"I can't remember where I was, here and there. I don't keep a diary. And if you're checking on Toyota's, I don't have a RAV4. We have a Suzuki S4, it's there on the drive."

"Do you own a caravan, Mr. Richards?" Whitehouse looked squarely at Harry. He faltered again. Smith scribbled notes.

"No, we sold it last week, actually. A dealer on Teesside gave us a decent price for it."

"The bin in your back garden contained dark grey ash. PC Wayman noticed a belt buckle in the bottom." Whitehouse was focused on Harry's eyes and body language. "How do you account for that?"

"I've no idea! There must be some mistake! I only burn garden rubbish in there." Harry was getting agitated, fingering his wedding ring, his breathing getting laboured.

"I'm afraid I'm going to have to ask you to come down to the station with us, Mr. Richards. It will be easier for both of us. It shouldn't take long. Are you OK with that?" Whitehouse detected some anomalies in Harry's story. He felt a streak of white lightning run down his spine. It was as though he was watching an episode of CSI on television – he was in it but it didn't seem real. Any time now he'd have somebody say it was all a mistake. It would not be Harry, but someone else that was involved. Time slowed down and Harry became nauseous. He remembered the trip to the waste ground and all that happened. Why did he grab the brown package? Blast, he should have damned well just left it!

"Excuse me a minute," Harry said as he rushed to the downstairs cloakroom. Smith was quick to follow him and stood outside while Harry vomited into the bowl. He wretched so much that he thought all of his insides were coming up. He stared down into the white porcelain cone below his face and *'Twyfords'* was looking back at him. What was he to do? Taking deep breaths he could deny it all, but then there was the belt buckle. Cursing under his breath, he should have simply said he'd accidentally burnt it. That was it, the belt must have been in a pile of leaves or branches and it just happened to be in the bin when he lit the contents. Harry's eyes looked back at him as he stared in the mirror after rinsing his face with cold water. His pupils were small and piercing.

"Come on, Mr. Richards. Time to go." Whitehouse was very matter of fact. It was his job. Smith had put his note book away and buttoned his jacket. Anxiously Anthea spoke.

"I'll be here when you have get back. I love you," she whispered as her husband was led outside. She kissed him on the cheek and squeezed his arm reassuringly.

"I won't be long," Harry smiled as he left, trying to comfort his wife. It was a feeble smile that said 'please forgive me.' Harry Richards walked down his drive between Whitehouse and Smith to an unmarked black BMW police car, a police constable in the driving seat. Harry was ushered into the back seat, Smith placing his hand on Harry's head to ease him into the car. Looking over at Anthea who was stood at the front door, Harry wondered when he'd see her again. He realised he didn't have his mobile phone with him, nor his wallet. In fact, apart from a few items such as chewing gum and a handkerchief, he was almost as naked as the day he was born.

Emptiness was what he felt. Total emptiness.

Chapter 22

"Hello, Mrs. Watkinson? This is Carl and Anna Jorgsholm in Kokkedal. We have something to tell you about Juliette." He got straight to the point. Anthea sat bolt upright as she detected the anxiety in his voice. No pleasantries, no 'how are you?'

The time had come on Sunday afternoon when Superintendent Jorgsholm, feeling he'd left it long enough, had no more news on the missing English girl. He used his professional judgement, and his moral standards, to make the decision to phone Juliette's parents. He explained the situation in as much detail as he felt was necessary. He painted a neutral picture. OK, she was missing, but it was only a matter of time before she was found.

"What do you mean 'missing'? How can she have gone missing? You are supposed to be looking after her, she's only a schoolgirl!" Anthea's voice was raised. Carl Jorgsholm tried the reassuring approach.

"We'll be in touch again when we have found her. Really, there's no need to worry. These things happen sometimes and I'm sure there will be some information on her whereabouts tomorrow. We're certain that she's somehow got lost in the area and she'll turn up unharmed."

"Unharmed? What do you mean unharmed?" Jorgsholm quickly realised he'd been careless in using that word. "How can she have disappeared? Oh, my God! You must do something soon! She's our daughter, we love her – she can't have gone missing!"

"Sorry, please try to calm down. It's very unlikely that anything has happened to her. I'm positive that we'll have some good news for you tomorrow. Don't hesitate to contact us if you feel you need to. You have our home number. Good bye." Jorgsholm put the phone down. He knew he'd been cold, very matter-of-fact, but he couldn't 'gift-wrap' the news about their daughter. Don't use one hundred words when fifty would do was his maxim. Anna was sat next to her husband and looked at him as though to say 'that wasn't the most diplomatic phone call in the world'.

Glym had called Carl and told him that the trail on Sven Longe seemed to have gone blank. There were no recent reports on the red Volvo nor on Longe. The girl who'd been seen putting something into the chocolate milk shake in the cafe had been interviewed - her name was Brigid. She had a record for drug selling and admitted to knowing Sven Longe whom she'd met in a night club and they'd dated for a few months. Brigid didn't know much about his background, but she knew he had links to the 'Chinese Liberation Brigade.' On further questioning it turned out that Longe had an arrangement in the cafe with Brigid. Like a tic-tac man at the races, he used hand gestures to indicate to her just when to add a sedative to a drink. That was clearly the case on the Saturday morning in the *Costa* coffee house in Kokkedal and Brigid was currently helping police with their enquiries.

Anna Jorgsholm was compassionate. She could understand what Jules' parents were going through right now. She thought about her own daughters and imagined getting news about either of them if they'd gone missing. News about the possibility of a lost one not being seen again? What on earth had happened? Anthea had told

Peter that she'd had a dubious feeling about Juliette's trip to Denmark. She was not too concerned about the Jorgsholm family, although the school had not answered all of her questions about the stay in Scandinavia. Juliette had only arrived the day before she'd disappeared. How on earth could a young girl go missing on a Saturday from a cafe in a Danish town?

So where had Juliette Watkinson gone? It was the waiting game, again, for everyone. The red Volvo, its registration number and pictures of Sven Longe were being circulated in Denmark. Carl Jorgsholm had connections with Interpol as well as PE and details of Juliette were being shown to other police forces in Europe. Jorgsholm knew there had been other cases where young girls had gone missing and in some instances they had never been seen again, or they'd been found after several years. A recent case in Cleveland, Ohio in the USA had shown that three women had been kept in a house by a school bus driver. He was one of three brothers. One of the women had managed to escape and alert the local police. Some of the details were still muddy but it showed that these things happened. Was Juliette a hostage in a Danish household?

Carl Jorgsholm had experience in human trafficking across northern and central Europe. The key question now was whether Juliette Watkinson had become a victim, after all she fitted the profile – young and beautiful. Jorgsholm did not want to share this with her parents and hoped beyond hope that she would be found – and soon. It was now surely only a matter of time. Other cases were on his workload, two murders in Copenhagen, a missing child in Espergaerde, and some drug dealing around Tivoli Gardens in the capital. Two ships docked in the harbour had been reported as having emigration issues, one recently arrived from Istanbul. All in a day's or week's work for Superintendent Jorgsholm, like the clown balancing the plates on sticks at the circus – none of them must fall, everyone had to be dealt with.

But for him the major concern was about their recently arrived guest from England. She had to be found. She simply had to be somewhere, didn't she? Juliette's parents had some time to wait before they would get any significant news. It was going to be a long time. But they didn't know that at the time. The days and weeks and months were to pass slowly...

And when the news came they weren't going to like it.

Chapter 23

Harry Richards found himself in a room at Cleveland Constabulary headquarters. He'd been asked if he wanted to contact his own solicitor but Harry had refused the offer. Whitehouse took charge of the interview in a small square room, while Sergeant Smith was sitting next to him. A glass of water was placed next to Harry. Whitehouse, who'd taken off his jacket and hung it on a peg in the corner, opened the interview procedure, sitting opposite Harry. Smith switched on the recording machine.

"Well, Mr. Richards. Do you want to give us your version of events? Start by telling us where you were on the afternoon that a mid blue Toyota RAV4 with a number plate beginning NX 59 was seen by CCTV cameras close to open ground where a man was murdered and a caravan had been left."

Harry gulped, his Adam's apple moving visibly. He had little time to decide whether to come clean, or give Whitehouse some concocted story that hopefully would seem plausible. He decided on the former. He was innocent – what was there to lose?

"Look, I want to be honest with you." The DCI smiled enigmatically. "It all started when I saw a 'post it' note on the caravan window when we were up in Berwick." The eyebrows of the Detective Chief Inspector raised towards the ceiling. "It asked if I wanted to sell the caravan. It was from a Chinese guy, he'd left a mobile phone number. I contacted him . . ." Harry continued the story, right up to the point where he'd spoken with Mao Tu Ying about the situation. The whole story had taken Harry about thirty minutes, but with added questioning an hour had soon passed. Whitehouse listened carefully, and Smith was taking notes. Being an experienced detective, Whitehouse prided himself on knowing if someone was telling the truth, it was intuition. Never taking his eyes off Harry, he actually believed his account.

"So why did you grab the brown package from the Mondeo car? You could have left it and driven away with your caravan in tow. Called it off."

"I don't know. I had such a short time to decide. It was just done on the spur of the moment. I'd taken the caravan there and just felt that I ought to have the cash after all the problems with the Chinese guy. If I could turn the clock back I wouldn't have done it, but it happened. I was gutted when I found that the package contained pieces of paper! It was a sort of set up, I suppose, I'm not sure why or how."

"Apart from your wife, did anybody else know you were planning the caravan delivery?" Whitehouse kept eye contact.

"No. At least I don't think so."

"Don't think so? You don't sound sure?" Whitehouse looked straight at Harry.

"Well, I'd been out to the pub for a drink a few nights before I was due to deliver the 'van. I'd met an old army buddy called Dave Wilks. We'd known each other in the services, but had our differences. He seemed to be generous in offering me a drink, said it was his birthday, but that drink turned into three, four, even more. I was drunk and couldn't remember what happened after that."

"Had your differences?" The Detective asked, as though posing a question at the local pub quiz.

Harry focused his mind. He told Whitehouse about the shooting and reloading exercise when he thought Wilks had scuppered his chances of passing the army test, the DCI weighing all these things up in his mind as he listened. He was trying to decide if the enmity between them accounted for what may have happened. How sure was Richards about the drink matter? Was he already tipsy before he went to the pub? Had he some psychological hang-up about Wilks? Or was the reality that Wilks had spiked his drinks? Whitehouse asked about the sale of the Toyota. Harry was open and honest and explained that blood from the murdered man may have been left on the driver's side of the Toyota, on the seat, door or the floor mat. He simply felt intuitively that had to get rid of it. Smith made a note to visit the car dealer and follow up on the RAV4.

Not having enough evidence to keep Harry at the police station, Whitehouse reviewed the evidence and told Harry what he thought about the situation - the circumstantial evidence surrounding the case, and that the investigation would be ongoing. As Whitehouse stood up, Smith concluded the interview and turned the machine off. Harry was told that he could go. An unmarked police car was made available to take Harry home, after all he had no wallet or mobile phone, and it would drop him off at his home in Yarm. Waiting for the car, he was drinking a cup of machine coffee given to him by Whitehouse as a constable walked in and shouted 'Richards'. He arrived back home just before 9.00 pm, and pressed the front door bell. He waited and waited. There was no answer. The house was empty.

Where was Anthea?

Chapter 24

Carl Jorgsholm became increasingly frustrated at progress, or rather lack of it, in finding Juliette. He'd asked Merete to organise a meeting for an update on what was happening. Twenty five police officers assembled in the main conference room, a combination of uniformed and plain clothes personnel. Standing in front of a flip chart Jorgsholm began.

"Let us summarise where we are in the search for Juliette Watkinson." He had done many similar presentations before, and everyone listened intently. He went over the details. The times, CCTV evidence, Sven Longe's background, input from the girl in the cafe. There were no reports of sightings at docks or airports. The red Volvo had not been seen. Nor had Juliette.

Clearly Longe had done this before. Brigid had confessed to having acted on his requests on over ten occasions. He had given her sachets of a sedative to use in drinks when he indicated by hand signs. She did not know exactly what Longe got up to with his victims. He had told her that they were taken to work in 'special places' that she did not need to know about and she was told to keep her mouth shut or else. Longe kept Brigid in smart clothes and jewellery, as well as good food and fine wine. She did far better than her paltry pay at the coffee shop would allow and she knew she was onto a good thing. Or so she thought, until she had been found out. The police had asked Brigid to reveal the whereabouts of Longe but she claimed that she didn't know where he lived. Picking her up at her place, they'd gone to a nightclub or restaurant, staying over at a friends' house or in a seedy hotel afterwards. Their relationship was off and on, but Longe had a strong hold over her, and, after all, she was neatly dressed and well fed.

The police had asked Brigid for Longe's mobile phone number. She stated that he had two phones, but she only ever had one number for him so she gave it to them. Glym told the meeting that she had tried the mobile number provided by Brigid but it had gone into voice mail. Glym had put a search on the number and was waiting for O2 to get back. She was also making enquiries on the 'Chinese Liberation Brigade' who allegedly had an office in Copenhagen and two detectives were on the case.

"We must get some answers!" Jorgsholm was still on his feet. He raised his voice. "I'm hearing comments on what is going on, but I'm not getting any positive feedback! Get onto the phone company again and tell them it's urgent! Where are the two detectives? How long does it take to check an office address in Copenhagen?" The veins on the neck of Carl Jorgsholm were standing out like strands of knotted cord. "And what about the car? Where is that? And who is the registered keeper? I want details - now!"

The meeting watched replayed CCTV taken from Saturday morning. Longe and Juliette were seen walking along like a married couple. Close, but not too close. It was difficult to tell if she was walking unsteadily. Her shoes may have been too tight, or a heel may have been loose? There was a hint of sway, but it was fair to assume that Brigid's handiwork was taking effect. The red car appeared behind them. It slowed down and then stopped a few metres in front. Longe opened the rear nearside door. He gave Juliette a gentle push onto the back seat. It took only a few seconds for the two passengers to get into the car before it drove away.

"Wait, hold the frame there!" Jorgsholm had spotted something. The CCTV images were replayed. As the car headed northwards out of Kokkedal a small piece of paper appeared to drop out of the rear window and float into the hedge on the roadside. "See that? Something came out of the window. Paper! Was it a piece of paper? I want that piece of paper found!"

As the meeting was coming to an end, Merete Glym took a phone call from the Danish licensing authority. The Volvo was registered in the name of Mao Tu Ying.

O2 had also replied. The mobile phone had been bought with cash in a mobile phone outlet in Copenhagen. It was a 'top up and go'.

Chapter 25

Fumbling in his left trouser pocket Harry didn't think he had a front door key with him. He felt some loose change in his pocket, and then a key! He and Anthea usually carried an extra key, it was an old habit of theirs, and Harry breathed a sigh of relief as he inserted it into the door lock and it clicked open. Going into the dimness of the entrance hall he switched on the light and then went into the kitchen. Twin neon lights flickered into life. There was a note from Anthea on the worktop. Unfolding it, he read the message.

'Harry, I've gone to stay with Jackie. I wasn't sure how long you'd be and I didn't want to be alone. You've got her number so call me if you need to. She has a spare room and we can catch up on business issues at the beauty parlour. I'll go straight to the premises tomorrow. Love and kisses, A.' Wondering if he should call her he decided not to – he wanted some time alone to think. Opening the fridge door he took out a can of beer, went into the lounge, and slumped down on the settee. His head was all over the place. Laying back on the sofa and closing his eyes, he took a mouthful of the cold amber liquid – it tasted good.

Harry was slowly recovering from the interrogation at the police station. Whitehouse had asked searching questions that Harry felt he'd handled well since he'd been totally open with the Detective Chief Inspector. He wasn't certain whether the visit of the two constables to search the back garden was part of checking up on him? Perhaps they'd done the same with the six other Toyota owners with similar number plates? Harry could ask the neighbours if they'd had any visits, but that would possibly require some explanation and raise queries? No, he'd leave it. Some of the other people living in the road would probably have seen him leaving earlier – he didn't want to have to answer any of their questions. Despite being a pleasant neighbourhood, quite a few of the people living in the same road were inquisitive by nature.

He thought about Hokun and Mao. By now, Mao will have told his brother about the discussion between him and Harry. Did Hokun believe what Harry told Mao? He'd have to. The police still had the caravan impounded, Harry didn't get his cash, and a man had been murdered. Whitehouse told Harry that the victim was called Mick Barrett, an ex-con from Darlington. Barrett had done time for petty theft and drugs, and apparently had met Hokun Tu Ying in 'The Flamingo' night club in Middlesbrough a few years back. Whitehouse had asked Harry if he knew Barrett. 'Absolutely not', Harry had implicitly told him.

Harry reflected again on how he'd got into all of this. From the note on the caravan window through to the tragedy on the waste ground. But there was more to all this... the red boat at Seahouses with privacy windows, Hokun buying and selling caravans, his monthly visits to Bamburgh Castle Inn. Harry felt he ought to be doing more. He'd been back to look for Hokun and met his brother instead. He had an email address and mobile number for Hokun, and vice versa. Harry was a little surprised that he hadn't been contacted by the Chinaman again. He wondered if Hokun knew where Harry lived? He hoped not! Was Hokun playing some sort of game? Biding his time . . .

Harry hadn't sold any second hand cars for a while and Anthea was clearly the breadwinner. She'd be talking to Jackie right now. Talking over the beauty business, whether to promote nails or facials, or to offer something more 'upmarket.' Did they need more staff, or were Jane and Rebecca sufficient for now? There'd also be the 'girlie' chat about shoes and clothes and TV soaps. In fact, Harry thought that Anthea would be getting some peace, mainly because she'd be able to relax a little. No hassle from her husband. Nothing to worry about just now. Harry recalled the conversation between him and Jackie at the dinner dance. Was Joan Bobbins a help or a hindrance to the business? 'Big mouth but a big purse.' Harry smiled inwardly. He liked that . . .'big mouth – big purse.' A key issue was whether the income from the business was growing or declining? Anthea was an astute person, and she'd kept records of monthly income year by year. The problem with Joan Bobbins was that her departure for another beauty treatment centre would leave a hole in the finances.

Jackie didn't tell her manager that she'd mentioned Bobbins to Harry at the dinner dance. She felt it wasn't important but if it came out in conversation, she'd simply say that they were just chatting. There was nothing to hide. What Jackie did tell Anthea was that Joan Bobbins had mentioned her 'boyfriend' yet again. Adam Tennant seemed the 'current love of her life'. She'd even taken a small photo out of her purse and showed it around. Bobbins had accidentally left the photo in the beauty parlour when her treatment was finished and Jackie had picked it up. She went to get it from her handbag and showed it to Anthea.

"What do you think of him, then?" Anthea looked at the photo. She wasn't totally sure, but she thought she may have seen that face somewhere before.

There was a familiar look about the man, though. No, perhaps not?

Chapter 26

The trail on Juliette Watkinson had gone cold. In fact, it was arctic . There were no leads at all, and the red Volvo had seemed to have vanished. There were no sightings of Juliette anywhere, and despite TV and newspaper reports, nobody had been able to help. The Copenhagen address of the Chinese Liberation Brigade was deserted, the tiny office in a back street was empty. Having been searched by the two detectives who had been there – they had found nothing of value in solving this case. Mao Tu Ying as the owner of the car, was no longer at the address he'd provided when he purchased the vehicle. The piece of paper that was seen falling from the rear passenger window of the Volvo on the CCTV might never be found but one police officer was still on the case. Jorgsholm believed in luck. Right now he didn't have any at all but he kept wishing for a four leaf clover, or a rabbit's foot . . . or anything

With other police cases in Denmark during his career, Carl Jorgsholm had been fortunate. Information from members of the public, comments from those who'd seen a television report, a forensic find such as a strand of hair, a stain on a discarded piece of clothing . . . These things had helped the Superintendent to solve difficult crimes – and get him promotion. But now there was nothing. Jorgsholm thought again about his personal involvement, and somehow that made it worse. From agreeing to host their English guest, collecting her at the airport, making her feel at home right through to her disappearance on that Saturday morning, he wondered what his colleagues thought? He didn't want to think about that part of it, not being certain if the odd strange glance he got was real or imaginary. Carl Jorgsholm needed a break in this case, just someone or something to come to the fore. A clue, however small – anything to give him a lead.

He spent the next few hours reviewing previous cases that had involved Sven Longe. Having been implicated in a number of criminal acts, he had begun as a petty thief after leaving school and graduated to drug dealing, car stealing, money laundering and other crimes. Jorgsholm had known him for a few years and Longe had only been given short prison sentences, behaving himself perfectly on the inside and that had resulted in early release. He'd never really done anything serious that Jorgsholm could nail him with for a long sentence. Yet, there he had been, in the coffee shop, seen leaving with Juliette Watkinson, and why was he a member of the C.L.B? The alleged owner of the Volvo was Chinese, but was that the only link?

Why had Longe picked Juliette up? Surely he must have had a plan. Was it kidnap? Was he going to ask her parents for a ransom? Right now Longe must be holding Juliette somewhere in Denmark. They could not have left the country; Jorgsholm refused to believe that. The airports and docks were still under surveillance and there were no reports of anyone matching their description having left the country.

Jorgsholm went onto his computer and began checking police files. He thought he'd remembered most of the cases involving Longe. But he had forgotten one important one. Longe had a visit to China in his personal file. He'd been there two years previously, but only for one week. With friends in England, Longe and Mao Tu

Ying may have known each other. Longe had been associated with a gang in Sweden which had abducted four young girls from Malmo some years ago. They were working for a company which was making flat pack furniture. It was a government scheme that gave young people an opportunity to learn work and business skills. Provided with board and lodging in a small hotel for a period of six months, the girls aged 17 to 21 had not come back from a day working at the factory. The mini-bus company which had the transport contract had denied sending a white Ford Transit to collect them at 5.00 pm on the day in question. When the official pick-up bus arrived at 5.15 pm, the driver had been told by another employee that they'd already gone. The Transit had been fitted with false number plates and one eye witness who had seen the Transit arrive reported noticing that it had a rusty roof rack with some blue rope tied to it.

Jorgsholm continued trawling through police files. The Ford Transit had never been found. The four girls had not been seen again, and even after some years there was no news of these young, innocent females. Was the disappearance of Juliette somehow connected? The police didn't have enough to put Longe away for the Malmo case. There was only circumstantial evidence. But there might be a connection, thought Carl Jorgsholm. Amongst the personal data stored on Sven Longe, however, there was no mention of his amateur dramatics experience. Longe had been involved in a number of stage productions while still at college and he was accomplished at make up and costume. In fact, Longe could change his appearance with little effort. Little did Superintendent Jorgsholm realise just how much that was going to be a factor in trying to find Longe. An average looking young man one day.

An elderly grey-haired gent with a walking stick the next.

Chapter 27

Anthea phoned Harry just after 8.00 am the next morning from Jackie's house. She'd had a restless night, believing that Harry would have phoned her if he was home. But she knew him well, and if he had been released may have wanted time alone. Anthea wanted to talk to her husband as soon as possible, find out what the police had asked him, was he under suspicion? Harry was a strong character in some ways, but with what might be called a 'soft underbelly.' Jackie had made coffee, but Anthea had refused anything to eat – she wasn't hungry, no growling stomach sounds telling her she wanted food.

"Hi, Hon." She rarely called him that – only when she was feeling concerned about something. "How are you? What happened at the station? What time did you get home?"

"Whoa, hang on!" Harry put a brake on her enthusiasm for answers. "It was all right down at the nick. Whitehouse was OK. I got a lift home in a cop car. I was totally honest with them. He didn't make it clear whether the back garden visit from the two coppers recently was a ruse, but I told him I'd burnt some clothes after what had happened. I decided I needed to some time on my own to think. Sorry I didn't phone you, but I just felt that we both needed some space. Hope you're all right?"

"Yes, fine. Jackie's been a big help. We had a girlie chat last night, caught up on all sorts of things. I didn't off-load too much about you!"

Continuing their conversation for another five minutes, Anthea felt more relaxed about the situation, and ended the call knowing she had to get to work. Saying she loved him, she did not want to tell Harry about the photo of Adam Tennant that Jackie had shown her. She'd tell him later. The name Adam Tennant didn't ring a bell with Anthea, however, the man with a moustache and nice eyes was someone she'd seen before, not being able to not place when or where.

Anthea bade her farewell to Jackie, thanked her, and drove to Marton to open 'Angel Face'. Jackie would follow shortly, and Jane and Rebecca would be in just before 9.00 am. Seven clients were in the appointment book for the day, but no Joan Bobbins. Sometimes one or two regulars would pop their head around the door to ask Anthea if they could be fitted in. Two of the seven scheduled for treatment were new, so Anthea would use her sales and people skills to create a good impression. Business was good, and the income was up almost twenty percent on the same period last year.

As Anthea and her colleagues got on with beauty matters, Harry showered and got dressed and put on blue jeans with a brown leather belt, a T-shirt and soft rope soled shoes. He went into the back bedroom cum study and switched on his laptop. There were 27 emails in his in-box. He recognised most addresses, and he had a handful of junk emails. He scrolled down and picked those he wanted to open first. Several previous customers who had bought a car off him had been in touch, one complaining that the car Harry had sold him was a lemon. Two others wanted Harry to source a vehicle for them. For a few seconds, Harry wondered where his Toyota RAV4 was? He wanted to convince himself it was being driven by someone who appreciated the vehicle. He hoped any blood stains on the car would have disappeared by now, maybe cleaned off if the garage had done its normal internal valeting. Swallowing hard, he didn't want to believe that the police were examining it. Why should they? He'd told them the truth, hadn't he?

He looked at another message half way down the screen. It was from Hokey! The subject box said 'Caravan?' Harry opened it and read it slowly, prepared for the worst news.

'I still have no caravan from you. I lose 14 grand. My brother tell me you no get money. Where it go? I give man package for you. We agreed. Man murdered. He my friend. You must get me another caravan. I need it by next week. You don't want your wife to get hurt do you? I will send you email with details. HTL.'

Harry gasped. *'You don't want your wife to get hurt do you?'* He didn't like the sound of that. Assuming that the matter was virtually closed, Harry really wondered if Mao had given his brother a fair interpretation of the circumstances at the waste ground after they'd met in Seahouses? Had Mao added his own adjectives to put Harry in a bad light? Whatever the situation was, Harry was now under pressure to get another caravan, and Hokey would email him soon.

Harry decided not to share this with Anthea. How could he? She had been worried enough about what had happened. And Hokey was threatening him, or at least his wife! *'What do I do next?' Harry mused. Should I arm myself with a knife, perhaps? Carry a heavy walking stick? At least I'd have a weapon to use if I was ever attacked!'* Scanning the remaining emails - holiday offers, supermarket deals, insurance policies - Harry closed down his computer. Blast! Hokey was after him.

He was a hunted man. Anthea was also on the list.

Chapter 28

One of the Danish policemen that had searched the area where Juliette was forced into the car had eventually found the piece of paper that had been thrown from the red Volvo. It was crumpled in a hedge back, damp and barely legible. It was eventually handed in to Jorgsholm. The squiggly information, written in thick red ink that looked like lipstick, said 'Help me'. Nothing more than that. It was only two words, but it said everything. An analysis of the red scrawl proved it was *Avon Carnation Red* lipstick, Juliette's favourite.

"This girl is in serious trouble," Jorgsholm knew that he was stating the obvious. It might have occurred to Juliette that being escorted along a road and then into a car did not seem right, but she was feeling groggy from the drugged chocolate milkshake. She must have realised that she was being forced into the back of the car, and an inner sense had shouted out to her to ask for help.

The question was 'where had Juliette been taken?' Jorgsholm continued going through previous case files but it seemed he had reached a stone wall – ten feet high and six feet thick. Half an hour later Jorgsholm came across some notes made by another detective. A case that went back three years involving an abducted girl who was found in a cellar in a house in Esbjerg on the west coast of Denmark. The kidnapper was in prison in Copenhagen and serving an eight year sentence. His name was Michael Brunander. The Superintendent wondered if there was any connection between Longe and Brunander? It was a long shot, but he was able to get

113

into the computerised files on both of them and soon Jorgsholm had found that the two in question were at the same college and studied Social History together. They belonged to an underground group called Frihed, the Danish word for 'freedom'.

Jorgsholm got permission from his superior to visit Brunander in prison to ask questions about Frihed and the objectives of the group. During the interview, accompanied by Glym, Jorgsholm suggested to Brunander that being helpful could result in a reduction in his sentence. Needless to say, Brunander was suspicious but finally agreed to help.

"Tell me what you know about Frihed?", Jorgsholm looked at Brunander.

"The ringleader of Frihed was Wang Xian. He was a student from Beijing and he set up the group by secretly recruiting people who had a corrupt sense of justice – of liberation and freedom. It was a sinister arrangement. They had to take an oath, and then a rat was tattooed on the right shoulder blade, the rat being one of the animals in the Chinese horoscope. Once you joined you were, well, sort of safe and protected. Some students who caused problems were tortured – just little things. A tooth pulled out, a finger broken, that sort of thing. They were threatened with further injury if they went to the police or the college authorities."

"What became of Wang Xian?" Jorgsholm took a sip of water from a tall glass on the desk.

"I don't know. He may have gone back to China, but I'm not sure." Jorgsholm wasn't sure if he believed him.

"Sven Longe was a student in your class, wasn't he?" Jorgsholm stared at Brunander as Glym left the interview room to take a phone call on her mobile.

"Yes, and he joined Frihed. He became a key member. He was virtually Wang Xian's deputy."

"Were you and Longe in touch often?" the questions persisted.

"No, we lost touch after we left college. I've been in here for three years and I've no idea where he is." Before he wound up the interview, Jorgsholm asked Brunander to expose his shoulders. A red rat tattoo was looking at him.

Jorgsholm decided he needed to find out if Wang Xian had left the country. Was there any way of determining whether Brunander was really telling the truth? The questioning came to an end. As Jorgsholm pondered his next lines of enquiry Merete Glym came back into the room.

"Sir, I need to talk to you." Jorgsholm nodded to the security guard who had brought Brunander into the room, and he escorted the prisoner back to his cell. As Brunander was leaving he shouted at Jorgsholm 'what about my sentence?' The Superintendent remained silent. Glym leaned over her boss and spoke to Jorgsholm in a quiet voice.

"A white Ford Transit van with flat tyres has been found in a disused warehouse on the outskirts of Malmo. It was a routine inspection by the health and safety authorities of a building with a dangerous roof. The van has a rusty roof rack." Jorgsholm knew immediately what the implications of this information meant.

What they didn't know, right there and then, was that a piece of blue rope was still tied around the roof rack. Internal inspection was to reveal even more. A lot more.

Chapter 29

Harry Richards was about to put the kettle on when the front door bell rang. Opening the door he was greeted, if that was the way to put it, by DCI Whitehouse and two uniformed officers. Harry was surprised. Whitehouse asked if he and his colleagues could step inside. One of the constables closed the door behind him.

"Mr. Richards, I'm arresting you on suspicion of the murder of Mick Barrett. You do not have to say anything, but anything you do say will be taken down and used in evidence." Harry was staggered, having already helped the police with their enquiries, he was a free man, wasn't he? "You'd better get some things together – we're going down to the station. We'll give you five minutes. You can contact your wife, but we need to be with you when you do." Harry turned ashen as he could feel the blood drain from his face and a million butterflies were flying in his stomach. Switching the kettle off, he went over to the telephone and called Anthea at the beauty salon. He kept the conversation short but gave her the facts - and told her not to worry.

"Listen, baby, the police are here at the house. They want me to go to the station with them. I'm under arrest. I'm leaving here now and being driven to the police station. Don't worry."

Don't worry, those famous words that were supposed to make everything all right.

Harry was just about to tell her to stay at 'Angel Face' when Anthea put the phone down. He went upstairs accompanied by one of the policemen and grabbed a few bits and pieces including his wallet, a comb and his mobile phone. Picking up the spare set of front door keys and a casual leather jacket Harry was on his way.

Ushered into the back of a police van, he sat alone in a small compartment the size of a portable toilet. This was a nightmare. He'd wake up soon, he convinced himself. It was a short journey, via the A66 past the Upper Teesdale junction and on into Middlesbrough. When they arrived at the police station Harry was taken straight to a cell after the Custody Sergeant had read him his rights. Although he was offered the opportunity to speak with his solicitor, Harry declined for the moment. Anthea came into the station after negotiating heavier than normal Teesside traffic and demanded to see Harry. She could not continue at the salon knowing that her husband had been arrested.

"Sorry, madam, that is impossible. He's been put away," said a chubby desk sergeant with a large moustache who could have modelled Michelin tyres. "No point in staying."

"I must see him! He's innocent! Has he spoken with our solicitor?" Anthea had raised her voice. A uniformed constable, after a nod to the desk sergeant, came across and placated her. She was distraught and looked around her as if she was asking for help from somewhere? The officer stood next to her and asked if she wanted a mug of tea. 'He has a kind face,' she thought, 'unusual for a copper.' She nodded.

"Sit down here. I'll be back shortly. White and sugar?" 'No sugar' Anthea indicated by mouthing the words and shaking her head. She began to calm down, but her pulse rate was high having driven very quickly from Marton and then rushing into the police station,

117

clearly concerned about Harry. The constable was back in minutes with a small steaming mug of tea.

"You won't be able to see him, I'm afraid," said the young policeman handing her the mug. Saying nothing, she stared at the opposite wall, therapeutically fingering the rim in circles as if to subconsciously clean it. Anthea was silent for a few moments, the events of the past couple of weeks grinding through her head. How on earth had Harry got to where he was now? From a note on the caravan window to this! Anthea knew he was innocent, and so did Harry. He never murdered Mick Barrett. Yet, here he was, in a cell at Cleveland Police HQ. There was plenty of room for Harry in this recently opened building – he was in one of 50 cells that could house criminals from all over Teesside and beyond. Anthea finished her tea, stood up and, and went over to the desk and spoke to the chubby sergeant on duty.

"What happens next?"

"He'll appear at the Magistrate's Court tomorrow. We'll have to see what the 'beak' decides. The case, at Teesside Crown Court, could be heard fairly quickly but it depends. We've got your details so we'll let you know of any developments." DCI Whitehouse was nowhere to be seen, nor was Detective Sergeant Smith. Anthea felt utterly alone.

Looking at the officer, she thought about a reply, but saved her breath. What more was there to do or say? Pushing her handbag firmly onto her shoulder she walked slowly out of the building and back to her car. Sitting in the driving seat she let out a long sigh and burst into tears. She was drained, utterly drained, as if she had been wrung out like a chamois wash leather by an angry window cleaner.

Chapter 30

The Magistrates Court in Victoria Square was busy, but not sardine-packed. Two petty thieving cases were heard, a case regarding the growing of cannabis in a sunroom, three hit and run incidents, and the case regarding Harry Richards. Harry appeared first after the lunch break at precisely 2.00pm. Anthea was sitting with other members of the general public in the tiered gallery. The presiding magistrate, Mr. Anthony Gourmand, listened to the case at this preliminary hearing against the defendant, Mr. Harold Richards of Yarm, Cleveland. Harry sat hand-cuffed between two burly G4S guards. There seemed to be a mountain of evidence against him. Whitehouse had prepared a statement that Gourmand had already read regarding the discovery of the dead body of Mick Bassett in the Ford Mondeo on the waste ground in Middlesbrough. It included the signed 'confession' made by Harry and his claim of innocence. However, Whitehouse firmly believed he had his man after further enquiries had pointed to Harry as the murderer. He was convinced that Harry had lied about finding Bassett dead in the car and in fact had murdered him, possibly after a struggle, then taken the cash, and made up the story about finding pieces of paper in the brown package. Harry's bank account did not show a deposit having been made. The police were still searching for the murder weapon, but Whitehouse was convinced it was only a matter of time.

Mr. Anthony Gourmand looked over his small, rimless spectacles and spoke "This is an involved case and the evidence against Harold Richards is strong. He will appear before Teesside Crown Court at a date to be decided. Take him away." Harry was led out of the courtroom, glancing at Anthea as he was closely guarded by the G4S heavyweights. Harry tried to glance around again before disappearing down the steps but he was taken away so quickly that it was impossible. Anthea sat there for a few moments, letting it sink in. It was almost half past two and she didn't feel like going back to the business in Marton. As she was about to get up she heard a man ask, "Are you Harry's wife?" She was taken by surprise, but replied positively. The man was tall and slim with a moustache, well dressed, and wore a Yorkshire County Cricket Club tie. He looked slightly familiar. Speaking clearly with a smile, but without a particularly strong accent, he said,

"My name is David Cresswell. I know Harry – we drink at 'The Bluebell'. Listen, there's a cafe not far from here, do you have time for a coffee? There's some information I have that you may find useful."

Anthea thought for a few seconds. Who was this stranger asking her to have coffee with him? He was very slim, she'd seen more meat on a jockey's whip. But was he a conman? She'd read or heard somewhere that they're often well presented – all part of the confidence trickster's persona – the smile, the pleasant manner, a non-threatening attitude. But on the other hand, what did she have to lose? The area was quite busy, the cafe would have people in it. It wasn't as though he wanted to drive her to a secluded spot in the middle of the North Yorkshire moors.

"Er, yes, that would be good, but I don't have long," she lied; she had all day. Anthea would limit the meeting to twenty minutes, then make some excuse to leave if she needed to do that. Cresswell walked alongside Anthea and they made small talk about the weather as they left the building in Russell Street and headed for a coffee shop. Once inside Anthea chose a table near the back of the cafe where it was quieter - it would be more discrete. It was a small place, but neatly decorated. Blue and white cotton tablecloths covered square tables. Cresswell pulled a chair out for her and Anthea sat down. Cresswell asked what she wanted, and then ordered for both of them when the waitress came over. They decided to leave the scones, cheese or sultana, and other pastries, éclairs, doughnuts, that were on offer.

While they waited for the coffee to be served, Cresswell began the conversation. "I've known your husband for about three years. We met in 'The Bluebell' and got chatting about football. We've been to a few 'Boro home games with some of the other lads. I was in 'The Bluebell' on the night Harry came in for a drink and he ended up getting drunk."

"He wasn't a heavy drinker," Anthea interrupted. "I remember him being ill the next day and it wasn't like him at all. It wasn't as though he was celebrating anything – at least that I know of?"

A waitress brought two cups of cafe latte to their table. Cresswell continued in a low voice, "I noticed a guy being particularly friendly towards Harry, buying him drinks and just fussing around him. It seemed strange, almost as if he might be a homosexual? I'm sure he wasn't, and I'm not suggesting Harry is." He added the last sentence quickly.

"So what are you getting at?"

"I saw this guy put something in a few drinks that he bought for your husband. He'd go to the bar, place the order and then pop something into the glass before taking the drinks over to where a few people were sitting. I wasn't sure whether to say anything, or leave it. The guy had a couple of big mates with him, one was called Don Wilson, and I didn't want to end up in the Tees with a pair of concrete boots so I decided to leave it. *Wilson was one sandwich short of a picnic, strong as a bull, and nobody messed with him. He'd been inside for GBH and his star sign was Scorpio.*

I was in court this afternoon because a friend of mine is up for a minor offence. Then I saw about Harry. As I looked around the courtroom I spotted you and from the way you behaved I assumed you were his wife."

"Would you be willing to testify in a court of law – tell them what you've told me?"

"There's more," replied Cresswell, not answering her question directly. "I heard Harry telling this guy about some arrangement he had with a Chinese bloke. He mentioned delivering a caravan in exchange for a bundle of cash. It seemed that his tongue was looser than it should have been, but he couldn't seem to help himself. Whatever that guy was putting in his drinks made Harry more talkative."

"Harry told me he couldn't recall much about the evening, except that an old army pal, Dave Wilks, was in the pub and was in a generous mood. It must have been Wilks who was spiking his drinks," replied Anthea.

"I'm not sure of his name, but I'd recognise him again," Cresswell offered.

David Cresswell knew Dave Wilks well only too well. He had been double-crossed by Wilks two years before and this was an opportunity for revenge. Cresswell was once going to kill Wilks but decided against it at the last minute.

"Would you give me your address?" Anthea asked him. "I'd like to let our solicitor know what you've told me, if you're OK with that?"

"Anything to help," replied Cresswell as he reached into the top pocket of his jacket and brought out a business card and handed the card to Anthea. She looked at it and noticed that a P.O. box address, email and mobile phone number was on it. He also gave her an extra card. They stood up together and Cresswell offered to pay for the coffee. Thanking him as they left the cafe, they went their separate ways, Anthea going to collect her car and driving home. On the way back she thought over the conversation with David Cresswell. He seemed a nice guy and obviously knew Harry. When she eventually got into the house the first thing she did was to make a phone call. Putting her handbag down, Anthea knew the number off by heart, she dialled.

"Hello, Lorimer, Blevins and Skerrit, solicitors. Dawn speaking, how can we help you?"

Chapter 31

The Ford Transit van had been towed on a low loader trailer to a police station in Kokkedal for examination. Forensic team members had been asked to go over the van with meticulous care. As far as Jorgsholm knew, this was the vehicle that matched the description of the one that had picked up the four girls working in Malmo. There were no number plates fitted but in any case they were false, taken from another van that had been scrapped a year earlier.

The inside of the Transit van was searched thoroughly. Two of the police forces' best forensic staff were on the job, their white suits and face masks hiding an ability gained over fifteen years of similar work. They'd both been involved in the infamous case of a female German student who was raped and murdered in Odense, a town in eastern Denmark. One fibre from a jacket and two hairs belonging to the killer were found on her body. A DNA sample from saliva following a bite to her neck, alongside the fibre and hairs, enabled Jorgsholm to eventually track down the killer. The evidence was conclusive and he was serving life.

The forensic officers spent over six hours going through the interior of the white van. Innumerable polythene bags were used into which they placed tiny fragments, fibres, hairs, and other minute items. Each bag was labelled with a code and position in the van from which the sample was taken. Once they had finished, the van was impounded and placed into a secure compound at the back of the police yard. The rusty roof rack, minus the blue rope, seemed to be mocking the police, its edge looking like a wide, grinning mouth. The blue rope was also bagged. It would prove to be a key aspect of the investigation.

Carl & Anna Jorgsholm had taken a telephone call from Juliette's parents. They were anxious to travel to Denmark to see where their daughter had disappeared and to get the latest news. The Jorgsholm's had to agree to meet with them. Carl Jorgsholm intended to treat their visit more from his perspective as a police Superintendent than as the Danish family who were hosts to a schoolgirl from England. Anthea and Peter Watkinson planned to arrive at Copenhagen airport on the following day. The aircraft landed at 12.10 pm and Carl Jorgsholm had offered to collect them. This was déjà-vu for him. It didn't seem that long since he picked up Juliette and taken to his home. How was he to position the current police enquiry? What positive news was he to offer? Could he tell them a few little white lies to placate them? No! Absolutely not! They would get the truth.

Anthea and Peter arrived on schedule. Carl was there with a small, discrete board to collect them, Merete Glym with him. This endorsed the fact that they were there on police business. As Juliette's parents came through the arrivals hall, they spotted their surname on the board held high by Carl Jorgsholm. They approached the two Danish police officers.

"Hello, we're Juliette's parents," Anthea spoke first. They looked drained. Weeks and weeks of waiting for some news of their missing daughter had taken its toll. Carl Jorgsholm shook their hands, as if to say 'welcome, but we haven't any news for you' – his expression almost blank.

"Hello, I'm Carl Jorsgholm and this is my colleague, Detective Sergeant Merete Glym. We'll go to the station and take you through what we have found so far. You're in time for lunch!" The last sentence almost took the edge off the seriousness of the situation, but Anthea was still very concerned. She had lost her appetite. In fact, she had lost three kilogrammes in weight since Juliette had disappeared. The not knowing, the daily anguish of wondering where her daughter had gone. It had taken it out of her and if it hadn't been for her own make-up skills she would have looked much worse.

Reflecting on how this had all happened, the school suggesting the visit, and her husband Peter agreeing to fund the whole affair had served to make Anthea feel uncomfortable. She had never been absolutely sure about some of the facts and details of the trip, but now, here she was, in front of the man who, alongside his wife, was willing to give Juliette an opportunity to sample Danish life and schooling. The whole experience was meant to be beneficial. It was nothing new, mature schoolchildren had visited families abroad for decades. Anthea couldn't blame the Jorgsholm family if facts were to be believed.

The journey to the police station took twenty minutes during which time very little was said. The odd comment about the greenness of the countryside and pleasant weather conditions were a shadow of what they all really felt. Looking out of the car windows, Anthea kept wondering why she hadn't seen any pigs in a country known for its bacon and pork.

"Follow me." Jorgsholm led the way and Glym followed behind. The four of them walked into the police station, stopped, and then Glym led them to a meeting room. A tray of drinks were on the central table, whilst a buffet table was laid opposite. Salad, ham, cheese, pickled herrings, and crisp-bread were laid out. Carl Jorgsholm waved for them to take a seat. The visiting couple sat down, almost exhausted. Glym offered them a drink. Both chose orange juice. Jorgsholm and Glym had water, and then Anthea and Peter were asked to help themselves to the buffet. Peter filled the plate with a bit of everything, and especially pickled herrings. He'd tried those once before at a conference in Billingham when ICI had entertained Scandinavian visitors – delicious! Anthea picked at one piece of ham, a sliver of Edam, and three water biscuits. Not many calories there, but she wasn't really hungry. Eating had become a habit, not a necessity.

While they ate, Jorgsholm took charge. He started to tell Juliette's parents about her arrival, getting settled into her bedroom, and then the Saturday morning bus trip into Kokkedal with his daughters. He ran through the details of what the CCTV cameras had shown, as well as what Agnatha and Louisa had said and gave them sufficient information for them both to get a very good idea of what had happened to their daughter. The follow-up action plan was also covered.

"So where do you think she is now?" Peter asked, eyeing Jorgsholm.

"That's impossible to say," replied the Superintendent. "We're going to begin further searching in a couple of specific areas of Denmark, but we still have so little to go on. We want to find the red Volvo car that was seen picking her up."

"What about the man who was in the cafe when she disappeared?" Anthea joined in the questioning.

"No sign of him, either. We know who he is and what he looks like, but there have not been any reported sightings of him." Jorgsholm looked at both Anthea and Peter with eyes that suggested he was both sorry and also doing his best. An uneasy silence followed.

"It's not good enough! You can do more, you must do more! Our poor daughter is out there – she's been taken from us!" Anthea was on her feet, her voice raised and her lunch barely touched. She began to sob, and Peter held her. She shrugged off his attentions, walked over to a window and looked out. The sky was cloudless. Somewhere out there their precious daughter was being kept against her will. The other three around the table avoided eye contact. Anthea stood for a while before sitting down again, picking at her ham and eating a little, breaking a water biscuit in half and taking a nibble. Jorgsholm felt the atmosphere change slightly and he stood up.

"If you want to, we can take you to the cafe and the places where Juliette was last seen. If it will help you?"

"No, there's no point in that. I've been thinking about it, I did feel I'd like to see the exact spot where she disappeared. But, a cafe is a cafe, and a road is a road. I can't see it will do any good. It's not as though she's dead." Anthea suddenly stopped herself . . . she's used a word that she didn't want to say. Dead. No, they both had to believe that she was alive! Still breathing, talking, walking, eating, drinking, her blonde hair blowing in the breeze somewhere. They continued chatting for a little longer, and then Carl Jorgsholm offered to take the Watkinsons to his home to meet his wife, Anna. Anthea thought for a second or two and then said she'd like that. Leaving the meeting room with bits of food left uneaten on plates, they arrived in the Kokkedal suburb and parked on the drive. Anna Jorgsholm came out to meet them and hugged Anthea like a long lost friend. They both shed a few tears before walking into the house, Anthea asking if she could see Juliette's bedroom. Anna led the way upstairs.

A few hundred kilometres away, Sven Longe had shaved his head and was wearing a wig. A newly grown small neat beard and pair of plain spectacles gave him an academic look, appearing nothing like the man on CCTV once seen in a cafe in Kokkedal on a Saturday morning. Nothing at all.

He had put his amateur dramatic skills to good effect, and they were to prove useful. He smiled at himself in the mirror – 'hello, Professor, how are we today?'

Chapter 32

Joan Bobbins took pleasure in telling the staff at 'Angel Face' that she was going on a cruise with her new boyfriend, Adam Tennant. She had made all the arrangements, booked the rail travel to Southampton, an outside berth on the MSC Costa Emerald, and over seven excursions. It was a Western Mediterranean cruise would be lasting just over a fortnight and they were leaving in ten days time. Although Tennant had offered to pay his share of the costs, Joan Bobbins had insisted that she would cover all expenses. She'd also been dating him for a while, but he always insisted on going out of the Teesside area. Even when they went to do some shopping as Bobbins had suggested. Tennant wasn't used to someone else buying his clothes, but he went along with Bobbins' suggestions.

His new wardrobe consisted of a new suit, several shirts and ties, casual 'Caribbean'-design short sleeved shirts, numerous T shirts with anonymous, uncreative designs on the front, and sandals and shoes. At the end of the day having trailed around innumerable shops in York, Tennant was absolutely tired out! Afternoon tea was at Betty's with a three tiered plate full of Betty's best cakes, sandwiches and scones.

Bobbins had looked after herself, too. She'd bought some new dresses and skirts, as well as blouses and underwear. She intended to enjoy this cruise – why leave her inheritance to others? She didn't love Tennant, but as a 'toy-boy' he'd do for now. She enjoyed his company, but she wasn't really sure how he felt about her. He always wanted to go to quiet places – small bars and restaurants out of the way, maybe up to Hartlepool or down the coast to Filey or Scarborough. She put it down to his shyness and introvert nature. He'd said he didn't like big crowds.

Jackie looked at Rebecca who was drying Joan Bobbins' hair and raised her eyebrows. She was wishing she hadn't asked the widow that standard question 'where are you going for your holidays?' It was a standing joke in most places like 'Angel Face', but when you made such a general enquiry of a customer you didn't expect to have the contents of a cruise brochure thrown at you! Bobbins went on about another cruise that she and her former husband, George, had once been on. The food, facilities and beautiful cabin were described in detail. Rebecca switched off mentally, but nodded or hummed politely from time to time as though listening to an old aunt telling her how to behave.

Eventually, Joan Bobbins stood up. She looked at herself in the full length mirror and breathed a sigh of approval. 'Oh, yes, very presentable' she whispered. Her VISA MasterCard was handed over and she entered her pin number. £85 for her treatment today seemed reasonable to her. She bade farewell to the staff, much as the queen might do on leaving the palace, slipping a tenner into Rebecca's hand as she strode out into the fresh air.

Across the other side of Teesside, DCI Whitehouse was following up the lead on Dave Wilks. Harry had mentioned Wilks during his interview and Whitehouse wanted to talk to him. Enquiries showed that he had lodgings with a woman called Mrs. Hardisty who lived in Stockton-on-Tees. When Whitehouse called at the premises, she said that Wilks had left five days before

131

and was going to see his brother in Aberdeen, taking a train from Darlington. He had one suitcase with him. She gave a description of Wilks to DI Whitehouse who then got Detective Sergeant Smith to go through CCTV from Darlington railway station for the previous Thursday – the day his landlady said Wilks had left for Aberdeen. There was no sign of anybody who answered to Wilks' description and carrying a suitcase boarding a north-bound train on that day. DS Smith also checked the details of everybody who bought a ticket to Aberdeen. No one bought a rail ticket to the 'granite city' with a credit or debit card on that day.

Whitehouse got in touch with Aberdeen police and discussed the situation with the most senior police officer in the Grampian force. He faxed a photo-fit picture of David Wilks to them. The photo-fit appeared on the front page of the 'Aberdeen Herald' the next day. It simply said that police were interested in interviewing the man shown in the picture. Members of the public were asked not to approach the man, but to telephone Aberdeen central police station if he was spotted.

Within half an hour of the 'Herald' being on sale, a woman telephoned the police station.

"Hello, my name is Miss Finlay, said a lady with a broad Scots accent. "I've seen the man on the front page of today's paper."

Chapter 33

Gerald Lorimer was a first class solicitor. He was the senior partner at the practice in the centre of Middlesbrough and had known Anthea Richards since she'd changed her surname from Watkinson. He'd been involved in her divorce from Peter, knew about Juliette, and handled one or two other matters for her, too. He'd once got her off a parking fine in Yarm when the two yellow lines were proven to be illegal. He was good. Anthea had made an appointment to see him while Harry was languishing in a cell.

"Hello, Anthea, how lovely to see you again, although the circumstances could be better." Lorimer's secretary had shown Anthea into the wood panelled room that absorbed the light. Lorimer wore a dark, double breasted pinstripe suit, white shirt and striped tie. His opal cuff-links were showing at a discrete level below his jacket sleeves and his gold Rolex watch glinted in the morning sun. His hair was almost in need of a trim, greying at the sides.

"Hello, Gerald," she replied. "Yes, things could be better, much better. However, we need to talk about Harry's predicament. He's totally innocent, and you've got to help him." Lorimer's secretary knocked and came in with a tray of coffee, cream and biscuits.

"Tell me what you know," began her solicitor. "Take your time and give me the facts, not opinions. Start right at the beginning." Lorimer was opening a small pad. He took his Mont Blanc fountain pen from his inside pocket. Anthea began telling him about the caravan trip to

Berwick and everything that followed. Lorimer jotted down notes. She also told him about David Cresswell and gave Lorimer his details from the business card in her purse. After almost forty five minutes, coffee finished, Anthea ended her account with 'and so we have it.' Lorimer screwed the pen top back on, replacing his pen inside his jacket pocket. Standing up slowly, he walked to the window but didn't speak for a few moments.

"I think we have a good case here to prove he's innocent. You've given me a lot to go on. I can understand how the police are thinking. I need to make some telephone calls, check a few things and then I'll get back to you. The Chinese involvement might muddy the waters, but all can be revealed. I know the boss of Whitehouse who's a member of Rotary, and I'll have a chat with him. I'll also get some indication of the date of the trial but it's likely to be in about a fortnight. Keep our conversation to yourself, Anthea." She put her handbag strap over her shoulder and Lorimer opened his office door, smiling politely at her as she strode out.

The morning was a little cool and Andrea pulled her collar up. The sun wasn't yet warming the air and Andrea felt like a walk to stretch her legs, get her blood circulating after sitting in Lorimer's office. She headed away from the town centre and found a small park with three wooden benches. One was empty so she sat down for a few minutes, a blackbird singing in a nearby tree. So much was going through her head. It had only been a few weeks since they'd been away in their caravan and yet so much had happened. She would be able to visit Harry tomorrow – it would be good to see him. He was still in Middlesbrough police station and visiting times were between two and four o'clock from Monday to

Friday. Anthea began to think how much she hated the Chinese. Their medicinal treatments and eating habits. She decided that she wouldn't buy, anything made in China from now on.

When Anthea arrived the next day, she was one of several visitors who were shown to a large room. A number of prisoners were sitting at a small table, each dressed in 'prison blue.' Anthea spotted Harry near the back and walked over to him. She held his hand, but was promptly told that there was to be no physical contact between prisoners and visitors! She felt like a school girl who'd been chastised by her teacher. Anthea sat down.

"Hi, how are you?" she said softly. Harry responded, saying he was fine, looking tired. His eyes had slight shadows and he resembled a negative photo of a Chinese panda. "Do you know a guy called David Cresswell?" she began. "He had a word with me after your court appearance. Wants to help." Harry sat up straighter.

"Yes, I know him, he's OK. Been to one Boro match with him and a few of his friends. He seems all right. What did he say?" Anthea told the story and Harry listened.

As Anthea spoke, Harry recalled the two thousand pound loan from Cresswell. Last year at the Riverside stadium Harry had asked Cresswell if could lend him some cash – things were slack with the second hand car business. Harry had heard that the well - dressed Cresswell was into lending, at a nice interest rate. He obliged but Harry hadn't repaid him, yet. Cresswell liked to have his debts repaid. The nice man did not like to wait too long . . .

"Harry, are you listening?" Anthea's raised voice brought him back from his thoughts.

"Yes, of course, but listen, there's something I want you to do," he whispered. He kept his voice down. "Hokey must know I'm in here. Check my emails when you get home. Hokey threatened me, us, about getting another caravan. I've got an idea. Ask Billy Bishop, if he can get a cheap 'van on ebay. Get him to fit a tracker to it and then email Hokey to ask where he wants it to be delivered? Tell Billy I'll pay him double what it costs him. I know he can do it. He's a 'techno' when it comes to things like that. Billy will be able to follow the 'van by using his laptop when he's downloaded a tracking programme. He's a whiz kid at those things! By the time I get out of here, Billy should have been able to keep a check on where the 'van is, and has been."

"Stop whispering, Richards!" said a stern voice from behind Harry. A short, bald security guard with a beer belly sponsored by Watneys was a few yards away. Harry changed the conversation to something lighter. He asked Anthea how she was, and they carried on chatting for a little longer until a voice shouted 'OK, five minutes!' Eventually the visitors stood up and made their way to the exit. No contact – Anthea blew Harry a kiss as she left. Anthea had told Harry about her visit to the solicitors, about Cresswell, and that Lorimer would have some positive news soon. The news about David Cresswell certainly gave Harry hope. He knew he hadn't been totally wrong about that night in 'The Bluebell', despite remembering little about what happened.

Billy Bishop was a good friend of Harry's. He lived in Eaglescliffe, just down the road from Anthea and Harry. When she got home at around 4.30 pm Anthea phoned Jackie at 'Angel Face' first, and then looked up William Bishop in the Cleveland telephone directory. Everything was OK at the beauty salon, Jackie was reliable, so she didn't need to concern herself. Anthea then dialled Billy Bishop's home number.

"Hello, Billy Bishop here!" He sounded as chirpy as Anthea remembered.

"Hi, Billy, it's Anthea Richards. How are you?"

"Goodness gracious, a blast from the past! I'm great. And you?"

"Have you heard about Harry?"

"Yes, and I'm sorry. I saw it in the *Echo*. Are you coping?" He sounded genuine. He was a diamond. A Christian.

"I can tell you better if you came round. Number 24. I'm putting the kettle on in ten minutes."

"I'll be there! Black coffee, no sugar!"

Billy Bishop had no idea what he was going to be getting himself into. But it was good that he liked an adventure. Anthea went upstairs to check the emails.

There were two from Hokun Tu Ying.

Chapter 34

Miss Finlay seemed confused. She fidgeted with a small handbag, and pushed her spectacles up her nose frequently. Dressed in tweed, she did not wear a ring on any finger. Inspector McTavish, a squat policeman with the face of a bulldog that only a mother could love, asked her the question for a second time.

"So where exactly did you see this man?" McTavish adopted a strict tone of voice, pen poised over a record sheet. He was a busy man and wanted to get on.

"I think it was in the newsagents on the corner of Airdrie Street. No wait, unless it was in the supermarket. He looked exactly like the pronto print." Miss Finlay pressed her specs up to the bridge of her thin nose.

"Do you mean the photo-fit?" He wasn't known for having a short fuse, but McTavish didn't suffer fools gladly. Miss Finlay was sitting in an office at Aberdeen central police station. She fingered the bracelet hanging loosely around her right wrist, her thin, pointed nose about to lose a drop of mucus under the force of gravity.

"How certain are you about seeing this man. I mean, did he really match the photo-fit?" McTavish had put his pen down, somehow feeling he wasn't getting far.

"Well, I think so. I only glanced at him quickly, but normally I do have a good memory. Let me have another look at it." McTavish showed her the front page of the 'Aberdeen Herald.' "Hmmm, now I'm not so sure. His eyes look different..." The police officer looked up at the ceiling in frustration.

"All right, Miss Finlay. We have your details so we'll be in touch if we need to be. Thank you for taking the trouble to contact us." McTavish walked to the front desk of the police station with Miss Finlay and bade her farewell. There were no other reports of anybody seeing a person that resembled Wilks. Inspector McTavish wanted a cup of strong coffee. Getting one from the machine in the station, he went into his office, closed the door and shouted 'balls' at the top of his voice. He felt better for that, it sort of cleared his system. 'Bloody time wasters,' he said to himself.

This was fed back to Whitehouse. After 24 hours no news on anybody who looked like Dave Wilks had been reported in the Aberdeen area. Had Wilks really gone to Aberdeen? Mrs. Hardisty reported that he was going to see his brother whose name she couldn't remember. The Grampian police had checked for males with the same surname but there were none on the electoral register, nor in the telephone directory. A dead end. So, had Wilks lied to his landlady? It seemed like it? If he left Stockton-on-Tees with a suitcase where had he gone? DCI Whitehouse wasn't going to let it lie. Although he was convinced that Richards was the murderer, he also wanted to talk with Wilks. The fact that Wilks had gone missing gave Whitehouse some concern. He also wanted more information on Barrett and the links across Teesside and County Durham that he had. Hokey was also listed for interviewing but Whitehouse only had a mobile phone number for him. Harry hadn't actually given Whitehouse Hokey's email address, nor had he asked for it.

Meanwhile, Billy Bishop had visited Anthea and she had told him of the discussion with Harry. He had some concerns, but as they were old friends, Billy agreed to help out. One of the emails from Hokey that Anthea had checked proposed a delivery address for the caravan to an area near Billingham. Billy went onto ebay, typed 'Caravans' into the top window box and clicked 'search.' He found a ten year old Lunar 'van at an address in Harrogate, priced at £4,750, described as being in 'good condition.' By borrowing a car powerful enough to tow it he could get it back to Teesside. An old pal who owed him a favour owned two 4 x 4 vehicles, one of those would be fine. The fitting of a tracker, or geo-location device, would be done at Billy's place - £90 would do the job. A web site relating to 'spy' products that included cameras in pens, microphones in lapel badges and other similar items had a link to tracking devices. Billy got this organised so that he would be able to monitor the movement of the caravan, a 'Lunar Onward' model, between northern England and any part of Europe. Once it was all ready, he told Anthea that he'd be taking the 'van in three days time. He suggested Anthea email Hokey to let him know.

What Anthea didn't tell Billy Bishop was that the second email from Hokun Tu Ying was threatening. He knew that Harry was inside, but that must not prevent Anthea from doing something. If a caravan wasn't delivered within one week, he would come and find her. Billy had seven days to get everything organised.

He would kill her. Anthea realised that Hokey meant business – the Chinese way.

Chapter 35

Jorgsholm concluded that the Transit van found in the disused warehouse was the one used by an unknown driver to collect the four working girls in Malmo. Forensic evidence pointed to several facts; blue rope fibres were found in four places, strands of hair from two girls were bloodied and stuck to the inside of the van, and there were traces of chloroform in cotton wool pads. There probably had been at least two other men in the back of the van where the girls were quickly tied up, or restrained in some way – very likely with cord as well as blue rope. Chloroform had been used to sedate them very quickly.

One, if not two handbags, had been opened – accidentally or on purpose, spilling some of their contents. A small comb, a lipstick, some coins, an eye-liner, a thin hair brush and a silver bracelet were found lodged in small gaps between the floor and the sides of the vehicle. Importantly, a mobile phone was found in the spare wheel well. Traces of semen were discovered, suggesting to Jorgsholm that one or more of the girls were possibly raped. Blood stains covered some of the floor, and finger prints were clearly seen on dried blood near the left side at the front of the van. Jorgsholm had a picture in his head of what had happened; the van had probably been driven to a secluded spot after the girls had struggled for their lives. Terror, total terror for the young, innocent passengers. If two men were in the rear of the van, they were strong. Holding and forcing the girls to the floor, fingers clutching at their throats, their finger nails had drawn blood.

Superintendent Carl Jorgsholm and Merete Glym drove to Malmo to visit the factory where the four girls had spent their last day. They had been in touch with the managing director, Bengt Soderstrom, and he was expecting them. Although it had happened three years previously, Soderstrom remembered the girls. He described them as bubbly, cheerful, and good workers. The meeting between the three of them took two hours over strong black coffee and pastries that were served, and the discussion was uninterrupted. Jorgsholm began by asking the MD about each of the four people involved. Soderstrom had a file on each girl – name, address, schooling, physical details and medical examination results prior to starting work, plus references. Jorgsholm asked for a copy of each of these. He or Merete could go through them later.

"Do you have any idea, any idea at all, who might have collected the four girls on that afternoon?" Although a trial had been opened and later adjourned through lack of evidence, Jorgsholm wanted to go over some details again. Soderstrom slowly shook his head.

"Do you still have anybody working here that knew any of them?"

"Let me think. Oh, yes. There is a supervisor – Frieda Rasmussen – she worked with them. She got to know them quite well, I think."

"Could we see her?" Glym chirped in. She'd beaten her boss to the question. Soderstrom asked his secretary to have Rasmussen join them, and she came into the room a few minutes later. Looking nervous, Jorgsholm used his interpersonal skills to put her at ease very quickly. Smiling in a casual manner, Jorgsholm looked at Frieda.

"Hi, Frieda," the Superintendent began, "we're here making some enquiries about the four girls who disappeared from the front of the factory just over three years ago. What can you tell us about them – anything at all?" Rasmussen looked down at her fingers that were held in her lap, playing with an imaginary ball of wool. She raised her head, her blond hair catching the light behind her, beautiful sky blue eyes looking at the police detective. She cleared her throat, composed herself, and smiled gently.

"They were lovely people. Full of fun, and hard workers. Nothing was too much trouble. All of them would do any extra little jobs that needed doing. They'd laugh much of the time but it never interfered with their work."

"Did they have any friends outside of work that you were aware of?" It was Glym's turn to ask.

"They kept themselves to themselves as far as I know. One of them, Nikola, had met a young man a few weeks before they went missing. We would pull her leg about him!"

"What can you tell me about this young man?" Jorgsholm asked.

"He was just a friend, I think. She spoke fondly of him. He had been a student in Copenhagen and was doing casual driving jobs in this area. I didn't know his name."

"Anyone else? Any other friends or acquaintances?" Frieda shook her head, her hair moving from side to side like a small pair of lace curtains.

They chatted for a few more minutes, and then Soderstrom thanked Frieda for her help. The short

143

interview had taken it out of her, the emotion showing in her eyes. He showed her to the door, opening it for her. As she was about to leave, Frieda turned around and looked at the two police officers.

"Oh, I've just remembered, the young man was Chinese, and he kept a pet rat. Strange really." Frieda walked away and the office door was closed behind her.

Jorgsholm's heart missed a beat, and Soderstrom looked confused.

Chapter 36

Billy Bishop had achieved his goal and helped his old friend out. He'd bought the caravan at a good price with cash that Anthea had given him, picked it up from an address in Harrogate near the hospital in Lancaster Road, and delivered it to a run down warehouse area of Billingham. Before then, on his driveway that was partly hidden by a tall hedge, he had fitted a tracker no bigger than a matchbox underneath the 'van, bolted securely to the axle. He'd wired it up to a silicon chip mother-board unit hidden beneath the floor, powered by a lithium ion battery with a six month life-span. Billy then checked it out on his laptop and when he looked at the computer screen he could see a small red dot that gently beeped. So wherever the 'Lunar Onward' went, Billy would be able to see it – the red dot and regular beep telling him of its exact position. A bit like Bo Peep and her sheep, he thought. It was still in Billingham where he'd left it, hitch lock fitted and the key in a polythene envelope on the top of a tyre. Hokey had been emailed again with these details. Billy would check the position of the 'van again soon.

Anthea visited Harry several more times in HMP Frankland where he'd been transferred and was based in a secure unit. Harry met some of the dregs of northern pond life in the prison, but he wondered if he'd make any friends? Perhaps there were one or two in there that may be useful when he got out? A big guy who was nicknamed 'King Kong' for good reason could come in handy. 'King Kong' was six feet five inches tall and weighed twenty two stone. He had biceps like a beer barrels and thighs to match. 'King Kong' was in for the murder of his wife's boyfriend, strangled with one hand apparently. He showed Harry once how he'd done it, his sausage-like fingers spreading wide enough to hold a medicine ball. Crushing a Granny Smith's apple in the canteen was one of his 'party pieces'. Nobody tangled with King Kong.

On the next available visit Andrea quietly told Harry what Billy had done on the caravan, and he smiled.

"Good work!" he muttered. "If Billy can keep tabs on that caravan that'll be a bonus. Hokey may not be with the 'van for long, but if it's kept in one place for a while it could be that that's where Hokey does his dealings. It should end up in Seahouses. Whoever eventually gets the 'van can be followed wherever it goes. I wonder what he's up to now?" Harry's eyes wandered as he was thinking about the cunning Chinaman. Anthea changed the subject.

She chatted about the beauty salon and how things were going. It seemed friends told friends – what Anthea referred to as MGM – 'member get member', and the monthly takings continued to grow. She hadn't heard from Gerald Lorimer but was confident that he was working on Harry's behalf. Having lost a couple of pounds in weight, Harry had used the gym and was keeping up his exercise routine. He had his routine of using a chest expander and weights as well as a jogging machine. Smoking was allowed in designated areas of the prison, but he'd cut down with a view to stopping if he could. He felt better for it, and Anthea told him he was looking good – fewer wrinkles, brighter eyes. What she really thought to herself was that he looked less haggard, but didn't want to put it that way. Anthea also told him that her 'least favourite' customer, Joan Bobbins, had just left on her cruise with her toy boy. That would give the staff at 'Angel Face' some peace for a while. Harry heard some of the details, but only pretended to be interested. How could he be when his view of the world was through bars and reinforced glass?

Bobbins was enjoying her trip with Adam Tennant. Cruising at a steady 25 knots southerly, a host of destinations were scheduled, and excursions to some cities on the way. The food was delicious, and this floating hotel left nothing to be desired. Bobbins had taken a couple of paperbacks to read on the sun-deck. *'The Broker'*, a John Grisham novel had been bought on a book web site and it promised to be a good read, whilst the other was the latest one by Dan Brown – *'Inferno'*. Joan Bobbins had taken a large amount of sterling, but didn't tell Tennant that she had £20,000 in used notes in a zipped bottom compartment of her hand luggage. She had some US dollar travellers cheques with her, but didn't like using credit cards. The cash was to come in handy for souvenirs, clothes and generally having a good time. Bobbins was definitely planning to enjoy herself!

The relationship between the two holidaymakers was slightly unusual, more like brother and sister than good friends. However, it seemed at times as if they didn't trust each other, Joan Bobbins eagle eyes followed his every movement. Tennant knew about Bobbins' past, but wasn't overly concerned about it. He also knew she was a white witch belonging to some coven in Cleveland and disappeared for a week-end from time to time meeting up with other witches. She didn't know much about him. He'd been in the army, but so had lots of other men. He was well spoken, and Joan Bobbins wanted somebody on her arm as an escort more than anything. They'd had

147

sex, but it didn't mean anything. It seemed to be over quickly – more 'lie back and think of England' than a mad passionate orgy.

Each day followed a similar pattern. Get up around eight o'clock, have a leisurely breakfast, read or sunbathe – or both, until lunch. The buffet usually served something different each day. Use of the pool in the afternoon, tea at four o'clock, and then relax before dinner with a gin and tonic in the bar prior to a five course meal followed by coffee and liqueurs. Tennant could put up with that – Bobbins was paying for everything – but he got a bit bored at times. One afternoon she asked him to pop back to the cabin to get a bottle of suntan lotion. He'd gone in and looked in the bathroom but couldn't see it. He tried a cupboard and then several drawers. In the wardrobe was her hand luggage. Tennant didn't believe it was in there but he decided to look. Opening a crimson case he saw that it contained a few small items – a note pad, some envelopes, nothing much. As he was about to close it he noticed a blue piece of paper sticking out of a small tear in the nylon fabric. Bending over to take a closer look he carefully tugged at the paper and eased it out. It was a £20 note! Tennant slipped it into his pocket. Then pulling gently at a discreet zip around the base of the case he revealed a large quantity of used £20 notes bundled together in one thousand pound wads, each wrapped with a brown paper sleeve. Tennant breathed out slowly as he closed the case after re-zipping the bottom.

'She really doesn't need all that money does she?' he whispered to himself.

Chapter 37

"Have you found it?" Joan Bobbins had come into the cabin. Tennant suddenly turned around after he'd put the case back into the wardrobe. "It's in the toiletries bag in the bathroom!"

"Sorry, I searched everywhere and couldn't see it. Anyway, you've got it now." He avoided looking her in the eye as he made his way out of the cabin. "I'm going back up on deck. Can I order you a cocktail?"

"Please, a bloody Mary, and ask that handsome Italian waiter to add an extra dash of vodka!"

Tennant left the cabin quickly. He hoped his body language hadn't given anything away. As he walked along the corridor on Q deck he wondered if his partner had suspected anything? Why was she carrying all that cash? He didn't know how much was there. His agile mind did a calculation as he ordered two cocktails up on the rear sun deck. Working out the area of the case and the depth of the £20 notes he arrived at a figure of between fifteen and twenty thousand pounds! He didn't know how close he was!

Why was Joan Bobbins carrying so much money? Did she have an ulterior motive – perhaps meeting up with a spy in Rome and paying him to shoot the Pope? Tennant paused his thoughts as the two drinks were placed on a small white table between the sun loungers. He gave Guiseppe the cabin number and signed the bill. Bobbins seemed to be taking her time coming back. Maybe she was applying the sun lotion in the cabin? With the £20 note still in his swimming shorts pocket, he felt ought to get rid of it. What if Bobbins came back and found the note on him, he wasn't spending anything on board right then so why carry money? He called Guiseppe over and the Italian was there in seconds. Adam Tennant handed the tightly folded sterling note to the waiter with a wink and a tap on the side of his nose - the international sign language right at that moment wasn't wasted on the helpful waiter. It was equivalent to asking for the bill by pretending to write on the palm of your hand.

"Hi, Adam!" Joan settled herself down on the adjacent sun lounger after kissing his cheek. "Sorry I've been a while, but I saw that couple from P deck as I came back. You know, those from Sheffield. They kept me talking – she can talk for England!" She took a long sip from her tomato red drink and purred like a kitten. "How's Guiseppe? I hope he's behaving himself. Hasn't he got a nice bum, though?" Smiling to herself with the thought of Italian buttocks in her head, Joan Bobbins picked up her Grisham novel and continued to read. Adam lay back and soaked up the sun for ten minutes prior to jumping into the warm, blue water of the pool. Swimming around as best he could, with too many other people getting in his way, he climbed back up the chrome plated ladder at the side of the pool, grabbed his towel and walked back to the sun lounger. Joan Bobbins was asleep, her breathing was relaxed and deep. The bloody Mary glass was empty. The novel was on the decking below her outstretched arm, pages flickering in the Mediterranean breeze, her bookmark a few feet away.

Tennant decided to return to the cabin. He wanted another look in the crimson case, just a quick look. He hadn't dreamt it, had he? Bundles of notes were stashed

150

away but why? Opening the wardrobe door he removed the luggage and placed it on the bed. He unzipped it and placed his hand on the base, searching for the wads of notes, but he couldn't feel them. Deciding to take a closer look, Tennant quietly and efficiently opened the bottom compartment but the case was empty - completely empty.

On the way back to the pool he met the couple from Sheffield. "Hello Adam, how's Joan? We haven't seen her since yesterday!"

"She's fine," he lied.

Chapter 38

Superintendent Carl Jorgsholm was unable to confirm or deny that Wang Xian was still in Denmark. The so-called leader of the Frihed group could not be traced by checking port and airport records, nor listings of foreign nationals on a database at police headquarters. Enquiries with credit card companies and the banks had drawn a blank. Jorgsholm was not going to believe, could not believe, that Wang Xian had left the country. He was becoming increasingly frustrated. There were people living in the country who did a whole load of menial tasks and were being paid in cash, illegal of course, but it was going on. Xian could be one of them. Denmark was fast becoming a multi-cultural society, and recent news reports suggested that it was high on a list of foreign countries where China was keen to invest.

The Volvo registered in the name of Mao Tu Ying had not been sighted. Perhaps it was stored in some garage or shed? It remained on a list of vehicles across Denmark that police continually sought. Passenger terminals at Copenhagen docks and other ports around the country were still on alert for several individuals including Xian, Longe and Tu Ying. Copenhagen international airport officials were also briefed on the same people. All Jorgsholm wanted, no prayed for, was a lead on any of these.

One summer's morning, about a week after Jorgsholm had been considering further aspects about the Juliette Watkinson case, a man was walking his spaniel on the outskirts of the fishing port of

Frederikshavn on the Kattegat in northern Denmark. A quiet stretch of green field with a small wooded area at the edge of it was ideal for dog walkers and ramblers. The man had let his dog off the lead for a good run and it had disappeared into a nearby wooded area. The dog began barking and the man, who was elderly with a slight stoop, went in after it. He was only about ten metres into the wood when he saw the dog standing barking near a mound of dirt, partly covered with branches and leaves. It looked somewhat artificial, although it could have been used by rabbits as a small shelter.

The spaniel eventually stopped barking as the man pushed back the dead branches with his walking stick. Recoiling, he saw three white, bony fingers sticking up through the soil. He searched a bit further, poking the soil with his stick and dragging leaves and branches away to the side. The skeleton of a foot appeared two metres away, facing in the opposite direction to the fingers. Tempted as he was, he resisted poking his stick any more into the mass of botanical detritus. He walked briskly towards the main road and stopped the first car that came towards him. Frantically waving his walking stick at the vehicle, a light blue Fiat slowed down as it approached the old man and a young couple in the car listened to his account of what he'd discovered. After a few minutes listening to him, they called the police.

Superintendent Jorgsholm was at the scene in under two hours. The local police had taped off the area and the crime scene was untouched, save for the old man's probing which was considered minimal. Jorgsholm slowly went towards the mound and carefully lifted some branches. He, too, saw the skeleton of a hand and a foot. But there was more buried in that spot. One and a half hours later, the skeletal remains of four young girls and their rotted clothing had been unearthed and carefully placed into body bags. There was absolutely no doubt in Jorgsholm's mind that these were the four missing girls from Malmo, and later forensic evidence would prove he was correct.

It was very likely that their lift from work in the white Transit van three years ago was their last day on God's earth. Jorgsholm vowed to solve this case. He felt even more determined now, and the search for Juliette would be intensified. He owed it to her parents.

Chapter 39

"Hello, Anthea." Lorimer sounded his usual efficient self on the telephone. "The chap you met at the magistrates court, David Cresswell. I've tried to contact him but I'm having problems. His phone has a voice mail message, just says it's an 'unavailable number'. Are you sure you got it right?" Anthea rummaged through her purse and found the business card of Mr. D. Cresswell. His mobile phone number was shown and she repeated the number to her solicitor. He agreed that the number she'd given was the one he'd tried. Anthea thought it was odd, but she'd try it herself later. Lorimer continued.

"I've been talking to Chief Superintendent Darren Savage at police HQ. He tells me, in confidence, that the evidence against Harry is a bit limited. It was good that Harry was open and truthful with DCI Whitehouse, although as a detective, Whitehouse was just doing his job, taking his comments with a pinch of salt. Clearly Harry acted inappropriately in grabbing the brown package that 'allegedly' contained the cash for the caravan. Burning his clothes was the act of somebody who was guilty, but that will be taken into account. The police have looked at the emails between Harry and Hokun and they indicate that Harry was again being honest, however they didn't appreciate the threats from the Chinaman. The two policemen, Wayman and Brass, that visited Harry have already reported that he was acting 'suspiciously'. Anyway, I'll be in touch again soon when I have a date for the hearing at the Crown Court. The key issue right now is being able to use your friend's offer to appear as a witness with regard to the incident in 'The Bluebell'."

"Thank you, Gerald. I've seen Harry a few times in the secure unit and he seems OK, just waiting for the court appearance. I feel I need a four leaf clover to bring me luck and I'm trying to keep sane about all this and it still seems like a dream. Anyway, thank you again. We'll talk soon. Bye." Anthea hung up.

David Cresswell? Anthea mused to herself. She was in no doubt that he was genuine. Maybe his mobile phone provider was having problems...Orange had taken over somebody, or EE had taken over Orange? Whatever . . . Anthea decided she'd try Cresswell's mobile phone number. She carefully put in the eleven digits – and waited. Nothing, not even a message this time, just a slight whirring sound like an egg whisk in the distance, but she would try again later. The front door bell rang and wondering who it could be, she peeked through the lounge curtains. Billy Bishop was stood at the door, laptop computer bag hanging from his right shoulder. Billy was a tall chap with a clean cut appearance and short hair, he could easily have been mistaken for a door-to-door salesman, or maybe a Jehovah's witness. She opened the door.

"Hi Billy. What brings you round?"

"Hello Anthea. I've got something on my laptop that you might be interested to see."

"Come in," she opened the door wider and casually glanced outside to see if any nosey neighbours were watching who could add two plus two and get five. She didn't see anyone. Offering Billy coffee, he shook his head and said 'no thanks' as he placed his laptop computer on the kitchen unit worktop and switched it on. In seconds it had booted up and he entered his password.

Anthea diplomatically looked away as he keyed in ten letters and four numbers. An icon appeared on the screen and a quick click revealed a little red dot within a few seconds.

"There's the caravan!" exclaimed Billy. "It's working! The tracker shows us that the 'van is in Seahouses. It was collected yesterday from the spare ground near Billingham. Hokey might even send you a 'thank you' email! I'll keep an eye on it for you and phone you whenever there's some significant movement. I just wanted you to see what it looks like on the screen and you can quietly let Harry know on your next visit."

"Thank you so much, Billy." She gave him a peck on the cheek and he blushed. "Harry will be so pleased. So, that means that we, or rather you, can follow the 'van wherever it goes. What about the police? Harry didn't want the cops to know. What do you think?" Billy moved a little uneasily. He wanted to help but obviously didn't want to be implicated in anything that was illegal.

"It's not up to me, Anthea. If Harry wants to keep it quiet, then that's up to him. I've only helped an old friend out. Anyway, I must fly – things to do." With that Billy closed down his laptop, re-bagged it and moved towards the front door. "I'll phone you when I see the dot has left Seahouses!" He was quickly at the gate, his long strides making him appear on stilts, and disappeared around the corner.

Going back inside, Anthea sat down and began to think about her only child, Juliette, who had never been found. Nearly nine years had passed since she had disappeared and Anthea missed her so much. She'd be almost 23 years of age. Anthea couldn't help but wonder what she would look like? Even though there was no

157

trace of Juliette, she had never given up hope. She continued to believe that she was alive, she just had to.

The contents of Juliette's bedroom from the Jorgsholm household were boxed and eventually placed in the loft in Yarm. Anthea kept Juliette's passport in her small bedside table. She went upstairs and into the bedroom and opened the top drawer. She took out the maroon document, opened it at the back and looked at her daughter's photo. A young, innocent, beautiful girl, Anthea sat on the edge of the bed and wept.

She cried until she couldn't cry any more.

Chapter 40

Tennant lay on his sun lounger. His eyes were closed, Joan was reading her novel. The sun was a bright daffodil yellow, shining down light an arc lamp. There wasn't a cloud to be seen in the blue Mediterranean sky.

"Where have you been?" she asked inquisitively. Adam Tennant composed himself.

"Oh just for a walk around the upper sun deck – really busy up there. Lots of people swimming. One kid nearly drowned until some guy pulled him out."

"You seem worried?" Joan put her book down at looked at him.

"Worried? Me? No. I'm fine. I was just considering our next port of call. We've got an excursion planned and we need to up early." Adam Tennant lied through his teeth, and Joan Bobbins didn't believe him anyway. A cat and mouse at play.

"There's nothing to worry about, Adam. We'll have an early night, and I'll keep off the gin and tonic. I ought to cut down a bit, I'll be getting more wrinkles." She'd been tipsy after drinking half a bottle of gin with a litre of tonic water the night before. Having been in the mood for a bit of 'slap and tickle' back in the cabin after dinner, a visit to the bathroom to do some retching put paid to that. Picking up her book up again she continued reading – the main character was living in Bologna and learning Italian, but he was a hunted man. Adam was sitting on the edge of the lounger gazing out over the azure blue sea wondering how she'd look if she did get

159

more wrinkles. He pictured a sheet of crumpled cellophane.

He had some thinking to do, some serious thinking. Tennant looked out at the slightly rounded horizon of the ocean, recalling that somebody once told him that it curved eight inches for every mile. The money had gone from the bottom of the case. Why? Was it because she suspected that he knew it was there? Maybe she knew that he knew. He wasn't going to say anything, how could he? But where had she put it? Was it still in the cabin? It must be. Or maybe Bobbins had taken it to reception and asked for it to be put in a safe. She stood up, closing her Grisham novel and picked up her handbag.

"I'm going to the cabin for a shower. It'll soon be time for cocktails in the Pompadour Bar before dinner. Are you staying here?" She looked at Tennant in an odd way. He wasn't certain if she wanted him to go with her.

"Er, yes. I'll be along in ten minutes. You go and sort yourself out. I'll miss you when you've gone!" He smiled as well as he could, wincing inside as he did so. She turned and walked away, her full length chiffon robe wafting around her long, slim legs as she left the deck and headed for their cabin. Bobbins hadn't seen the smile in his eyes, only across his lips and the edge of his cheeks.

Tennant was hatching a plan. His wicked mind was working overtime. He thought about the excursion tomorrow; they would be docking at Civitavecchia for a visit to Rome. 'Ah, Rome. The eternal city,' he thought. 'It won't be eternal for Joan Bobbins, but something else would be.' Mrs. Bobbins, the white witch from Middlesbrough, wouldn't be seeing Rome. No Coliseum,

160

no Trevi fountain, no Spanish Steps. In fact, nothing at all. At least, not in Rome.

After dinner that night Adam Tennant suggested a walk around the top passenger deck. He'd persuaded his partner, with no difficulty, to have one or two extra glasses of a very good, full bodied red wine. Joan Bobbins was slightly unsteady on her feet as they wandered around the perimeter of the deck, holding onto Tennant's arm with two hands. Eventually they stopped to look out at the reflection of the silver moon on the Mediterranean sea, resting against the teak and chrome rail. She giggled and chuckled as Adam told some silly stories and jokes . . .

"Did you hear about the two peanuts walking down the Strand? One was assaulted."

"Our paper-boy has a small round. A small round what?"

It was getting late as Adam Tennant glanced around the deck noticing that there was no one else about, and it was quite dark. The moonlight cast shadows across the wood underneath their feet.

In less time than it takes to say 'over you go' he'd lifted her slight frame over the edge of the chromed railing and gravity did the rest. He didn't hear her scream, nor the splash as she hit the water. Adam Tennant prayed that nobody else had either. Davy Jones' locker, or some other 'eternal' world awaited Joan Bobbins. The fish could be in for a treat.

Tennant ran his fingers through his hair, adjusted his cuff-links, made sure his tie knot was straight and took a few deep breaths. It was time for a drink. Heading for the bar, he took one last look at the gentle wake behind the cruise ship. The gentle churning of the white water

161

drifting away for over a mile looked peaceful under the moon.

He wondered if seawater would cause more wrinkles.

Chapter 41

The bodies of the four girls underwent extensive forensic examination. Rotted pieces of clothing, personal jewellery and their dental records revealed that these were definitely the workers from the Malmo factory. It was difficult to say whether they were brought here directly, or whether their corpses had spent some time elsewhere. Jorgsholm believed they were probably taken directly to the wooded area to be buried as soon as possible. Strands of blue rope were found around the wrists of the girls whilst two had been gagged with a pair of tights. Hands had been tied behind their backs and a grey coloured cord had been used to tie their ankles. Without a doubt they must have suffered pain and torture in the back of the Transit van prior to their death, screams and cries for help having gone unnoticed.

The underside of several finger nails revealed minute flakes of skin, and the tissue would be examined for DNA. Of the items found in the abandoned van, Frieda Rasmussen confirmed that the items, including a bracelet, did belong to the workers. However, the mobile phone discovered near the spare wheel had not yet been checked. Jorgsholm called a press conference after phoning Soderstrom at the factory first. He told him the news, limiting the information to basic details, and asked him to keep it to himself until the next day when the newspapers would be full of it. Soderstrom was very upset. He'd liked having those four cheerful girls around the place, and he wondered what effect the news would have on business? The parents of the four were also contacted by police, and home visits made by trained counsellors.

Jorgsholm did not mention the mobile phone. He knew this could prove crucial in the ongoing investigation of what became known as the 'Four Blondes Case.' The press conference was held in Alborg, the capital of North Jutland province, just south of Frederikshavn. It was a town with a population of two hundred thousand and a small airport. Jorgsholm took charge of the meeting which was attended by over 30 reporters from all over Denmark. Glym and several other senior officers from Copenhagen were present and after introductions, Jorgsholm started things off.

"Ladies and gentlemen. Thank you for coming today. Danish police have found the bodies of four young girls, aged between 17 and 20, following a report by a member of the public who was walking his dog near Frederikshavn. The girls had worked at the Carlsson factory and were there on a six month work experience programme. Details of exactly how they died is not totally clear yet, but forensic work continues to take place. At this moment we do not have any strong leads on the motive for the murders, nor who was behind this."

Jorgsholm was bombarded with questions about each of the girls, where they were from, why had it happened in a quiet place like Malmo, what were the police doing to find the perpetrators? Jorgsholm and Glym handled the questions well. The usual, non-committed answers gave the reporters enough to go on for the moment. They would approach the Carlsson factory to ask for pictures of the four girls and make other enquiries themselves. That's what reporters do – everyone a frustrated detective. Press photographers would converge on the wooded area on the outskirts of Frederikshavn, as well as Danish TV. There would be a melange of activity for several days. Jorgsholm was under the spotlight. He was well aware that he had to produce results. And soon.

However, it was the mobile phone that was to give the police the next lead. It belonged to Nikola, one of the working girls with a boyfriend, the information that Rasmussen had volunteered. She didn't know his name but she had said he was Chinese and had a pet rat. Although the mobile phone was about three years old it was still possible to retrieve data from the SIM card. Some of Glym's staff examined it and after a couple of hours a number of facts had emerged. Firstly, there were three voice-mail messages from her Chinese boyfriend whose name was Li. Secondly, two text messages had been sent to Nikola. The first voice message suggested she spend a week-end with him in northern Denmark, the second gave details of a place he wanted to take her to, and the last one described a house on a quiet road north of Frederikshavn. The text messages told Nikola that the sender was 'fond' of her, one being quite suggestive.

Glym was able to let Carl Jorgsholm know the possible whereabouts of a light blue wooden building located on a narrow, little used road to the west of Skagen, some 30 kilometres north of Frederikshavn. Li had described it – three bedroomed, gables at the windows and a slate roof with grass on it. It was now apparent that Li had wanted to take Nikola to this place, kilometres from anywhere, as a 'holiday' for her. He also described the outstanding beauty of the countryside. 'Some holiday that would be', thought Glym.

It seemed to Merete Glym that Li was a persuasive individual with low morals who may have had a history of luring young girls to this spot. They needed more to go on. Glym wasn't sure if Li was his real name. Nor was she certain whether he was a loner or part of a gang. Frieda had recalled that he had been a student and had a driving job at the time. Jorgsholm made contact again with Brunander in prison, and Brunander told him that he remembered a guy called Li Wong who was a member of Frihed. So, Li Wong was involved and had been, or still was, a member of the group set up by Wang Xian in Copenhagen. Brunander had also heard on the criminal grapevine that Li Wong was getting concerned that Nikola was beginning to ask awkward questions about him – where was he from, what did he do, and that tattoo? Did he need to get rid of her? Was she talking to her friends at the factory?

Jorgsholm needed to drive out to Skagen and look for a light blue building on the narrow road. He planned to do it with two armed policemen along with Glym. The timing crucial, Jorgsholm wanted to do it at night. Dim the car headlights, drive slowly along the road, see what they came upon. The next evening, the plan was put into action. It was a moonlit night – dark and somewhat eerie but with enough light at that time of year to see. The VW Passat carried the four members of the police force towards the area Li had described. Two of the uniformed police were armed with high powered rifles. They drove slowly along the road, not being totally certain if they were in the right area. Suddenly, Glym said. "Look, there, over there!" In the distance they could make out a building that had lights on. As they got nearer it fitted Li's description –it seemed light blue in colour, had gables at the windows and a roof covered with a growth. It was a bit too dark to be sure about the roof, but it was either grass or moss.

They parked the car half a kilometre away. Using sign language, Jorgsholm indicated to the two armed policemen to go around the back of the property as they approached it. Jorgsholm rarely carried a firearm but tonight he was wearing a H&K 9mm pistol in an underarm holster. Crouching, he carefully and slowly crept up to the front window. The curtains were not drawn. Glym held back, standing at the front gate. He peered inside. It was not often that Jorgsholm felt frightened but tonight was different. Trying to look into the room, he accidentally stood on a thick, dry stick that he hadn't seen. It made a loud 'crack'.

Suddenly, the lights in the house went out.

Chapter 42

The date of the trial of Harold Richards had been set. It was to take place at Teesside Crown Court on 1 August, Yorkshire Day. 'A little ironic', thought Harry to himself when he was told the date. Although he was born on Teesside, he 'felt' he was a Yorkshireman. However, true '*White Rose*' supporters would tell you that all parts of Teesside south of the River Tees were once part of the North Riding of the county.

Anthea had given Gerald Lorimer, her solicitor, as much information as she could. Lorimer had been busy collecting data and sifting through reports and other material. He had been in touch with an experienced barrister called Jonathan Cleasby who was to take Harry's case for the defence. Cleasby had accumulated what he considered a substantial amount of evidence – dates, times, places, witnesses. He had retained an eminent surgeon to give evidence with regard to the murder of Michael Barrett as well as a psychologist who specialised in stress and trauma.

Dave Wilks had not been found despite police surveillance across the region as well as one or two other places that friends in 'The Bluebell' had mentioned. Nothing more had been forthcoming from the Aberdeen area. Wilks would be a key witness, especially after what David Cresswell had told Anthea. Gerald Lorimer was becoming anxious about Cresswell – he had not picked up on his mobile phone despite several calls and correspondence to the P.O. Box number had remained unanswered. Lorimer had spoken with the Cleveland

Constabulary recently and was waiting for a response on the P.O. Box number. He had initially been in touch with the Post Office but they would not reveal contact details – 'company policy', he was informed.

Anthea had been to see Harry several times at Frankland. He was in good spirits and had put on a little weight. Pumping iron in the prison gym twice a day and eating more protein and less carbohydrate made him look better, his eyes not looking so panda-like. She quietly fed back information on the tracker in the caravan that had been delivered to Hokey. Billy Bishop had phoned Anthea that morning to say that the red dot was flashing on the north sea! It was slowly moving north eastwards and Billy had again promised to keep Anthea informed, especially when the red dot 'struck' dry land. Anthea brought Harry up to date with her conversation with Lorimer and gave him all the news. Harry Richards felt positive about things. After all, he was innocent, wasn't he?

When Anthea got home she made herself coffee and then noticed the 'message waiting' light was flashing on the phone. She picked up and pressed the play button. 'You have two new messages'. Anthea listened. They were both from Gerald Lorimer. The first one was about Dave Wilks. Lorimer's secretary had been scanning news items on her computer in the lunch break when she had seen the first report. Wilks had been sighted in Keswick where his sister lived. An Aberdonian, holidaying in the Lake District saw Wilks after recalling the photo-fit picture in the local newspaper. He reported it to the Cumbria police and within a few hours, Wilks had been arrested and was now in a cell at Cleveland police HQ. Lorimer considered this a 'one in a million' chance. The phone message ended.

The second message, sent ten minutes later, was far less positive. Lorimer told Anthea that the P.O. Box number for David Cresswell did not exist. It was pure fabrication. The email address on the card that Anthea had given her solicitor was also false. He was still trying to determine whether the mobile number was, too. Putting the phone down she'd ring Lorimer back after she had her 'caffeine perk' and made time to take in what she'd just heard. So, if Lorimer was correct, who was this likeable chap called Cresswell? Why would he volunteer the information about Wilks in 'The Bluebell'? What else did this so-called David Cresswell know? Anthea couldn't come up with any answers at that moment. She finished her coffee and phoned Lorimer.

"Hello, Gerald, I got your two messages. So, where do we go from here?"

"Good morning! Good question. The good news is that Wilks is being held in custody. I assume Whitehouse is giving him a good going over. As for your friend, Cresswell, well I can't understand that. Have you tried his mobile again?"

"No, I'll try later. Can't we find out from the mobile phone company who owns the phone?" Anthea was getting into her detective mood.

"It's possible, everything is possible. I'll have a word in the right places. Meanwhile, how's Harry? I hope he's keeping his pecker up. You can tell him that my staff and I will be doing all we can to prove his innocence. The trial starts very soon and we're dotting the i's and crossing the t's. I know the jury has been selected, and lawyer for the prosecution is an old friend, Denzil Penberthy. Despite that he's a cunning old fox and I know he'll have some tricks up his sleeve. Anthea, I must go, I've got a client coming in for an appointment. Bye."

Lorimer didn't tell Anthea that his client was a well respected surgeon from St. James University Hospital, Leeds. His name was Sir Wyndham Honisett. Lorimer and Honisett had been at Oxford together. The surgeon had over forty years of experience in forensic medicine and some of his evidence would prove crucial.

But Mr. Denzil Penberthy Q.C., the 'cunning old fox' was also working on his case, working very hard.

Chapter 43

The Rome excursion left the Civitavecchia quayside at
9.00 am bound for the 'eternal city', one and a half hours
away. The coach had 39 passengers on board – Adam
Tennant and 38 others. The tour guide did a head count
and told the group there was one passenger missing.
Adam Tennnant shouted out that his partner wasn't
feeling too well and would not be coming. The trip took
the cruise passengers through the green countryside of
Lazio, eventually pulling into the underground
designated coach parking area in Rome just after 10.30
am. The passengers followed the tour manager up five
escalators to ground level and fresh air. A few more
paces from the last set of moving steps brought the
group out to a wonderful view of the Vatican and St.
Peter's Square on their left hand side.

Tennant was carrying a small case, but nobody
thought much about it. Inside he had his clothes, at least
the ones he wanted, and a few other personal belongings
including his passport. Not only those items, but he had
the money that Joan Bobbins had tried to hide from him.
Tennant had found it in a designer label polythene carrier
bag under the bed. With one objective, he now had to get
away from the cruise, away from Italy, and back to the
UK. He had six hours to get out of Rome before the
group returned to the coach park and headed back to the
ship.

The tour guide had given them directions to various
parts of the city and suggestions for visits prior to
meeting back near St. Peter's square at 4.00 pm prompt.

172

As the guide went on her own way, small groups diversified towards the Vatican, the Vatican museum, and a bus stop across the road where an open top red bus would take them around Rome for under ten euros. It was a 'hop-on, hop-off' deal and, with a map, it was a perfect way to see this wonderful place in the time allowed. The audible buzz of excitement from the cruise ship passengers, the china-blue sky and an agreeable temperature in the low thirties Centigrade all added up to a great day in store.

That was, for the tourists, but Tennant no longer saw himself as one of them. He wanted to place as many kilometres between himself and Rome as he could, but first he needed to exchange some sterling notes for euros. Although he had his own credit card, he did not want to use it. It would be traceable. Cash was best, and he found a small agent with a flashing euros sign that offered a reasonable rate of exchange. He went inside and walked over to a young man with jet black hair who appeared to be about 16 years old. He changed five hundred pounds, but needing to show some ID he got out his passport. Everything was fine, and he placed the wad of euro notes into his waist bag.

Not wanting to waste time, he asked a travel agent about flights to London Heathrow. The young girl behind the desk brought up the timetables for Rome to LHR. There was a departure at 1325 hrs. with four empty seats. Tennant took one of them. The agent printed off the ticket, took the cash for the flight, and handed the ticket to his newest customer. Tennant smiled, his grin wider than the mouth of the Tees estuary. Outside a taxi rank was a two minute walk away. Tennant strolled to the waiting cars and jumped into a taxi. 'Fiumicino airport, please!'

The maid who made up the beds and tidied the cabin used by Bobbins and Tennant had let herself in. She was a small girl called Ola from Tenerife with long dark hair tied up in a pony tail, thin fingers and a chirpy grin. There was nothing that seemed out of place as far as Ola could see. Footwear was still under a side table, cosmetics in the bathroom, one damp bath towel on a rail, a bracelet and two pairs of earrings in a small glass tray. A glance in the wardrobe showed clothes hanging up – everything was normal as far as the maid was concerned. She did what she was paid to do - make the beds, tidy the cabin and bathroom, change the towels and leave the place smart. Glancing around the room as she left she had one nagging thought. She couldn't think why, but something was different. It was late, Ola had twenty more cabins to attend to, things to do before changing and working in the kitchen before lunch.

Tennant's taxi pulled up in front of Departures at the airport. He paid the driver, gave him a good tip, and got out. 'Av a good flight', the taxi driver shouted in broken English as Tennant strode to find the check-in desk for the Alitalia flight to London. He looked up at the departures screen and saw the flight. 'Desk 28. Checking in now.' The desk wasn't busy and Adam Tennant felt good as he handed over the piece of paper that would get him to London by 1520 hrs. that afternoon, local time.

"Any luggage to check in?" asked a beautiful, raven haired check-in girl who spoke excellent English. Her perfect white teeth showed as she smiled at her customer.

"No, just hand luggage," he smiled back at her, wondering if she'd have said 'yes' if he asked her out for a drink? Tennant was prone to thinking women liked him. Somebody once told him, after a few drinks, that he

174

resembled a young Erroll Flynn. Maybe because he also looked like Robin Hood.

"Seat number 12A. Boarding time 1255 hrs. Have a good flight, Mr. Tennant." As the passenger turned away, the check-in attendant thought to herself 'what a creep!' He walked down to a coffee bar and ordered a cafe machiato – a milky coffee, and a sandwich. He realised he hadn't eaten breakfast. The fewer people he saw on the cruise ship that morning the better. He didn't want to bump into 'Mr. and Mrs. Sheffield' who would have asked questions about Joan. Tennant would have had to make up some story as to where she was. He didn't want that. Sitting munching his ham salad sandwich, his conscience wasn't troubled. He sipped his tea. Able to clear his mind about the night before, he found some of his training in the army had helped. Move in on the enemy, destroy, get away, keep a clear head.

In Civitavecchia a cabin maid, now on kitchen duty, was peeling potatoes and generally helping in the galley on board the large cruise ship. As sometimes happens, when she wasn't thinking about cleaning cabins, a thought suddenly came into her head. Normally there were two damp bath towels in the cabin occupied by Bobbins and Tennant. That morning there was only one.

'Strange?' she thought, but dismissed it as quickly as it had occurred to her.

Chapter 44

On command from Jorgsholm the two armed policemen entered the building via the back door, forcing entry. The lights were switched on.

"Hands up, hands up and don't move!" One of them screamed. Jorgsholm rushed in behind them holding his pistol directly in front of him with two hands. Glym, although unarmed, was at the front door in case they tried to escape that way. She was primed to use her martial arts training, it had come in handy on a number of previous occasions. Inside the house there was nobody about. It was as though the occupants had just gone out, maybe they had? As quietly and as stealthily as possible, Jorgsholm went upstairs. The third stair creaked slightly, sounding like an rusty door hinge. He went from one room to another, his 9mm handgun at the ready, held out in front of him with his finger on the trigger. Suddenly there was a shout from downstairs.

"OK, come out from behind that settee!" screamed a police officer seeing three fingers protruding at the side. Carl Jorgsholm turned quickly and ran back down the stairs two at a time and into the lounge. An elderly couple were hiding behind the brown three-seater settee. The man, a Dane aged at least 80, slowly moved out from behind the furniture and raised his hands. His wife remained cowering on the floor. Jorgsholm moved towards him. The man, still on his knees, looked at the detective.

"Please don't kill me. We've no money but you can take what we've got!" His eyes were wide with fear and his hands shook. His brain didn't register that a police uniform usually meant safety. "My wife is blind and my sight is poor. Please don't kill us!"

The room was silent. The members of the Danish police force looked at each other. Jorgsholm swallowed hard. He spoke.

"Who else is in the house?"

"Nobody but us," replied the old man. One of the policemen helped the elderly lady to her feet. She eventually sat down, frightened and breathing heavily. Her husband sat next to her and held her hand for reassurance. "Please, please . . ." he continued.

"It's OK," Glym said having run into the property from the front garden. Her voice sounded more comforting than any of the other three. "So you live here alone? How long have you been here?"

"Twelve years. We moved here after I retired from business. My wife slowly lost her sight because of glaucoma and we get regular visits from our family – two sons and their wives. We have seven grandchildren and three great-grandchildren." He volunteered more than Glym expected. She was certain that they were telling the truth.

"What's are your names?" Glym continued.

"Carsten and Lisbet Halskov."

"Mr. Halskov, we are police officers and are following up on a lead regarding missing persons." Glym did not mention the murdered girls. "We had reason to believe, it now seems wrongly, that this house may have been used by someone involved in that. We are very sorry to have caused you this grief. We shall arrange to have your back door fixed first thing tomorrow, but in the meantime one of our officers will remain with you overnight for your safety, if you wish."

She paused, allowing Carsten Halskov to absorb her statement. "Is there anything else we can do right now?"

Carsten Halskov shook his head. He didn't want a policeman in his house. Halskov was from the school of independence – a tough Dane with an iron constitution. He'd nail some planks of wood across the door – make it safe enough. Getting up he made his way to the front door with the police officers, unbolted it and showed them out. As they walked down the path Halskov coughed to clear his throat before he spoke.

"Others have made the same mistake. There is another property very similar to this house further towards the coast. It's in that direction and about four kilometres from here." His gnarled index finger pointed west. "We pass it once or twice a month. They have a red car parked on the drive."

Chapter 45

Alitalia flight AZ 204 landed at London Heathrow right on time. Tennant undid his seat belt before the 'unfasten seat belt' sign had been switched off. As soon as the aircraft had come to a halt he was out of his seat and getting his small case from the overhead locker. Other passengers quickly followed suit. Within seven minutes Tennant was striding towards the exit signs and 'Underground'. He'd gone through Customs without a hitch and he felt good. The Piccadilly line would whisk him to King's Cross and from there he'd be on a train to Darlington. He could be back on Teesside by 8.00 pm that evening. No problem.

Tennant had his mobile phone in his jacket pocket but he had not switched it on for quite a while and the battery was probably flat. He decided to leave it switched off. Joan Bobbins had used hers for most of their needs whilst on the cruise, and Tennant had made a couple of calls himself from her phone. The Piccadilly line got him to King's Cross in about an hour and he was soon buying a ticket for his northern destination on the east coast line. W.H. Smith provided him with a newspaper, paid for, of course, with money from Bobbins. As he settled back in his first class seat, Tennant found time to reflect on what had happened over the last few weeks.

He'd met Joan Bobbins in a pub, they got chatting and became friendly. He'd been careful how much he'd told her about himself. She, on the other hand, was all talk, and soon told him about her prison sentence, her

179

husband George's lottery win as well as her inheritance. When she told him about witchcraft he was a bit scared, hairs standing up on the nape of his neck. The rituals, the drinking of strange potions, the chants, and their strange clothes made Tennant listen intently, his bladder asking to be emptied before it did it involuntarily. But it was nothing he couldn't handle, he was tough, or so he thought. She'd been generous with her money, paying for lavish meals, often with champagne. He'd never *really* fancied her. She had a reasonable figure for her age – which she never openly divulged – and liked to kiss and cuddle. Tennant always thought she had a look of a cross between Angela Rippon and Twiggy, sort of attractive in a way, but a bit too mature for him - mature in the sense of a good wine.

The train passed through Doncaster, and continued to the next stop, his getting off point. He wondered what was happening on the cruise ship. Being aware that the head count on the coach returning from Rome would be one short, he asked himself what the guide would do? Wait for him? He wasn't bothered. Joan Bobbins was feeding the fish in the Mediterranean, and it might be some time before she was missed. Tennant felt fairly secure. So he'd not returned to the coach. Maybe he had been abducted in Rome? These things happen and nobody could prove what had gone on. No, everything was going to be OK. Tennant felt it was now time to move on, make some new resolutions as though it was New Year's Day.

The train slowed as it came into Darlington Bank Top station, once the home of Stephenson's 'Rocket', and he got out of the carriage. As he walked towards the exit, he had a sense of concern as, ahead of him, police were stopping people at both the route down to the taxi rank and the side exit at Bank Top. There seemed to be a queue forming as police were checking those that were leaving the railway station. There couldn't be a problem, could there? Tennant remained calm and approached the exit barrier.

"Excuse me, sir, but do you have any identification on you? Just a routine check for security reasons." There had been earlier reports of possible Al Queda terrorist activity in the north east and airports and railway stations were on alert. Tennant reached into his pocket and pulled out his maroon coloured passport. He handed it to the police sergeant.

"You don't look like Joan Bobbins, sir?" said the policeman after scrutinising the document.

He'd totally forgotten that he was carrying both passports with him. Tennant was detained for questioning and taken to the police station across the road from the Civic Theatre.

Chapter 46

The tour guide had waited for an hour in Rome before deciding to get on the coach to return to the port of Civitavecchia. The passengers who'd been tolerant for up to sixty minutes had got cheesed off. Where was the guy who had a small case with him? It had been made clear to everyone on the tour that if they were not at the meeting point within half an hour of the appointed time the coach would leave without them. It was then their responsibility to get back to the cruise ship as best they could.

Once back on the ship, the tour guide made a phone call to security on board ship to inform them that they were one passenger short. A senior receptionist then headed straight for the cabin of Adam Tennant, aware that Mrs. Bobbins was reported as feeling unwell. There was no answer from the three knocks on the cabin door so she decided to leave it for the moment and headed back to the main reception desk on G deck. Details of the missing passenger, Mr. Tennant, was passed to other administrative staff on board. If he phoned the ship, the senior receptionist wanted to know immediately.

It was later that evening when the Purser saw the tour guide to say that one of the maids, although she didn't think it was important, had mentioned the towels. A tannoy request was made for Mrs. Joan Bobbins to come to reception as soon as possible but she never showed. Ship's security were alerted and the cabin that Bobbins and Tennant had booked was entered. It was exactly as the maid had left it. No sign of use during the day, nothing touched or used. Security called Joan Bobbins' mobile phone number - no reply.

The next port of call was Naples, further south along the west coast. Security thought Tennant may show there, but he didn't. The head of security had become anxious. Only once before in his twenty years experience had this happened. They had full details of both passengers, and he decided to contact the Metropolitan Police. The Met, in turn, then got in touch with Cleveland Constabulary. This occurred two days after Tennant had arrived in Darlington. He had been detained, and the police were unhappy with his account of how to came to have another passport. He had said that he'd been over to France on the Dover to Calais ferry for a few days and found the passport at the ferry terminal. A pack of lies ensued, including winning the large cash sum at a casino which he had changed from euros into sterling.

The passport office in Newcastle upon Tyne confirmed the name and address of Joan Bobbins. Further enquiries by the police revealed that Adam Tennant was friendly with her, and eventually it became apparent that she had taken him on a cruise from Southampton. Tennant was a compulsive liar but broke down under persistent questioning. He did say, however, that he had no idea of the whereabouts of Bobbins. He was fed up with the cruise and wanted to come home so he had left her on the ship, and later Tennant said he must have accidentally taken her passport, saying he was confused.

The cabin that they had booked on the cruise ship was thoroughly checked by Italian police when it came into Naples. It was apparent that Joan Bobbins had not used the cabin during the past 48 hours. They were now looking for a missing person. That was one thing that the MSC shipping line did not want to become news. But it did. Newspapers across Europe reported on the missing English tourist, and that included *The Northern Echo*. And the face of Adam Tennant appeared on the front page of Wednesday's edition.

Anthea Richards hadn't yet seen the photo, but when she did she would get a shock. A very big shock.

Chapter 47

"The caravan is in Sweden!" said Billy Bishop over the phone. Anthea was surprised.

"Sweden! What's it doing there?"

"No idea. All I know is that the red dot is flashing on the laptop screen near Malmo."

"I've remembered, Harry did say that the Chinese guy, Hokey, once told him that he bought 'vans to sell in Scandinavia, especially Denmark. He got a good price for them there."

"But Malmo is in Sweden. I wonder if the Chinaman will take it over that long bridge to Denmark, then?" Billy was getting involved, which Anthea appreciated. It also sounded as though he knew something about the geography of the area. The emails from Hokey seemed to have dried up so Anthea was beginning to feel more relaxed.

"Probably. Can you keep an eye on it for us over the next couple of days, like every three hours or so, or breakfast, lunch and tea if that's easier? We must find out where it ends up. Harry has a theory that there may be a link with some sinister activities in Denmark – drugs, kidnapping, things like that."

"He's got an imagination, hasn't he?" Billy sounded interested. "He should write a book!"

"Well, his brother Mao gave a little more away than perhaps he ought to have done when Harry met him in Seahouses. They're certainly a shifty pair!" Anthea reinforced the point. "Anyway, Billy, thanks for the call and do keep me informed. Have you heard that Harry's case will be heard on 1 August?"

"No. Can I come along? If you want some support I can be there."

"Billy, of course you can, you're very welcome. I'll be on edge, but I'm confident he'll be found innocent." Anthea hoped beyond hope that he would be. She simply did not want to think about her husband being put away for years and years. Thirty maybe? What on earth would she do on her own? She'd gone through the trauma of losing her daughter on the Danish trip – and hadn't got over it – even after all these years. Anthea still had to believe that Juliette was alive. Of course she was. It was just a matter of time before she was found.

Dave Wilks was still being held in a cell at Middlesbrough police station although time was running out. He'd have to be charged if they wanted to keep him in much longer. DI Whitehouse and DS Smith had spent some time going over the events in 'The Bluebell' on the night Richards got drunk. Whitehouse had details of what appeared to be Wilks spiking the drinks that he bought for Harry Richards.

"Come on, Dave, we have at least one eye witness who said you had been seen (a) buying drinks for Harry, and (b) putting something in them. What have you got to say for yourself?" Whitehouse sat opposite Wilks and eye-balled him straight on.

"It was a bit of fun. It was my birthday and I'd won some cash on a lottery scratch-card. I've known Harry for a long time. He's all right. I'd bought drinks for other lads, too. He used to say he wouldn't get drunk, so it was a challenge." Wilks seemed to be telling the truth.

"Harry said the drinks tasted awful. What had you put in them?"

"I'd asked Les the barman to put in a shot of 'grappa' first, then one or two other things after that. It gave the drink an extra kick, but it's got a bit of an unusual taste. Ask Les, he'll tell you. I'd slipped him a tenner to do it." Wilks kept eye contact.

"Someone said you'd put a packet of something into one glass?"

"That was saccharin, just to sweeten one bitter tasting drink – a Jagermeister." Whitehouse wasn't getting far. Wilks kept cool. Smith asked Wilks if he wanted a coffee to which he nodded. "Milk and two sugars." When the coffee came into the interview room, Smith placed it on the left hand side of Wilks. The interviewee moved it over to the right, and he stirred the mug with his right hand. Whitehouse continued.

"How many drinks do you think you bought for Harry?"

"Maybe eight to ten."

"Were you surprised that he could hardly walk?" Smith threw in the question.

"No. I'd be on my back after that lot! Some other lads were getting merry, too, but it was all good natured. Nobody got annoyed or anything."

"Can you recall who else was in the pub that night?" Smith was poised with pen and pad. Wilks closed his eyes for a few seconds to aid his recall.

"I don't know all their second names, but I remember Ed, Jim, Don, Ray, Ken, Dick, Ron, Kevin, Joe and Harry, himself. Les in the pub probably knows some of their names."

One of those did hear what Harry said, and one of those wanted the money.

Smith wrote them down with a view to popping into 'The Bluebell' soon.

"Do you think any of the others you've mentioned will have picked up on anything Harry might have blurted out after he'd had a few? Apparently he was talking about the sale of a caravan."

"Selling caravans! They're a blinking nuisance! Always hogging a lane and a half on the roads, you can't overtake them! I heard him mention a few thousand pounds that he was getting for a 'van after he'd delivered it somewhere. To be honest, I wasn't interested."

"Did anybody else listen in to the talk?" Whitehouse was standing up now, adjusting his cuff-links and flattening his gravy spotted tie against his shirt front.

"Well, yes, anyone of those I mentioned could have done. I can't recall anyone in particular, although there was a guy called David somebody who seemed to be earwigging."

"Why did you run away from your digs, and why did you tell your landlady you'd gone to Aberdeen?"

"I'd borrowed three grand from a guy called Eric 'Axeman' Mowbray a while back. I couldn't afford to pay him and I knew he was looking for me. I had to get away, so I told Mrs. Hardisty I was off to Aberdeen but went to see my sister Doris in the Lakes. She's got a place near Keswick. I needed space and time to think. I told Doris about my situation and she gave me the money. Her old man – my brother-in-law – had passed away six months ago and left her a tidy sum. I can give you her address in Keswick if you want." Whitehouse looked at Smith as if to say 'so far this makes sense.'

"So, would you say you struggled to make ends meet financially?"

"Dead right I do. My job doesn't pay well and I can't save for toffee!" Wilks smiled.

"OK, Dave, that's all for now. Don't go too far away from Teesside. We might want to be in touch. Where are you staying now?"

"A mate has a four bedroomed house in Redmarshall. I'll jot down his address for you, and then I need to find Eric Mowbray to give him his cash." Wilks was passed a sheet of paper and he wrote his new address down. Whitehouse noted he was right handed. Smith showed Wilks to the front door of the police station and Dave Wilks walked down the steps, looking straight ahead of him. Wilks headed to a local bar for a drink and smiled to himself. He was relieved. He bought a scotch and fingered the money in his inside jacket pocket. 'Axeman' Mowbray could wait a bit longer. Just a bit longer.

Meanwhile a body had been found washed up on a beach on the west coast of Italy. It was a woman wearing a tattered evening dress, but no shoes. There was bruising on her body, and part of her face and lips had been eaten away, giving her a gruesome appearance.

Even a visit to 'Angel Face' wouldn't have helped – Anthea was good at her job but she wasn't a miracle worker.

Chapter 48

Jorgsholm decided that they would drive over to the coastline further west of Skagen the following day. He met with Glym for breakfast in the small hotel they were using in Frederikshavn. The place wasn't busy - there were a few visitors, identifiable by their casual clothes and a camera slung around their neck, plus a handful of business men, laptops open on the table. Jorgsholm glanced around and found a table in the corner. Over a light meal of fruit juice, toast and coffee they discussed where they had got to in this investigation. Jorgsholm pulled a pad out of his pocket and reviewed notes he'd made over the past few weeks. Glym listened, leaving her notepad in her handbag, as she spread a small pat of butter over the golden brown toast. He spoke.

"There is still no sign of Wang Xian. Should we assume he's back in China? No sightings of Sven Longe. Where is he? And what about Li Wong?" Jorgsholm sipped his black coffee.

"Sven Longe cannot be far. He must still be in the country," replied Glym, chewing her toast. "We could increase surveillance in the Kokkedal area. After all, that's where he picked up Juliette – he may be back there. As for Wong, he had a driving job around the Malmo area. We haven't really spent much time checking out the sort of companies that employ drivers. And with him being Chinese, that shouldn't be too difficult. If he was a member of 'Frihed' then he'll have a tattoo on his right shoulder blade." Glym took another bite of her toast and then sipped her juice.

"Get two of your staff to check out companies in Malmo that employ drivers – either full time or part time. Check what type of vehicles they use. Get somebody to review the CCTV footage around the shopping mall in Kokkedal on a daily basis. Keep a look out for Longe. Have someone increase intelligence on Wang Xian. Check everything . . .where he went after college in Copenhagen, did he take a driving test here, any credit card or bank applications. I know we've followed up on some of that, but we may have missed something. You know how it is, Merete, often it's the tiniest piece of information that could be key to this whole affair. Let's go!" They both finished off their coffee, pushed back their chairs and strode out to the car park.

Jorgsholm's plan that day was to drive up to Skagen to look around. They'd try to find the light blue house that was similar to the one belonging to the Halskov's. Carl Halskov said he'd passed it and seen a red car on the drive. It was unlikely that Jorgsholm would do anything more than survey that part of north Denmark. The rugged coastline, bird life and fine settled weather made this a part of his job that he liked. He still had to keep tabs on a number of other cases he was dealing with and used his mobile phone regularly throughout the day. He continued to carry a handgun in his shoulder holster but Glym remained unarmed.

The road became narrower as they slowly drove along. A few small houses dotted the landscape, none matching the description they were looking for. Most were white, with small gardens and maybe a shed. A few had cars parked at the side or in front. Some had a small boat, probably used for fishing or pleasure. After twenty kilometres of a casual drive, stopping only occasionally to check the area through binoculars, that Jorgsholm always carried in the car, they headed back towards Frederikshavn. A man was digging in his front garden wearing ragged trousers, brown lace-up boots and a check shirt. Looking as though he was just off a Viking longboat, he was also smoking a pipe. Jorgsholm stopped outside the front gate and got out of the car.

"Hello, good morning. We're looking for a friend of ours who lives around here somewhere. We wondered if you could help?" He'd walked up to the man while Glym stayed where she was. The old man stood up, breathing heavily as he did so and grimacing as his back creaked.

"What does he look like?" The old man placed both hands on the handle of his spade and his left foot on the edge of the spade.

"Well, he's Chinese and drives a red Volvo. He may live alone these days, but I'm not sure about that. It's a while since I've seen him and his wife may have left him?" The old man paused to consider the question as Jorgsholm stared at him.

"No. Nobody like that around here that I know of. Volvo is a common car, but I haven't seen a red one. A dark blue one goes past once or twice a week. I don't think I've ever seen a Chinaman in my life." He puffed on his pipe and Jorgsholm caught the heady aroma, not unlike cigar smoke. "There is a man, I think he might be a schoolmaster, moved into the area a month back. I saw him in the village shop last week. Academic looking, maybe teaches around here somewhere?"

"OK, thanks. What's your name by the way?" asked Jorgsholm.

"Schmidt, Johann Schmidt. And yours?"

"Call me Carl," said the Superintendent.

"Good luck with your search for your friend, Carl."
Schmidt smiled, took another puff on his briar, and
continued digging. Jorgsholm got back into the VW
Passat. Glym looked at her boss.

"Any news?"

"Not really. A blue Volvo sometimes goes by but it's
not the one we want. He's never seen a Chinaman in his
life." They both laughed out loud. "A guy looking like a
teacher moved into the area recently, but nothing else.
Let's go back to the hotel and use the laptop, check the
emails, and make some more phone calls." He pulled
away from the roadside and within half an hour they
were pulling into the hotel car park.

"I'd like to freshen up for five minutes, then we can
meet in that quiet part of the lobby," Glym proposed.
They had adjacent rooms on the first floor and they took
the lift. "I'll bring the notes and folders I've got from my
room and see you downstairs." Jorgsholm smiled and
nodded in agreement. She thought he had a lovely smile
and straight white teeth, but she could never tell him.
Glym put that down to his habit of chewing gum nearly
all the time. She slipped the key card into the slot,
entered her room and immediately let out a loud,
piercing scream.

"Carl!"

"What?" He came running from his room next door.

"I've been burgled, my room's been ransacked!"

Chapter 49

A screech of tyres came from the car park below. Jorgsholm rushed to the window and saw a white BMW leaving the parking area at speed. Black marks were left on the tarmac as it raced away towards the south. He wasn't certain, but the driver could have been oriental.

"Stay here and report this!" he was gone. Jorgsholm was fit. He ran down the staircase, his car keys in hand. He didn't have time to put anything down when he heard the scream, nor kick his shoes off. He ran across to the VW Passat, jumped in and fired up the two litre turbocharged engine. He could see the BMW in the distance, but Jorgsholm was not going to lose it. As he got closer he could see it was an M3, the sports version with a top speed of about 200 kph. Jorgsholm had always enjoyed driving, and had done some car rallies in his youth. He'd passed the Danish Police Advanced driving course and could do 'hand-brake' turns if a situation required it.

The roads weren't busy and Jorgsholm kept up with the BMW, losing sight of it from time to time when it went over the brow of a hill or round a long bend. However, he was not far behind. The Passat engine roared as he accelerated, the powerful engine doing its job. Rarely had he driven like this but he was enjoying the thrill of it, adrenalin now pumping through his body. Ahead lay a cross roads with a Give Way sign. The BMW had to slow down, didn't it? The brake lights would come on. No brake lights showed. The driver went straight across at high speed but Jorgsholm was more cautious and slowed, just enough to check that there was nothing coming from his right or left. The road was clear, he sped over.

'This guy's a maniac!' he said to himself. And damned dangerous, too!' The road opened up, the countryside flat with grass fields on both sides. Ahead was a light industrial zone, the type often seen across Denmark. Both cars were doing over 120 kph, dust billowing into the air like a mini tornado. On the right about two kilometres ahead an articulated lorry was moving slowly from right to left to join the main road where the chase was taking place. Jorgsholm used anticipation and eased off the accelerator slightly. The BMW was not for slowing down. Whether the driver of the artic had not seen the cars, or was on his mobile, or otherwise engaged, he did not stop at the road junction. The fifty metric tonnes of steel kept going. As the haulage company truck straddled the road, the BMW's brake lights came on, but it was too late. The white car went right under the middle section of the articulated vehicle.

Jorgsholm braked hard and pulled to the right, coming to a stop only metres from the green and white lorry on the roadside. He jumped out and ran to the BMW, thirty metres on the far side of the truck. The car roof had been taken off completely, like an opened sardine can but without the fish contents. A headless torso lay slumped back in the leather driving seat that had lost its headrest. Blood covered the rear of the car, the back seats and boot. Thick, red rivulets slowly ran down the side of the bodywork, glooping onto the alloy wheels and tyres. Blood pooled around the car, contrasting nicely with its 'Antarctic Ice' paintwork.

Jorgsholm walked back down the road for a short distance. In the middle of the road was a head. It was definitely oriental, very probably Chinese. Short cropped, black hair, and almond eyes that were still open as though looking for something. A small, enamelled red cross stud was fixed in his pierced right ear. Jorgsholm walked back to the BMW as the lorry driver was stood at the side of the road, speechless. His face was snow white, and he was holding his hand over his mouth, his blue eyes open wide. Jorgsholm went back to the car, looked at the torso, and putting his hand into the top left shirt pocket of the dead body he took out a thin black plastic wallet. Opening it slowly, he saw it contained two 50 euro notes, a receipt from a liquor store, and two petrol receipts. There was also an identity bracelet on the left wrist of the torso. Jorgsholm turned it around.

It read 'Wang Xian'.

Jorgsholm ambled over to the side of the quiet road, his stomach knotted but churning. He bent over and wretched, and, despite not having had any lunch, he could have filled a bucket. Looking down at his spattered black shoes he was thinking to himself 'I'll need to clean those'.

But right then that was the least of his worries.

Chapter 50

"Have you seen today's *Echo*?" Jackie asked Anthea as she walked through the door of 'Angel Face'. "You won't believe this!"

"No, I didn't have time to buy one. Anything interesting?" Anthea put her handbag down and switched on the kettle for her second caffeine fix of the day. Jackie showed Anthea the front page. The photo staring at Anthea was that of David Cresswell. She had to sit down as she suddenly felt light headed, her hands trembling slightly.

"Anthea! Are you all right?" Jackie rushed across, placing her caring hand on Anthea's shoulder. "You look as if you've had a shock!"

"What's this all about?" asked Anthea holding the *Echo*. Jackie told her about the report of a missing woman on a Mediterranean cruise, her body found on an Italian beach. The comprehensive report covered the story and the body was thought to be that of Joan Bobbins, but was yet to be confirmed.

"But she had gone on the cruise with Adam Tennant", Anthea said, looking at Jackie. "And can this be *our* Joan Bobbins?" as though there was another one!

"It must be her!" Jackie walked over to the side unit and made the coffee as Anthea took in the news, staring at the front page again.

"I'm confused. That guy is David Cresswell. I met him after I'd been to the magistrates court a while back. He gave me his business card. It's here in my purse." Anthea got the card out. She showed it to Jackie as well as Jane and Rebecca who had just come into the salon looking concerned as they picked up on the situation – their boss sitting ashen-faced. Her gaze returned to the front page of *The Northern Echo* as the other three passed the business card around. Anthea read the whole article. They all knew that their prime customer was off with her toy-boy to the Med. She'd bored them with it enough! But there was a mistake here, there had to be. The police had somehow mistaken Cresswell for Tennant. Anthea didn't know how they'd done that, but Cresswell needed to be made aware of this if he didn't know already! The kind, well spoken young man had helped Anthea, and offered to be a witness in Harry's court case.

Anthea needed to phone Cresswell to tell him of this mistake. Previous attempts to contact him had failed but she'd give it another go. She picked her mobile phone out of her bag and rang Cresswell. She waited for a few seconds. She heard his phone ringing. Meanwhile, a mobile phone was buzzing in a cardboard box in a locker at Cleveland Constabulary HQ.

Chapter 51

The White Rose flags flew on Yorkshire Day from a handful of buildings in Middlesbrough. The gentle breeze blowing them enough for the white petals to be seen. People were making their way to Teesside Crown Court on Russell Street on a sunny August day. It was a murder trial – the trial of Harold James Richards of Yarm in the county of Cleveland. The public gallery soon filled up as gowned and wigged barristers and other legal officials went about their preparatory business. There was a hum of anticipation in the air as folk wondered if Harry was guilty? As usual there were members of the public who knew the accused, and then there were the 'nosey parkers', those with little else to do but turn up and listen to the cut and thrust of legal debate, especially the gory bits. Newspapers were folded, and mobile phone switched off or turned to silent mode.

Jonathan Cleasby walked in looking resplendent in his black gown, and a tidy wig covered his short, black hair. The court recorder took her seat at the front, and then Denzil Penberthy entered. He nodded to Cleasby, more out of courtesy than respect. They'd met before. Members of the jury took their seats and the last remaining visitors of the local population sat down in the upper public gallery. Anthea was there with Billy Bishop as well as many others who knew Harry. Harry Richards was brought in between two G4S guards, and handcuffed to one of them. The ticker-tape chatter of human noise declined as the judge entered. Everyone stood. The presiding judge, Mr. Evelyn Lionel Sinclair-Armstrong

D.Litt., Q.C., stood for a few seconds, looked around, and sat down. He particularly eyed Cleasby and Penberthy. The courtroom was silent, the atmosphere expectant.

Sinclair-Armstrong opened the proceedings. He briefly explained to the court the reason as to why Richards was appearing, and the charges against him. He emphasised to the jury their role and that they were under oath not to discuss the case with anyone until a verdict had been reached, not even their spouse. Sinclair-Armstrong also reinforced the fact that under the British legal system all those accused of a crime were innocent until proven guilty. An officiating clerk handed Harry the Bible and he took the oath, repeating after the clerk - "I promise to tell the truth . . .and nothing but the truth, so help me God."

Jonathan Cleasby began by telling the jury how Mr. Richards had been arrested for the murder of Michael Barrett, wrongly in his opinion, and the circumstances surrounding the event. Cleasby continued, informing the jury that Harry Richards was an honest man with a fine army record, showed his goodwill to his fellows and had an all-round good character. Cleasby would later call Harry's previous army Major, Clive Purdy, to vouch for him as a soldier and his response would be extremely positive. Harry had also done voluntary work and had made a significant contribution as a member of the 'Yarm Community Organisation.' Cleasby's initial strategy of getting the jury to see his client as a 'good person' was taking effect.

Cleasby opened the questioning by asking Harry to tell the jury about the note left on their caravan window and the ensuing events. This continued for twenty minutes, Cleasby prompting Harry when needed.

Eventually, Cleasby thanked Harry – calling him Mr. Richards all of the time – and sat down.

However, Penberthy, quickly on his feet like a jack-in-the-box, countered some of the positives about Harry's character when he told the jury, unusually to begin with, of two minor crimes that Richards had committed. One took place in a shop three years ago when he'd stolen a loaf of bread, and the other referred to failing to stop when a police car attempted to pull him over for speeding. Penberthy made a meal of both of these as Cleasby moved uneasily on his hard wooden chair.

"Let's get to the reasons why Mr. Richards is here!" barked Sinclair-Armstrong, looking hard at Penberthy.

"Yes, m'lud." Penberthy replied, pupil to master.

The two barristers began arguing the points about Richards' case, getting down to the serious business of the case itself. Penberthy went over the details of why Harry had gone to be at the waste ground in the first place. He accused him of being confused about the post it note and making it up, suggesting that if indeed there had been a post it note, where was it now? Surely, he would have kept it?

Had Harry Richard's ever owned a sharp, long bladed knife? The murder weapon had not been found.

Richards had adopted an aggressive attitude towards the potential buyer, perhaps because he was Chinese, if the note *was* genuine.

He had taken the brown package after murdering Mick Barrett. Why? Because Barrett wasn't going to hand over the cash. Penberthy intimated that there had been a struggle, that Harry was armed with a knife, or sword, when he arrived at the waste ground.

And why did Richards say that the envelope contained pieces of paper? He'd taken the £50 notes out and hidden the cash, making up the story about equivalent sized pieces of paper. Where was the paper now?

Why had Richards burnt his clothes if he was innocent? Because he'd murdered Barrett and was getting rid of the evidence.

Why did he change his car at that time? Because it had blood from the dead body inside of it and this had been shown to be true.

Why did Richards visit Seahouses in the first place? Because he was in league with a Chinese dealer who allegedly sold caravans to Scandinavians and the meeting place was a harbourside cafe.

Why had he later met with the dealer's brother? Because he was hatching a plot - possibly something sinister?

Time after time Penberthy looked at the jury, slightly doe-eyed, saying 'And I put it to you . . .'

Penberthy went on and on and on. He brought witnesses to the stand who confirmed many of the points made by the QC. They included several police officers, the car dealer, the waitress from the Bamburgh Castle Inn, Dave Wilks and two other regular customers from 'The Bluebell'. On two occasions he asked Anthea Mary Richards to appear as a witness and he 'went to town' on her, accusing her of being involved with her husband. Anthea was close to tears at times as Penberthy pummelled her with searching questions. Dave Wilks told the jury about the night in 'The Bluebell' when Richards got drunk and 'blabbed' about the caravan deal, overheard by those nearby, suggesting that several people had overheard the details.

Yes, someone had overheard.

Sinclair-Armstrong had to intervene often, with Cleasby standing to shout "Objection, m'lud" as Penberthy made the most of what evidence he had. He'd certainly done his homework and Cleasby knew he was up against a crafty barrister. After a period of intense questioning, the presiding judge called for an adjournment. He said that a 30 minute break would be taken, with a prompt restart on the hour.

After the break, welcome for a drink, smoke and use of the toilet by some, Cleasby was on his feet. He began slowly, reminding the jury again that his client was innocent until proven guilty. Bit by bit Cleasby pieced together the case and countered the points made by Penberthy.

He used emails sent between Richards and Hokun Tu Ying and text messages on his clients mobile phone to indicate that there was genuine contact between them. An offer had been made and accepted – normal business practice.

There was no evidence that Richards had ever got the £14,000. His bank account, nor that of his wife, did not show such a sum of money being deposited. He had never met the Chinese guy before the post it note was left on the caravan in Berwick and there was no collusion between them. Harry had certainly never seen Michael Barrett before his body was found in the Ford Mondeo.

He argued that his client had panicked when he opened the car door on the waste ground and Penberthy used a psychologist to confirm that that was a perfectly normal reaction given the stressful situation at that very instant. He also reinforced the issue relating to Richards burning his clothes and putting his car in part exchange for another. All perfectly normal human survival responses, inbred from Neanderthal days.

The case continued, like a game of tennis. Backwards and forwards, ball in and ball out, advantages, deuces, and double faults played. Witnesses came and went, and the time passed. The jury were led one way, and then the other. Both barristers were professional and persuasive. The jury had to sift the data mentally, their brain cogs turning round and round. At first it seemed that Richards had murdered Barrett – clearly. On the other hand there was mounting evidence that he had not done it, he just could not be guilty.

But Cleasby hadn't finished, yet. There was more . . .

Chapter 52

Cleasby called Sir Wyndham Honisett, the eminent surgeon from Leeds. He was wearing a dark suit, light blue shirt and yellow bow tie. After confirming Honisett's credentials in medicine, his years of surgical practice and his experience in forensic cases similar to the one being heard, Cleasby began questioning him.

"Sir Wyndham, you examined the body of the deceased within 24 hours of death, did you not?"

"That is correct. I'd been asked by the Cleveland Constabulary forensic medicine team to come to Middlesbrough and look at the body of Michael Barrett."

"And would you say that you examined the body thoroughly?"

"Absolutely. I was particularly interested in the modus operandi of the killer. In other words, the way that the throat of Barrett had been cut." Honisett stood upright and presented the facts clearly and concisely.

"And what conclusions did you reach?" Cleasby looked straight at the surgeon and then at the jury.

"It was clear to me that the killer had reached in through the passenger door and slashed the throat of Barrett, from right to left, using his or her left hand. The right hand was very probably used to hold his hair to lift his head. One could tell that from the angle of the cut across the throat and the way that the cut angled downwards. Neck muscles, blood vessels and the windpipe almost down to the spine were severed. By the depth and gape of the cut, I would say it was definitely a

male, because of the strength needed, to make the cut."
There was a slight murmur from the public gallery.

"Are you absolutely certain – beyond any shadow of a doubt?"

"Absolutely."

"So," continued Cleasby, "the killer was left handed, male, and had opened the passenger door, front nearside door, of the car to carry out his crime?"

"Correct, I have no doubt at all."

"And do you have a view on the instrument used in this murder?"

"I would say a long bladed, single-edged, very sharp instrument. Not serrated. Consistent with an army bayonet, a butcher's knife or a small sabre. Perhaps even a samurai sword."

"Of those weapons, which do you think is the most likely one that was used?"

"I've had experience of examining the bodies of soldiers killed in battle. The deep cut and the line along the edge of the wound would suggest a sharp bayonet."

"Thank you, Sir Wyndham, you may stand down." Cleasby breathed a gentle sigh of relief.

He then asked Harry Richards if he was left handed. Richards said 'no'.

The barrister asked Richards if he had opened the passenger door of the Mondeo. Again, he replied 'no.' In fact, Harry's fingerprints were only found on the driver's door. Another set of prints, not belonging to Harry or Mike Barrett, had been discovered on the passenger door, in three different places.

Prints from somebody who was in 'The Bluebell' that night.

Cleasby's final question at this stage was to ask Harry if he had ever owned a sharp, long blade knife like a butcher's knife, a bayonet or a sword? The third 'no' ensued, although he confessed to having a blunt penknife as a boy scout. There was a slight chuckle from the assembled members of the general public.

Penberthy stood up and asked Harry some more questions, but it seemed that they were of limited consequence.

Cleasby had questioned Les, the landlord, about the situation regarding the drinks on the night that Harry got drunk. He confirmed that it was a prank that had potentially serious consequences. Confessing that things were being added to Harry's drinks, he knew it was Wilks' birthday and he was in a party mood. As a publican he was aware that he was in the wrong and apologised. When asked if there was any other particular individual who seemed interested in Harry's caravan story, Les replied that Wilks himself seemed to have been listening as well as a customer called David.

Cleasby called Adam Tennant to the stand. Still being under arrest, Tennant was brought in handcuffed to a G4S guard. Tennant stated his name and took the oath. Within seconds there was a kerfuffle as a number of people began asking questions. One man near the back shouted out.

"That's not Adam Tennant!" Another joined in.

"No, it damn well isn't!"

"Silence in court!" bellowed Sinclair-Armstrong, as feet shuffled. Confusion reigned.

"Silence in court!" The presiding judge shouted out again. "The court is adjourned. We shall take a ten minute break!" This was most unusual – here was a witness that was causing mayhem.

So here was a man with two identities. He is Adam Tennant and also David Cresswell. In fact there was a business card. It had the name David Cresswell on it and it belonged to Adam Tennant. A clerk took the card and handed it to the jury to look at. Cleasby knew about the fact that Tennant was being held on a charge relating to a missing person but was unable, because of the legal position, to elaborate further on that matter.

"Mr. Tennant," Cleasby recommenced his questioning, "how long have you known Harry Richards? Two years was the answer, and Cleasby continued, the replies from Tennant all being positive towards Harry. However, Cleasby raised a question relating to a loan that Harry hadn't yet paid back. The barrister then probed further.

"Are you left or right handed?" *'Left handed.'*

"Have you ever been in the armed forces?" *'Yes, the army.'*

"Have you ever owned a weapon like a bayonet?" *'No, well yes. When I left the army I took my bayonet with me.'*

Tennant was perspiring, beads of sweat appearing on his temples. His eyes darted around the courtroom. He desperately needed Penberthy to help him.

"Do you have any blank A4 paper from the army in your possession?" *'Yes, a few sheets that I took when I left, just for making notes and things'.*

"Can you recall where you were on the day that Michael Barrett was murdered?" *'No, I'm not sure. I might have gone to the Teesside Showcase cinema?'*

"Do you remember what you saw?" Cleasby was grilling him as a headmaster would query truancy by a young pupil. *'No, my memory isn't very good.'*

Cleasby thanked Tennant and asked him to stand down.

He called Anthea Richards, asking her questions about the first encounter with Tennant, posing as David Cresswell. Anthea gave her full story in detail.

"So, Mrs. Richards, Adam Tennant told you in sufficient detail what he had gleaned in 'The Bluebell' on the night in question. From what you have heard today, do you think that Adam Tennant could have been telling you lies when he met with you?"

"Objection, m'lud!" Penberthy moved faster than a rattlesnake.

"Objection overruled," replied Sinclair-Armstrong. Anthea nodded and replied 'yes, definitely.'

Cleasby had no further questions, and Anthea Richards stood down.

After five days of hearing at Teesside Crown Court, with eight witnesses taking the stand, the jury adjourned to consider the evidence presented to them. Twelve members of the jury sat and considered every fibre and crumb of information and evidence. Two hours and eighteen minutes later, they came back into the courtroom and took their seats. Court was reconvened and the slight murmur turned to silence.

"Have you reached a verdict?" Sinclair-Armstrong asked the jury foreman.

"Yes, your honour," replied Jim Smith the jury foreman, standing up and looking directly at the judge.

"What verdict have you reached?" Sinclair-Armstrong bent forward, head down.

The court went as quiet as the grave. Nobody moved, in fact, everybody was holding their breath – it could have been a waxworks museum.

The man who murdered Michael Barrett was sitting in the courtroom. Smiling.

Chapter 53

Wang Xian had been in the hotel on the morning when Jorgsholm and Glym were having breakfast. Despite normally being observant, the Superintendent had not spotted a Chinese guy. Xian had heard on the 'grapevine' that police were in the area asking questions. When the two police officers left the hotel and placed their keys on the desk he was loitering and he noticed their room numbers. When the receptionist was occupied later that morning, and the room had been serviced, Xian took the key to Glym's room. He was looking for any information and assumed Glym would have most of any documentation that they were likely to have with them. He was right – and Xian took anything he could that may help in finding out what information the Danish police had. Jorgsholm wondered how he could have known they were there?

Two important folders were found in the passenger foot-well of the crunched BMW that were returned to Glym by the local police. Although a post mortem was not necessary for Wang Xian, one was undertaken and a rat tattoo was found on his right shoulder blade. His head had been cleanly severed at the second cervical vertebra. The BMW, fitted with false number plates, was searched thoroughly but not found to contain anything of significance. No mobile phone, no other items other than those in Xian's shirt pocket, nothing. In fact the car had been reported stolen two weeks earlier in Copenhagen. The liquor store receipt was for a place in Frederikshavn, while the two petrol receipts were for two fuel stations over three hundred kilometres apart. The first was an Esso garage on the northern outskirts of Alborg, 65 km south west of Frederikshavn, and the other was a BP station south of Odense.

So, Xian, or one of his gang, had stolen the BMW. It had been driven from the capital northwards to the Skagen area via Odense and Alborg. It was fair to assume that Wang Xian lived in this very northern part of Denmark. But where? Jorgsholm decided to drive back to Frederikshavn and visit the liquor store on Margareta Street. It was a long shot, but the owner might recognise Xian from a description that Jorgsholm would give him. The VW Passat headed to the coastal town, Jorgsholm found Margareta Street and parked up around the corner. He and Glym walked into the store and looked around at the hundreds of bottles of wine and spirits. Cans of beer and lager were stacked high at the far end. Jorgsholm went up to a middle aged man behind the counter while Glym browsed the store. The man was of medium height with blonde hair that needed brushing, wore a goatee beard, and was dressed casually.

"Hello," said Jorgsholm showing his police ID badge. "Are you the owner of this place?" The man behind the counter nodded. "Have you had a Chinaman come in and buy liquor recently? In fact, last Monday." He had the receipt in his hand as he asked the question.

"No, I don't think so. My wife was working here, but let me ask her, she's out the back." The owner's wife came in and Jorgsholm repeated the question.

"Yes, I remember a Chinese man. He came in about half past ten and bought two bottles of Scotch whiskey, paid cash and left." That tallied with the receipt. "I saw him get into a white car parked outside and I recall that he drove off very quickly."

211

"Has he been in before?" The owner's wife nodded.

"Yes, with another Chinaman and a dark skinned man." Glym was now standing next to her boss. She had a folder with her and she took out a picture of Sven Longe.

"Is this the dark skinned man? Glym held up the photo.

She looked at it carefully, taking it from Glym's grasp to examine it more closely.

"Well, not really. His eyes were a little like that, but he had spectacles, and fair hair which I thought was unusual as his skin was light brown. If I was to guess his occupation, well he reminded me of a teacher." That sounded a little odd, but Johann Schmidt had mentioned someone who had moved into the area that looked like a teacher. Just at that moment a customer walked into the store, but immediately turned around and hurriedly left. Glym glanced round at him, but only saw the back of his head.

"Here's my card," said the Superintendent, "give me a call the next time either of those two come in. If you could get a car registration number plate that would be very useful, too." Jorgsholm thanked them as he and Glym turned and left the store. They walked back around the corner to their car. However, what they didn't know was that they were being watched from a vehicle parked about a hundred metres down the street. And the occupants of that car were killers.

The next morning when the liquor store hadn't opened by ten o'clock, a customer phoned the local police station. Two policemen arrived at the store ten minutes later, deciding to force entry at the rear of the premises. Inside the back room hung the bodies of the owner and his wife. They had multiple stab wounds and both were hanging by the neck from a beam across the room. His tongue had been cut out and neatly laid on a plate. The letters C L B were daubed on a mirror in blood.

Their hands were tied behind them with blue rope.

When Jorgsholm got the news he knew he was involved with something bigger than he'd previously thought. Something that was going to test his detective skills to the limit.

Chapter 54

The body washed ashore near Naples was confirmed by
Italian police as that of Joan Bobbins. Her white
witchcraft had been unable to save her. Collaboration
with Cleveland Constabulary with regard to her
dentition, and a small scar from an appendix operation,
had proven that it was her. A fall of almost thirty five
metres into the cool Mediterranean sea after a nice
dinner with extra wine had done for her. Her partner, if
he could be called that, had swiftly eased her body over
the side, albeit with a struggle, and bruising on her neck
and arms was consistent with a tussle. The survival
instinct is very strong, even in those who are weak.
Cause of death was cited as drowning, the bruises on her
body were considered to have been caused by hitting the
railing and the fall into the sea.

A boy called Peter had gone up to the top deck that
fateful evening. Playing there earlier in the day, he had
lost his red plastic whistle that his parents had given him
to keep around his neck in case he got lost, when he was
to blow it as loudly as he could. Searching for it that
evening, he had seen Bobbins and Tennant amble along
the side of the top deck and so he'd hidden behind a
small stack of sun loungers.

When he was later questioned he told the Italian
police that he'd heard them arguing about money and
after a few minutes he lifted her up by the waist and neck
and threw her over. The man had then said something
like 'good riddance, witch' as he walked away chuckling
to himself. Peter, aged twelve, stayed hidden for another

five minutes before he found his whistle and went back to his cabin where his parents were getting ready for bed. He never told them because he thought they'd be annoyed if they knew he was on the top deck at that time of night. Peter told them he was with friends playing on the fruit machines in the games area and had lost track of time.

Bobbins' body was flown back to Teesside for post mortem analysis that showed she had also incurred a broken neck, and that it was likely to have occurred as a result of the fall into water from the side of the ship. But who could really be sure? The body had bruises that were still marking her neck, throat and left leg despite being in the water for several days - seawater can be a good preservative. The coroner recorded a verdict of death by drowning, and that's what was shown on the death certificate.

So, poor Joan Bobbins had died at sea after taking her boyfriend on a cruise. She was no angel and had served time – as Tennant knew. But what Bobbins didn't know was that Tennant had searched through her bank statements and found all of her bank details. She'd left a password for internet banking on a note stapled to her last statement. She'd trusted him too much, allowed him into her home, given him a front door key, he'd even been in her home when she was lunching with important friends. He'd betrayed her! Adam Tennant deserved to be 'strung up' as they say. He'd moved one million pounds into a bank account in Guernsey that he'd set up, hoping that she'd never find out, and she never did.

Meanwhile, at Teesside Crown Court, Jim Smith, diminutive and balding with a thin black moustache like a piece of liquorice, was standing in front of Mr. Sinclair-Armstrong.

So, with the jury having reached a verdict, Sinclair-Armstrong asked for a response.

"And what is your verdict?" Sinclair-Armstrong looked down at Jim Smith like a hawk eyeing its prey, his eyes focused and fixed on the jury foreman.

"Not guilty, your honour."

"And is that the verdict of you all?" The presiding judge peered at Smith over his spectacles.

"It is, your honour." The court erupted, hugs and kisses taking place all round as family and friends expressed their relief at the verdict. Anthea was sitting next to Billy Bishop in the public gallery and hugged him, more as a reflex reaction than through a feeling of love, but she knew he was helping Harry and she really appreciated that.

There was eyeball contact between Harry Richards and his solicitor that said it all, and Gerald Lorimer allowed himself a slight smile of self-congratulation. But the moment belonged to Harry. Having been found not guilty, Anthea was already planning a party for him. Sinclair-Armstrong eventually managed to calm things down, banging his gavel like a cobbler mending shoes. He summed up. Once he'd finished, the press exited the courtroom as rapidly as possible and everyone sought sunlight and fresh air outside of the Crown Court on a warm August day. After a short wait, Harold Richards was allowed to leave the court with Anthea walking by his side. Television reporters and cameramen were all around, as well as the local and national press. Being confident of a non-guilty verdict, Harry had prepared a short written statement.

"I'd like to thank my wife, Anthea, for her unstinting support during the past few weeks. Thanks must go to all of my friends who have believed in me, and now we just

216

want to go home, get on with our lives, and put the kettle on." A waiting car, that Anthea had organised, was parked at the front of Teesside Crown Court. The black limousine slowly pulled away, Harry and Anthea in the back, and the driver headed towards Yarm, carefully avoiding the gaggle of media men struggling to get more details from Harry on how he really felt. The posse of cameramen may have got a few good pictures, including the cream of *The Northern Echo,* but tomorrow would tell. Pictures sell papers.

Meanwhile, hundreds of miles away, a caravan was moving across Denmark. Slowly but surely, the 'red dot' headed north.

Chapter 55

A few days later, Harry and Billy were looking at the laptop in Billy's front room. The dot fascinated Harry. To think that little, almost insignificant red pinhead was showing them where the Lunar caravan was located was a marvel – at least to Harry. Obviously the red dot seemed to hardly move, but over hours and days it was easy to note that it was slowly creeping across the screen. The map indicated the lines of longitude and latitude, and when the zoom button was tapped the geographical area enlarged. The dot was north of Odense and at that stage Billy and Harry agreed to switch the laptop off.

"I need to go, but thanks for that, Billy. You're a pal. Keep me informed and I'll talk to you soon." Harry got up, patted Billy on the back and left. He walked home. It was another sunny day, birds were singing and it felt good to be alive. Anthea was at work and he had the day to himself. He knew Anthea's takings at the beauty salon would be down but he knew that secretly Anthea was glad not to have Joan Bobbins as a customer any more. The conversation about her gradually decreased over the following weeks and months.

Harry made himself a cup of coffee in the kitchen and sat down in the lounge to think about things. He thought back on the events of the past weeks. 'Almost like a dream' he said to himself, 'a nightmare.' It certainly had been. A caravan trip to Berwick in early Spring resulted in a court appearance on a murder charge – that was how he summed it up. Harry had information on a number of matters that he had not shared with the police. He knew that he now had to be careful as to how he used the details on Hokey and his 'business dealings'. The 'van tracker was between him and Billy. He sensed that Hokey and his brother were involved in something more than selling caravans to Scandinavia. How could he find out more? He thought about another trip to Seahouses, but what would that achieve? Unless he stowed away on the 'Kwangsi Chuang' boat ... but he dismissed the idea immediately. He could fly to Denmark and hire a car, drive up to where the red dot was situated. Find the Lunar caravan . . . but so what? Suppose it had been sold to a genuine caravan-loving couple and Harry banged on the 'van door demanding to know what was happening. He could envisage the scene, almost like a Bruce Willis film! How embarrassing would that be?

No, he needed to come up with a plan for his next move. He went onto the internet and went into google. He typed in 'caravan sites Denmark'. Several links were shown and he clicked on one of them. A park called 'Sun and Smiles' came up and he looked at some photos of the site. Approximately fifty touring caravans were on the site and it was possible to book a pitch between the beginning of April and the end of October. There were three sites in the area where Harry had last seen the red dot but maybe he'd wait a little longer and see where the dot stopped. Why didn't he and Anthea take a week long break in Denmark? They could catch a ferry from Newcastle to Esbjerg on the west coast. Nowhere in Denmark was more than about 300 km from the port of Esbjerg so they could take their Suzuki over and take a look around.

Anthea had not been back to the country since she had seen a man called Superintendent Carl Jorgsholm almost nine years ago. At that meeting he promised to let Anthea and her first husband, Peter, have any updates on their missing daughter. She'd had several, but there wasn't much to report, most being more like courtesy calls. There was no news on Juliette. Simply none. She had gone somewhere, but where? Anthea had continued to believe she was alive. She had to. There were other cases of missing persons that had made the headlines. Madeline McCann was one such instance; her parents believed that she was still breathing. And there were more. Whatever happened to Suzy Lamplugh? People who were there one minute, gone the next. How did parents cope? Photos stood on shelves or mantle pieces, with a frame holding their loved one - forever looking into the room. Parents, possibly grandparents and other family members thought about their missed one every single day that God sent. A piece of clothing, or a tatty teddy bear was all that kept the flame burning. And the saddest thing of all was that those that were grieving sometimes went to their grave not knowing the outcome.

"We're going to Denmark!" Harry hit Anthea with the news as she walked through the front door at the end of a busy day. She put some shopping down and kicked off her shoes.

"What? When?" she moved right up to Harry and kissed his cheek.

"When the red dot stops!" She knew what he meant, but anyone listening in would have been confused. "Billy is going to let us know when it comes to a halt. I guess another couple of days, then we can book a ferry from Newcastle." Harry had given this some consideration.

"So are we looking at next week? It'll be busy won't it?" Anthea went into the kitchen and poured herself a glass of wine.

"I've checked the ferry timetable and availability. Bookings are down this year, people seem to be staying at home. The hotels are not fully booked either. Once Billy lets us have the news we'll go ahead." Anthea smiled, sipped her wine, leaving the glass on a small table, and went upstairs to change. Harry knew she had agreed without speaking – he just knew. "And I've ordered a Hawaiian special from the pizza house in Yarm so don't be too long!" He topped up Anthea's glass and tugged a ring-pull off a can of beer. Harry was feeling much better. He'd given up smoking, continued his exercises and felt good. A trip to Denmark was going to be a tonic. He was really looking forward to it.

As Anthea came down stairs, dressed casually and with her hair tied back, the phone rang. Harry picked up.

"Hi, Harry, its Billy here. I've got some bad news."

"Oh, what's that?"

"The red dot has disappeared."

Chapter 56

Carl Jorgsholm worked hard on the case of the murder of the liquor store owners. He and Glym had toiled tirelessly after the gruesome killing, the bodies found hanging as if in a butchers deep freeze cabinet. A witness in Margareta Street had taken the registration number of the car that had contained the two killers, simply because they were sitting in the car as though spying on somebody. In a small town like Frederikshavn people don't just sit in cars looking around. They get on with life, go about their own business.

Jorgsholm had followed up on the registration plate and traced the car, an old Ford Cortina, to an address near Skagan about 40 km north of Frederikshavn. The door of the house was opened by a Chinese guy who turned out to be Li Wong. Although Jorgsholm did not know what Wong looked like, after a few questions Wong was running out of the back door of the house as if training for the Olympic 1500 metres. He was caught in open countryside by sniffer dogs two hours later. Jorgsholm had caught one of the killers of the couple from the liquor store. Being questioned by Jorgsholm in the local police station, he would not say who his partner was – only that he was a member of the CLB. After further intensive questioning, Wong confessed to being involved in the murder of the four girls from Malmo. He tried to excuse himself by saying he was acting under instructions. It wasn't him that committed the murders, it was a command on high – from a 'god' that he obeyed. A 'god' that spoke for the C L B, the Chinese Liberation

Brigade, and he had used Wong as his instrument. Jorgsholm came to realise that Wong had to get rid of Nikola, and her friends, before they spoke to the police about their suspicions. Wong stated that Nikola was much cleverer than he'd first thought – she had to be killed.

Li Wong had heard of the death of Wang Xian and saw that as a signal from 'on high' that his future was mapped out. Having been caught, it did not seem to bother him. This was his destiny, going to another world in due course . . . but not until he'd served a minimum of thirty years behind bars.

After many years of service, Jorgsholm was promoted to Chief Superintendent. His dark hair had greyed, he needed to wear spectacles all of the time, and his frame had aged. Walking was slower, and his slightly decreased reactions meant that his driving skills were not as good as they once were. His daughters, Louisa and Agnatha, had grown up; Louisa had graduated in medicine and was starting her training at Copenhagen Hospital whilst Agnatha read law at university and was to become a solicitor in Kokkedal. Anna and Carl Jorgsholm were very proud of them. Neither of the girls had forgotten Juliette and a photo of her always hung on the wall in their front room. Beautiful, blonde, smiling – full of fun. Where was she? Where on earth was she? Out there somewhere. The years had not dimmed the enthusiasm of the Chief Superintendent. He would never forget the day he collected her from the airport. He had sensed then that she was vulnerable – her beauty and radiance said it all. It had been a personal challenge for him to find her, and he felt guilty, always carrying the burden with him.

But before Jorgsholm retired from his police work there was to be a revelation that he could not have

223

predicted. It was something no one could have known, except one.

Just one.

Chapter 57

The case of Adam Tennant came to court. He was found guilty of the murder of Joan Bobbins and sentenced to thirty years.

There was insufficient evidence to convict him of the murder of Michael Barrett. The murder weapon had not been found.

Several weeks later, a regular at 'The Bluebell' took a bayonet into an antique and collectables shop in Middlesbrough. The weapon had the initials DW inscribed on the handle.

The owner of the premises telephoned the police.

Chapter 58

Billy had explained to Harry that if the caravan with the fitted tracker was being stored under a metal roofed warehouse or similar, then the signal would be lost. So, had the Lunar 'van now reached a destination in northern Denmark where it was being kept? That was a distinct possibility. The trail had gone cold but Billy was able to identify the last time the tracker was showing. It was at a place 20 km west of a small town called Jerup. From the map on his laptop it seemed to be in the middle of nowhere! However, Harry decided to book the ferry and hotel. Scanning the details again, within ten minutes he had booked the Newcastle to Esbjerg ferry and a double room in a hotel north of Frederikshavn.

At the end of August they would take the ferry and be travelling around northern Denmark. According to a holiday weather web site conditions were settled and at that time of year the Skaggerak and Kattegat waters between Denmark and Sweden were calm, beaches were generally busy, and they'd blend in with other visitors in this beautiful part of Scandinavia. Harry had printed off details of some caravan sites, but the clear challenge was to try to find the caravan sold to Hokey. The red dot had stopped showing within 25 km of where their hotel was situated so some exploring was on the agenda. Harry had an idea of what to look for – a large building, metal roof perhaps, signs of caravans nearby?

They drove off the ferry and headed east. Denmark is such a clean country - no crisp packets blowing about, no empty cans in hedge backs, so clean. Not like parts of

England that Harry could think of. The little Suzuki purred along like a sewing machine, fuelled up and recently serviced it was happy travelling at about 80 kph. They passed a *Morris Minor* centre – in the middle of nowhere! Harry slowed down, U-turned and went back for a look. There were over twenty cars for sale, all left hand drive and in immaculate condition. Two door, four door, station wagons and convertibles! Right here in the centre of Denmark! Harry got down on one knee and looked underneath one of them. Absolutely immaculate and not a speck of rust. As clean as a whistle! He could not believe his eyes, these 'Moggies', as some enthusiasts called them, had been completely renovated and were for sale. Anthea nudged him as if to say 'come on, time to go.' If he'd had time he'd have bought one! But he had other much more pressing matters that needed his attention.

After a couple of stops for coffee, fuel and the loo, they eventually arrived at their destination. Skagen had a small harbour and the rows of low coloured houses with red tiled roofs dotted the beaches. They'd passed a couple of groups of *'Hell's Angels'* on Harley's and Honda's but they hadn't been any trouble. The 'Hotel Petit' on Holstvej 4 was a charming hotel with a small car park. It was only a six minute walk to Sonderstrand beach, although they weren't planning much time there. Red flowers grew in window pots near the front door. Harry lifted the luggage out of the boot and carried it to the front of the hotel. They were travelling light, it was summer after all, and neither Anthea nor Harry needed many clothes. They were both practical – crease-proof shirts and blouses, shorts, jeans, decent footwear – and that was about it.

"Good afternoon", said the receptionist to the holiday couple. "You must be Mr. and Mrs. Richards?" Natalia had eyes as black as jet and a lovely smile. "It is nice to see you. We don't get many English visitors in this part of our beautiful country." She entered their details onto the hotel database, confirmed the total cost for bed and breakfast for seven nights, and gave them a key card to room eight. Harry thanked Natalia and picked up the key. On entering their room they noticed that the curtains were half drawn to keep out the warm afternoon sun, and the air-con was set to low. A queen sized bed with a light bedspread in autumnal colours, two bedside lockers and an open wardrobe made it attractive and welcoming. A small, flat screen television was in the corner, and the curtains matched the bedspread. Anthea went over to the window and pulled back the curtains slightly.

"What a lovely place!" she exclaimed. She was looking out onto open countryside. The near cloudless sky was light blue and a few large sea birds swept the skies. Wooden cottages in different pastel colours were dotted around. Anthea had also been told that sometimes Danish film stars could be seen in this part, holidaying away from the capital. Gazing out across northern Denmark her eyes misted over slightly as she thought of Juliette. She could be near here, couldn't she? But then she could be anywhere. Was she alive? Yes, she was alive. Anthea could feel it. It was one of those feelings only a mother could feel for a daughter, the bond so very strong.

"For the second time, do you want a cup of tea?" Harry raised his voice slightly. Anthea hadn't heard the question first time round, nodding as she blew her nose and pretended that she might have a cold coming on, then reaching for two paracetamol tablets as Harry poured the tea.

"We'll have this and then take a drive around the area, get to know it a bit better. What do you think?" Harry was in 'Go' mode and he wanted some action during their stay.

"Yes, good idea. I'll hang a few clothes up first, finish my tea and freshen up." Harry opened a map of the area that he had brought with him and spread it on the bed. It covered north east Denmark and had a scale of 1km to the centimetre. He looked at it carefully, identified the hotel position, and scanned the local area for anything that might be useful, finding four camping and caravan sites in the immediate vicinity. A magnifying glass in his hand luggage helped Harry see some of the map icons more easily and he used a pencil to mark three sites. Once Anthea was ready they left the hotel for their exploratory drive, taking a quick look at Grenen, the sandy beach right at the northern tip of the country where it was said you could stand in the water and have one foot in the Skaggerak and one in the Kattegat.

The first two sites were small, about 10 to 15 pitches for 'vans and motor-homes. Limited facilities for washing and toileting meant that they didn't appear too popular, but it was the third site that gave the Richards a useful lead.

It would turn out to be a very useful lead.

Chapter 59

Within minutes of driving onto the site, a warden came over to the Suzuki. Harry put the window down.

"Can I help you?" he asked in a dark brown voice as though he might have been a cigar smoker. The warden wore denim shorts, a cotton open neck shirt and had a full Viking beard. All he was lacking was a double headed axe and a large shield.

"Oh, hello. We're here on holiday and some friends of ours from England said they were staying on a caravan site in the area. We don't know which one for certain, but we thought we'd try this site. They have a Lunar Onward caravan and a silver coloured Nissan X-Trail." Harry thought his comment seemed plausible. It was only the 'van he was interested in, blow the towing vehicle.

"We don't have any guests from your country. Sometimes we get British caravans here, though. We have storage in two large sheds over there." He pointed across the site towards a small supermarket sized warehouse. "We have people who pay for annual storage, they come and go, and it's not my business to get involved as long as they pay."

"If we wanted to store a caravan with you could we put it in those sheds?"

"Of course, we have room for several more. It would be the larger of the two, the other is kept locked."

"Kept locked?" Harry frowned. He tried hard not to show any real interest.

"Yes, it is rented by a man who comes once or twice a month. It is also used by a local dealer. He buys and sells caravans so he needs somewhere to keep them. He pays me good money so I don't ask questions."

"Thank you," replied Harry and eased the Suzuki into first gear, "we'll take a look around elsewhere." Anthea and Harry drove slowly towards the main gates. As they turned left onto the main road, Harry noticed a small single track road that went alongside the site. Deciding to take a look, they drove down the narrow road. At the end was a wide metal gate, easily big enough for a large caravan to pass through. Harry stopped and switched off the engine. It was eerily silent, not a sound of any sort to be heard. Anthea told him to be careful as he got out of the car. She stayed behind, almost as a look-out.

Harry went up to the gate which was padlocked, a heavy chain secured around the steel uprights of each gate. The 'large shed' was about five metres high, sixteen metres wide and almost forty metres long. Tracks of tyres were clearly visible in the soft ground leading from the gate to the shed door, a distance of approximately twenty metres. The building was made of corrugated iron with steel girder supports. Was it the sort that could block out Billy's tracker unit? Harry walked back to the Suzuki and grabbed a reel of black cotton that Anthea kept in the glove box. He pulled a small length of cotton from the reel and tied it around the bottom of the two vertical gate uprights. In that way he'd know when the gate was next opened, as long as he checked it regularly. He wasn't sure how often the gates were used, but he planned to return tomorrow. This would be called 'Shed One'.

Anthea and Harry drove around the lovely countryside for another hour before returning to the hotel. Getting back into their room, they kicked off their shoes, and opened the mini-bar in the fridge for a cool drink. Anthea had a gin and tonic while Harry checked out the local beer - a Carlsberg, brewed in Copenhagen, was perfect. They relaxed before dinner, took a shower, and went to the restaurant at around 7.30 pm. A tall, fair haired waiter took their order. Over their delightful meal they discussed their current situation.

"What do you think we should do now?" Harry opened the more serious part of the conversation. He wanted to hear what Anthea thought.

"We could phone Billy first thing tomorrow, see if he's picked up the tracker signal again. If not, it may be fair to assume the Lunar is in the large shed where we stopped. You could see if there is a small side door to get in, or even hide up somewhere nearby and wait for any comings or goings, but you'd need to be careful. We could also take a trip to the nearest port to see if we can see any sign of 'Kwangsi Chuang'." Harry was pensive for a few seconds before replying.

"Well, it's what we've come for. Seems a waste of time hiding in the long grass when we could be more active doing something. Perhaps we can check the black thread first after we've phoned Billy, and then go along the coast and find out where the smaller boats are moored."

Anthea and Harry talked over their evening meal, weighing up the options. They were well aware that they had not involved Jorgsholm. In fact, he didn't even know that they were there. But that was soon to change. Twenty five km from Frederikshavn a red Volvo was towing a caravan along a quiet road. The police had continued for look for a particular model of a Volvo, a 240 with a registration number of HTY 247. Two police officers passed the car and 'van travelling in the opposite direction. The number plate was not HTY 247 but one of the policemen suggested turning round and checking the driver. They followed the car and caravan for a couple of km until it was safe to stop the vehicle. The police car overtook the Volvo and signalled for it to pull over. Inside the red car were a respectable looking couple, maybe a husband and wife holidaying in the area. The Volvo came to a halt. One of the policemen got out of the white police car, put his cap on, and walked back to the Volvo.

The driver was middle aged, with short cropped hair and spectacles. Although he'd had a small beard, his clean shaven face made him look about twenty. As the police officer approached the car the driver fumbled under the dashboard as if to look for his driving licence. He put his window down and the officer peered in, sniffing slightly to detect any odour of alcohol. With the policeman's face 30 centimetres from the driver, and before he could ask any questions, a bullet from a Magnum pistol went through his forehead and out of the back of his skull, bone fragments spitting into the air like confetti at a wedding.

His colleague jumped out and ran back towards the car, drawing a hand gun as he did so. In an instant the Volvo driver leant out of his open window and shot the second officer through the chest, blood spattering over his white shirt and onto the ground, the liquid gathering around him like an oil slick. The Volvo driver put his window up, indicated to pull away, and continued on his planned route. In his driver's door mirror he saw the bodies of the Danish policemen, lying in the warm sun. Flies would soon be buzzing around, eggs laid, and maggots would be doing their job. He smiled to himself, looking in his rear view mirror and thinking how well his wig fitted. Yes, his disguise was good.

The blonde girl sitting next to him didn't say a word. She was far too drugged to do much of anything, her pupils wide, her eyes staring.

Chapter 60

"Let's get out there now!" Jorgsholm bellowed to Glym. The Chief Superintendent got the news about an hour after it had happened. A car had driven along the quiet road, spotted the grisly scene where the two officers lay facing the sky, and phoned the police. Although the air temperature was hovering around 25 C, flies didn't have time to lay too many eggs. Carl Jorgsholm had a police driver these days and he was good driving rapidly, but safely. His use of gearbox, brakes and four wheel drifts around corners would have made an impression on any rally driver. Jorgsholm felt the G forces as they reached 130 kph, but he trusted his driver. Merete Glym was in the back, tightly belted in, but looking a bit ashen faced.

They arrived at the scene of the murder after local police had been there for half an hour. The bodies of the two dead officers were untouched. They knew that the Chief Superintendent always wanted that. The black covers were lifted off the bodies and Jorgsholm looked at both of them. It was clear to him that they had been murdered by a killer who had no sense of remorse. A simple, quick shot to the head and chest had been enough. The killer knew what he, or she, was doing. Scene of crime officers were on the scene as quickly as possible and did their usual, professional job. As well as checking out the bodies and the immediate scene, one of the S.O.C. officers took a photograph of the tyre marks that were in the soft dirt behind where the police car had stopped. They were also able to tell that the car was towing a trailer or caravan. A small ruler placed next to

235

the tracks helped with sizes as he snapped a dozen shots with his Minolta camera. Back in the lab they would be able to use a new 3D scanner to identify every ridge, wave and detail of the tread. That would be put through a car tyre *TreadMate* database to reveal the tyre make and size.

The bodies of the two policemen were put into body bags and lifted carefully into the back of a Mercedes Benz Vito police van. They'd be taken to the local hospital for an autopsy and Jorgsholm insisted on a report on the weapon used within 24 hours. Glym stayed in the background as the work went on. Jorgsholm knew she had become increasingly squeamish. Was it her age? Was it a female thing? It wasn't the time to worry about it. Jorgsholm wanted to know who had done this and set up an enquiry office in the police station in Frederikshavn. Motorists within a thirty km radius of the murder were stopped and questioned. Police presence increased and men were armed with high velocity G36 rifles. TV, press and radio coverage was extensive. Any relevant CCTV information was reviewed.

The scanner did its job back in the lab. After scanning hundreds of tyres, the screen suddenly showed 'match' in the top right hand corner. The tyre marks of the car belonged to a new Vredestein Sessanta 225/45 R17Y tyre, size 17". Jorgsholm asked Glym to check out suppliers of this tyre in the country. After spending an hour on the internet looking for Danish suppliers of that Vredestein tyre, she told Jorgsholm that she had not found any. The strange thing was that there *was* one supplier. A garage in Odense was the *only* national source of these tyres. The car that was driven by the killer had been fitted with these tyres at the garage within the last month.

Anthea and Harry saw the six o'clock TV news and the murder report made them feel uncomfortable. Very uncomfortable.

Chapter 61

DCI Whitehouse was reading the forensic report on the bayonet retrieved from the antique and collectables shop.

Tiny fragments of dried blood and one hair had shown that this was indeed the weapon used to murder Barrett.

A man with the initials DW had been questioned by the police. He had paid £13,500 into his Santander bank account two days after Michael Barrett took his last breath.

He was ambidextrous, but signed cheques with his left hand.

Chapter 62

Harry phoned Billy at just after 8.00 am, and was told the red dot was still absent from his laptop screen, but he'd keep looking. Harry and Anthea left the 'Hotel Petit' early and pulled up at the edge of the fishing port in Skagen soon after. This small, northern-most part of the country had seen boats for centuries. It had a flourishing fishing and pickling industry, albeit on a small scale compared to other ports scattered around the country. Herrings by the million were caught annually to provide the virtually insatiable appetite of Danish palates. Across the water separating them from Sweden was Gothenburg and the docks there were busy as usual. Harry thought that if Hokey was up to anything he'd use a quiet part of the coast, not a busy harbour. He wasn't wrong. There in the marina in Skagen was a red fishing boat. It was the Kwangsi Chuang! He and Anthea slowly walked down to the water's edge. The boat was securely tied up and looked deserted. They stopped next to it for a few minutes. Time stood still. It was as though they were still in Seahouses – it didn't seem five minutes since they'd had lunch at the Bamburgh Castle Inn and first seen the boat. Anthea had images in her head of the old man mending his nets, pipe in his mouth . . .

"Can I help you?" A voice came from nowhere. About ten metres away a short, stocky man aged about sixty was stood leaning against a wooden shed. He had a peaked cloth cap on his head, and he was wearing wooden clogs. Anthea was tempted to take his picture but resisted.

"We're on holiday," replied Harry straight away. "This is a delightful harbour. Do you work here?" The stocky man looked at them suspiciously. "This looks an interesting boat. Different. Does it moor here often?" After some consideration, Mr. Clogs replied.

"I'm retired. The boat comes and goes. It's for sale, though. The man who owns it wants to get rid of it. I was talking to him last week. He's asking sixty thousand euros for it."

"Why does he want to sell?" Harry didn't want to appear too keen, keeping calm and relaxed.

"His brother, Wang, was killed in a car accident recently. Decapitated. Nasty business. It left him in a state of shock."

Harry didn't know Hokey had another brother apart from Mao. And he certainly hadn't heard that his other brother's name was Wang Xian. Harry wondered how many relations Hokey had, and where did they fit into what was going on between north east England and Scandinavia?

As the Richards' bade a farewell to the Dane, still resting against the wooden shed, Anthea suddenly smelt a perfume. Often in her past she'd picked up odours in the air, orange blossom, honey, candy floss. But there were no other women about. Detecting the unmistakeable odour of a Miss Dior perfume, Anthea knew it was Juliette's favourite.

She wondered if it was an omen? She prayed that it was and kept it to herself.

Chapter 63

Billy Bishop texted Harry the next morning. He'd seen the red dot on his laptop the night before when he was surfing the net. It was around midnight local time that it had appeared, and it was in the area close to where the hotel was situated. Billy was able to note the latitude and longitude and quoted those. Harry's sat-nav could handle the co-ordinates and he would enter them later. Did this mean that Hokey or one of his men were moving the Lunar 'van only at night? That was a possibility. The gates of 'Shed One' at the edge of the third caravan site they'd visited had been opened since Harry had used his method of fastening the thread around them. What was in there? How often was it used? The other major question Harry and Anthea asked themselves now was 'do we involve the Danish police?'

They were going it alone, but for how long could they realistically do that? They had a few more days. So what if they came across some illegal or immoral dealings, what could they do about it? If Hokey were buying and selling caravans to prospective, bona fide customers in Scandinavia – so what? Harry needed to find a key to something that he could use to go to Jorgsholm that would get his interest. Was the tracker enough? Harry wasn't aware that the evidence gained after the murder of the two policeman pointed to a vehicle that was towing something, and that Jorgsholm made an assumption – it was a caravan. CCTV pictures that had been made available showed three car and caravan combinations in the area on the day in question.

Only one of the images could have been the car of the killer. The two other vehicles had tyre sizes of 16" and 18" – a Renault Megane and an Audi A8. The third picture showed a Volvo 240. The plate number was AKW 152. The Danish licensing authority confirmed that the registration number belonged to a Saab that had been scrapped some years previously. It was totally clear to Carl Jorgsholm that this was the car that must be found. An alert was put out across the whole country.

Harry decided to take a look at 'Shed One' after dinner that night. Anthea tried to dissuade him but he was adamant that he'd drive out there. They'd finished eating by 8.30 pm but it was still light outside. A coffee and brandy in the lounge of the hotel helped them to relax, and the night sky began to darken about two hours later. Harry didn't want Anthea to get involved and he firmly suggested that she stay in the hotel, and anyway there was a good film on channel eight. She always enjoyed *'Roman Holiday'* with Audrey Hepburn and Gregory Peck and it was worth watching again. Harry changed into his dark jeans and a black sweatshirt. Kissing Anthea, he grabbed a dark windcheater and he was gone. She told him to be careful, he promised he would. Audrey Hepburn was about to make an appearance as he left the hotel room. Once he was out in the car, he entered the co-ordinates Billy had given him into his sat-nav.

Harry drove over to 'Shed One', switching to sidelights when he entered the narrow road. As he neared the building he parked up and turned off the car lights. The night was lit by a new moon, and a few cumulus clouds passed overhead. An owl hooted in the distance but Harry was as stealthy as he'd been trained to be in the army. He moved slowly, avoiding anything under foot that might make a sound. The gates were still padlocked and the cotton thread was intact. He placed his strong fingers into the 5cm wire mesh squares and hauled himself up. Over the top, just like an army exercise at Catterick Garrison, and he dropped to the ground. Carefully going over to the main door, the night air was silent but Harry heard voices . . . coming from inside the shed. He eased closer to the door, a slight crack to one side allowing him to see through. The inside of 'Shed One' was dimly lit. He put his left eye to the slit and gasped, hearing someone shout 'Yes. Yes.' It sounded like a man's voice . . .

Harry hadn't heard the footsteps behind him. Suddenly his world went black.

Chapter 64

Regaining consciousness a couple of hours later, Harry had the mother of all headaches. He slowly got up, feeling groggy. Looking through the gap in the door again he noticed that the inside of the shed was pitch black. His luminous watch showed it was nearly 2.00 am. Climbing back over the wire fence, and stopping every few seconds, he knew he had to get back to the hotel. He'd be there late and he prayed that the main door wouldn't be locked. Starting up the Suzuki he drove back slowly, his head throbbing. Anthea was asleep and breathing deeply. He'd crept into the room and then rinsed his face in the bathroom washbasin as quietly as possible. Undressing, he slept on the floor, the thick pile carpet was soft, and a cushion for a pillow was adequate for his needs. The spare blanket on the top shelf in the open wardrobe would keep him warm. Laying there staring into the darkness, he tried to work things out. The green digits on the radio alarm clock showed 02.48 but he didn't feel tired. His mind felt like it was on a grand prix racetrack somewhere, and he needed some paracetamol.

Harry thought about what was going on inside the big shed? He hadn't seen much, but the outlines of 'white blocks' he'd seen may have been caravans. The dim lighting could have come from inside the caravans. So were they occupied? No, maybe they were just security lights. But who had hit him? A night watchman perhaps, just doing his duty, and had the police been informed?

'Harry, you're a bloody fool!' he said to himself as he lay looking at the ceiling light unit as his eyes became accustomed to the darkness. A sliver of moonlight was coming through a slit between the curtains. 'What are you getting into? Hokey, prison, a courtroom, now this! Bloody hell!' He was annoyed with himself. He could be in Yarm wheeling and dealing cars on the internet, having a quiet drink in 'The Bluebell'. *A quiet drink in 'The Bluebell'!* Wasn't that where it had kicked off? Harry and his mouth. He wondered how Les, the barman, was doing. And the other lads – Kevin, Dave and particularly Dave Wilks – if he was still around? He'd pop back in soon. Soon? How long was soon? He and Anthea were here in northern Denmark getting involved with something that may be too big for them! They had a few days left before the return ferry from Esbjerg would take them back to Newcastle. Harry dozed on and off throughout what remained of the night. He felt that he was in a state of flotation – as though in a dentist's chair floating on a cloud.

"No, no!" Anthea woke herself up. She'd been dreaming. She sat up in bed, fully awake. Harry woke, too, Anthea's voice making a good alarm clock.

"Are you OK?" he asked, getting up off the floor and going over to the bed.

"Yes, I had an awful dream, that's all." She sat up. "What time did you get back last night?"

"Not too late. Well to be honest, I'm not sure," he fibbed. Harry sat on the bed and went on to tell his wife about the events between leaving and returning to the hotel. She reached for a foil pack of paracetamol on her bedside table, holding them out for Harry.

"Here, take two of these and tell me what *you* think we should do now?" Harry went into the bathroom and filled a tumbler with cold water. The drink felt good and he hoped the analgesic effect of the tablets would kick in soon. It was 7.25 am and breakfast was served from eight o'clock.

"Let's shower and talk over croissants and coffee," Harry suggested, being practical as usual. "You go first."

"What was your dream about?" Harry casually enquired as Anthea went into the bathroom.

"I'll tell you later, let's get ready to face the day, whatever it has to offer." She closed the bathroom door and stepped into the bath, turning on the shower. The day was going to offer a lot.

When Anthea had finished, Harry went into the bathroom and took his clothes off. As he was about to get into the shower he looked down at his arm. In red ink, a rat had been drawn on the inside of his right forearm.

Chapter 65

Over breakfast Harry suggested that the time had come for them to speak with Jorgsholm. The police detective would have information that they did not have, and vice versa. If they pooled their knowledge they'd be far better off. The Richards' had no idea about Frihed and all those involved, nor about the death of Wang Xian. Carl Jorgsholm was not aware of Harry's caravan tracker activities, nor about Hokey and Mao. Yes, it would make sense to get together. But was there anything that Harry and Anthea wanted to hold back on? Should they tell Jorgsholm about Harry's court appearance after being accused of murder?

They'd keep the information to the necessary detail – Hokey, the tracker, their current activities. However, they'd need to tell him about 'Shed One'. It could be worth storming the place, but that would be up to the police. Harry hoped Jorgsholm take their news as positive, and not that they were trying to do his job. Anthea still had a telephone number for Jorgsholm. She phoned him on his mobile.

"Hello, Carl Jorgsholm," he said in Danish.

"Hello, Carl, it's Anthea Richards here. How are you?" Jorgsholm remembered that Anthea had re-married and changed her name from Watkinson.

"Goodness, how are you and where are you?" He sounded genuinely surprised.

"Harry and I are in the Skagen area on holiday. It would be nice to see you. Can you spare a little time for coffee?" She spoke casually with no hint of nervousness in her voice.

"Of course! What about this afternoon. Where are you staying?" Anthea told him. The detective proposed three o'clock at the hotel. Anthea agreed and ended the call. Jorgsholm decided to get all of the latest facts on the search for Juliette. He wasn't certain whether Anthea had heard or read about the four girls from Malmo being found near Frederikshavn. He'd let her mention it – there was no point in raising it first. He wanted to give Anthea something positive on her missing daughter and he would pick out a few points, focusing on the old adage that 'no news is good news'.

Anthea and Harry tried to relax a little, and after a stroll near the hotel they headed south towards Frederikshavn, stopping off on the way for lunch. The day was fine again with just a hint of a breeze, the air as clear as crystal. Anthea kept an eye on the time. They didn't want to be late for the meeting with Carl Jorgsholm. Lunch consisted of roll-mop herrings, slices of ham and fresh bread with a good brown crust. Slightly salted butter was available and their bread was coated with a thin layer, Harry putting it on as if trowelling cement onto a brick. Choosing still water to drink, they took their time over their lunch and chatted about the area and the weather. However, Anthea wondered if Jorgsholm would have any news on her missing daughter. Surely he must have something to tell them. After all these years, the search had never stopped despite the trail drying up at times. The phone calls had lessened from both parties, Anthea finding it hard to ask for more news when there wasn't any. She sensed that Carl Jorgsholm was trying to find different ways of saying 'we are still on the case', or 'we are hopeful that we'll have something in the coming weeks.'

The bill was paid, Anthea feeling that it was rather expensive for what they'd eaten. It was Denmark, after all. The pair set off the return journey to Skagen, allowing themselves enough time to arrive at 3.00 pm. Within about ten kilometres of their hotel, and making good time, the Suzuki got a puncture, Harry sensing that the steering was pulling to the right. He slowed and parked up at the side of the road. Reassuring Anthea that he'd only be five minutes he got out and looked at the flat front tyre. It would be a 'piece of cake' he told her, kidding himself. Anthea got out and Harry opened the boot, removed the jack and raised the Suzuki. Lifting the spare wheel out he saw that the tyre was flatter than an Indian chapati. Anthea gasped as Harry stared at the useless spare wheel.

"Oh, no!" What do we do now?" She was starting to panic. Harry tried to remain calm.

"Phone Jorgsholm and tell him we've had a puncture, tell him we're ten km south of Skagen on the main road to Frederikshavn and we'll be there soon!" Ever optimistic, Harry wondered if a passing motorist might help – take him and the spare wheel to a garage?

Anthea got her mobile phone out of her handbag, but the tyre wasn't the only flat thing around at that moment – her mobile phone was dead, too. It hadn't been charged since they'd arrived! She hadn't given it a thought. Carl Jorgsholm was sitting in the hotel reception area, but he couldn't keep smiling at Natalia at reception without her wondering what he was doing. He waited an hour, glancing at his watch every five minutes or so. 'Where was Anthea?' He then left the 'Hotel Petit' and got into his car. Jorgsholm had other things to do.

Lots of other things to consider. He'd waisted sixty valuable minutes of his day.

Chapter 66

A Volvo 240, now resprayed blue, drove slowly across Denmark towards the eastern seaport of Arhus. This university town had a wonderful Gothic cathedral but the occupants of the car weren't going to church today. They had other plans. The car was driven by Sven Longe. He had three other occupants, Mao Tu Ying, Hokey and a woman. One of them had been based in the Chinese Liberation Brigade office in Copenhagen – now totally empty. Frihed was still operating in the country, and a small but active group continued their subversive activities. Totally ruthless, they consisted of youths with misdirected ideals. They had the 'I must belong to a gang' ethos. Longe had visited Beijing on a college project and been brainwashed whilst there. He loved and approved of Chinese culture and all that went with it. Laughing at those who disapproved of using rhino horn or tiger parts for medicinal purposes, he didn't care what they thought. 'They are only animals' was his counter to criticism from the western world. He abhorred the comment that 'ivory looks best on elephants'.

A caravan was being delivered to Arhus from the UK. Longe and his henchmen were going to collect it. Mao had been involved with the logistics of the 'van in the north east and the Kwangsi Chuang had brought it over, delivering it to Arhus before going north to Skagen to 'hide' for a few days. Hokey did want to sell the boat as the 'Viking' had told Harry, but the news of his brother's death and the circumstances under which he lost his life had made him very angry. Wang was ruthless, but

Jorgsholm knew he was better off going to his so-called 'next life'. The detective had made enquiries on Xian and his curriculum vitae was a blueprint for wickedness. Hokum Tu Ying wanted revenge and had made it clear to his brother, Mao, that Jorgsholm was to be killed, no matter what the cost.

Anthea had managed to contact Jorgsholm and explain the situation regarding their meeting. A passing motorist had stopped and helped Harry put air into his spare tyre which didn't have a puncture – Harry had never checked it since he bought the car off Ron Jones at the second hand car dealership some time ago. He'd remember to give Ron a call when he got back and chew his ears about it! Jorgsholm was understanding and agreed to meet Anthea and Harry again the following day. They agreed a breakfast meeting would be good, so coffee and croissants at 8.00 am at 'Hotel Petit' was the arrangement.

Merete Glym had phoned in sick. She told a colleague that she'd caught a bug from a friend, who was full of cold, who'd come over from to Norway for a few days. Jorgsholm knew those things happened, he'd had a chill himself recently, and he'd asked another colleague to go with him. It was a detective sergeant called Karl Knutson. Knutson was an up and coming police detective in the Copenhagen City force. He'd studied law and achieved a second class honours degree, but wanted to join the police rather than become a lawyer. Jorgsholm and D.S. Knutson arrived at the hotel the following morning just before 8.00 am. Parking up, the two detectives marched into reception.

"Good morning, Anthea." Jorgsholm looked into her eyes as he spoke, and then turned to Harry. "Hello, Harry. I hope you are both keeping well? This is

Detective Sergeant Karl Knutson." Jorgsholm shook their hands warmly, as did the sergeant. They meandered to a table in the corner of the dining room so as not to be too close to the other hotel guests. Apologising again for not being able to meet with the Chief Superintendent the day before because of the flat tyre, Harry looked embarrassed, but Jorgsholm waved away the apology as if to say 'don't worry about it'.

Over a light breakfast the Richards' and Carl Jorgsholm discussed a number of matters, each being open with each other. Knutson listened carefully, his computer-like memory retaining virtually every detail. Jorgsholm congratulated Harry on his 'tracker initiative' but Harry gave credit to his friend, Billy. The follow up activities with Hokey were covered and Harry was surprised with the news from Jorgsholm's side, although of course, the detective didn't tell the Richards' everything. The police never did - a card would always be kept up a policeman's sleeve. After an hour and a half they had almost exhausted the facts and figures as to what had happened over the past few months. Although Harry had not tried to find the Lunar 'van from the co-ordinates that Billy had given him, he gave them to Jorgsholm from a notepad in his pocket.

Jorgsholm was very keen to visit 'Shed One' with a number of armed police and asked the Richards not to divulge any details to anyone, nor to visit the shed again. The Chief Superintendent stressed that this was now a police matter. Harry reluctantly agreed, he had been so involved with all of this so far, and he didn't really want to give it up. He enjoyed the amateur 'tec role he'd adopted. Jorgsholm had mentioned the Frihed group and Wang Xian's role as well as the rat that each member had tattooed on their right should blade. Harry mentioned the rat that had been drawn on his forearm after he was knocked unconscious, almost confirming that Frihed had something to do with 'Shed One'. He looked down at his arm as he told Jorgsholm, but Harry knew he'd scrubbed the image of the rodent off in the shower. It was like those who need to look at a clock when asked what time they did something.

Jorgsholm and Knutson bade farewell to the Richards', Carl again asking them to keep matters confidential. Little was said about Juliette, but Jorgsholm had taken Anthea aside to say that their search for her was ongoing and they had not given up hope, holding her hand as he did so. They were continuing to do all that they could. After the detectives had driven away with Knutson driving, and leaving some dust billowing up into the air, Anthea's mobile phone rang.

"Hello, Anthea Richards."

"Hi, Anthea, it's Merete. How are you? I was wondering how the meeting with Carl had gone?"

Chapter 67

"You never told me about your dream, or was it a nightmare?" Anthea and Harry were sitting in a cafe in Skagen near the beach front, not far from the art museum. They'd ordered two coffees. Harry had remembered that Anthea had woken suddenly the morning before and said she'd had a dream. Composing herself, she took a deep breath.

"Well, I was walking along a footpath on a cliff top. It might have been in England, I'm not sure. The sun was bright and there was a mild breeze. Below me was a long, sweeping sandy beach – totally empty. I'd walked about two miles and the path was getting narrower. There were parts where the path was very close to the cliff edge and I needed to be careful. A large bird like an albatross flew overhead, nearly touching my hair, and I ducked to avoid it. As I bent down I slipped and felt myself falling. I was descending through the air, tumbling over and over. I waited for the thud, the sickening sound of my body hitting the sand and rocks, my neck probably broken. But before that happened Juliette took hold of me in her arms. She'd caught me and she looked just the way I'd last seen her. I looked up into her beautiful face and she spoke to me. 'You're all right now. You're with me. You're safe. You have nothing to worry about.' Then I woke up."

Anthea was sobbing quietly, tears rolling down her cheeks. She took a tissue from her handbag and dabbed her eyes. Reaching for her hand, Harry took it and squeezed gently in a reassuring manner. Other customers in the cafe looked at her for a few seconds, but they got on with chatting and drinking their coffee. Anthea didn't notice the moistness in her husband's eyes, Harry was desperately trying to be strong for her.

"What do you think it meant?" Harry spoke softly as Anthea sipped her coffee.

"She's alive, Harry, she's alive. I just know it!" He kept hold of her hand. "Seeing her as she was almost ten years ago was fantastic. I love her so much, *we* love her so much." They sat for a while saying nothing, eyes now much drier. Looking out to sea, a flotilla of small yachts with white billowing sails were scything across the small waves about two kilometres off shore. The Danes loved sailing, their country was made for it.

"I'm hoping you're right. No, I'm sure you're right." Harry instantly gave Anthea a more positive response. No doubt about it, he wanted to see Juliette again, too. He'd met her a few times at parties when Anthea was still married to Peter, remembering her smile, full heart-shaped lips and whiter-than-white teeth. Juliette possessed beautiful eyes, an aquiline nose, high cheekbones. Any of the major cosmetic companies would have offered her a modelling job for lipstick, make-up, eye-liner or toothpaste. She also walked like a model, one foot in front of the other as though stepping on a long piece of string. Harry asked himself 'what did she look like now?' Would her looks have diminished? He couldn't bear to consider his own questions . . .

"What did Merete want?" Harry asked, wanting to change the subject. Naturally Anthea was feeling down and Harry decided to talk about something else. He did actually *think* sometimes. Sipping her now cold coffee, she continued looking at the white sails bobbing past.

"She just wondered how our discussion with Carl had gone and was sorry she couldn't make it. She had a cold or something. Maybe flu."

"She must be keen. If she's off sick, phoning you to ask about things." Harry had a quizzical look about him.

"She's a good detective and has worked with Carl for a few years. They get on well. I quite like her. She's professional and anxious to get things done. I told her most of what we'd discussed with Carl and Knutson."

Harry was looking out to sea, the boats gradually becoming more distant. A touch of indigestion made him burp a couple of times, and he asked for an antacid tablet. Anthea always carried half a pharmacy in her large handbag. He put it down to the roll-mop herring he'd eaten earlier, although he felt a little uneasy about something.

He just couldn't put his finger on it. There was a slight nagging thought somewhere in the back of his head, as if trying to find the answer to a cryptic crossword clue.

Chapter 68

A blue Volvo 240 pulled a caravan into a compound in a wooded area halfway between Skagen and Frederikshavn A small hanger, that had been used for the storage of agricultural vehicles, had its door slid open by Mao. The 'van was towed inside. Large double doors were closed, creaking slightly as the rusty metal castors rolled through the grooves on either side. Inside the building were seven other touring caravans, parked at a 45 degree angle to the main side walls, three down one side, four along the other. They were all in good condition and clean, with a step outside the door that enabled anyone seeking to enter a caravan to do so easily. The caravans were connected by orange cables to the mains supply at the far end of the hanger to provide electricity as needed. There were two shower cubicles in the far corner of the building, as well as a fully equipped kitchenette. It was as if this place could be lived in . . .

Sven Longe spent some of his time here. The other three occupants of the blue Volvo, got out and stretched their arms and legs. The caravan was unhitched by Longe. Mao Tu Ying helped him move it across to one wall, angled perfectly in line with the other three on that side. The woman who had been in the back seat of the car went along to the kitchenette, filled a kettle, switched it on, and made coffee for the four of them.

Meanwhile, Jorgsholm was planning to visit 'Shed One' on Harry's information. He would take three armed policemen with him, as well as Knutson. He'd wanted to have Glym there, too, but she was still off sick. He'd spoken with her on her mobile and briefed her on the plan. The five of them would go at midnight, telling no one else in the police force. Jorgsholm named it *'Operation Sting'* and he hoped he would catch one or more of the Frihed gang in the building. To find Sven Longe was the best he could pray for, along with the Tu Ying brothers. As Carl Jorgsholm neared retirement this would be a pretty good way to go out on a high note, along with a gold watch and a party at police headquarters in Copenhagen.

Harry and Anthea were due to catch the ferry back to Newcastle the day after tomorrow – how the time had flown since they'd arrived in Esbjerg. However, it seemed things were developing and Harry didn't want to go back too soon. He wanted to be a part of the action. Anthea had spoken with Jackie at 'Angel Face' and everything was under control there so she felt a few more days would be all right. Harry went onto the internet, got into the ferry line and clicked on 'manage my booking'. He was able to change the scheduled departure date for another three days later although there was a £10 administration fee, but so what? The reservation was confirmed. Writing down the new booking reference number they now had another 48 hours in Denmark.

At 11.30 pm., Jorgsholm and four others approached the shed. They had left their vehicles half a kilometre away and walked quietly to their objective, Jorgsholm leading the way with Knutson to his left. The three armed officers walked behind in single file, their high powered rifles held in readiness. When they reached the gate, Knutson used a pair of bolt cutters to cut through the padlock. Quietly holding the chain to prevent it falling to the ground, the gate swung open in the still

259

night air. An owl hooted eerily somewhere away to the north as Jorgsholm tiptoed to the main door and listened. Nothing. The armed policemen had been told to spread themselves out, one going to the rear of the building, the second staying at the gate and one was to be next to Jorgsholm. Knutson stood next to his boss, both armed with a H&K 9mm handgun. The whole area had the atmosphere of an eerie cemetery.

Jorgsholm got hold of the vertical door handle with both hands and slowly slid it across to his right. It moved easily making a gentle sound, almost like the miaow's of a kitten that had seen a bowl of warm milk. Jorgsholm peered inside, the place was gloomy and he crept in. Turning on his small, powerful torch, he found a light switch just inside the door. He braced himself as he pressed down on the metal knob protruding from the wall. The shed lit up brightly as a multitude of neon strips came to life. The two detectives and the armed officer rushed in.

It was empty, the place was completely empty! Jorgsholm wondered if Harry had been dreaming, or taking something like 'wacky-backy'?

Harry knew he hadn't been dreaming, and he hadn't smoked pot for over twenty years.

Chapter 69

Harry took a call on Anthea's mobile phone from Carl Jorgsholm. He sounded pleasant enough, but there was a slight edge to his voice when he told Harry what they had found the night before. In fact, if truth be told, Jorgsholm felt exasperated since he really believed that he was very close to finding Longe and his gang. Harry was very surprised that they'd found nothing in the hanger, he had seen lights of some sort – they weren't flying saucers! He placated Jorgsholm by offering to call Billy Bishop and to ask him to check on the latest positioning of the Lunar caravan tracker, praying that nothing was going to prevent Billy from finding the red dot. Harry could then give the Chief Superintendent a definite fact that he could follow up. Hopefully Billy could obtain the latest co-ordinates and return the phone call. Jorgsholm mumbled something in Danish, thanked him, and hung up.

"Hello, Billy here," said a tired voice on Teesside. Billy'd had another late night playing games on his computer. He was addicted to games like 'Zappo & the Barbarian Invaders' and 'Cataclysmic Cacophonies.'

"Billy, it's Harry. Sorry to bother you so early but can you give me the position of the red dot on your laptop? It's really important, otherwise I wouldn't have phoned you this early. I've got a Danish detective breathing down my neck, not literally, and I need to keep him happy."

"I'll call you back in a few minutes." Billy sat up, yawned as he rubbed his eyes and reached for his laptop on a small table near the bed. Within minutes he had tracked the Lunar caravan, the little red pin-prick of a dot almost burning a hole in his screen. The exact position was shown, and he wrote down the latitude and longitude on a piece of notepaper.

Anthea's mobile rang and Harry picked up. It was Billy, trustworthy as usual, phoning back to give him the details. Thanking him, Harry immediately rang Jorgsholm who was sitting at his office desk. He gave the detective the co-ordinates which Jorgsholm immediately put into the police computer. Within a few seconds a place midway between Skagen and Frederikshavn was shown. That was where Jorgsholm wanted to go, and right now! He spoke with Knutson and the same three armed marksmen were recruited to join them to travel to the 'red dot' area. To minimise drawing attention to themselves all five of the policemen travelled in two unmarked police vehicles, a two litre Ford Mondeo and the turbo-charged VW Passat.

Merete Glym could not shrug off the flu, apparently. She was going to miss all the fun. As the two vehicles were heading from Frederikshavn northwards towards Skagen, Jorgsholm's mobile rang. He picked up immediately, it was Glym's number.

"Carl, please help me, help me for God's sake!" It was Merete Glym, her voice strained and high pitched.

"What's the matter? Where the hell are you?" Jorgsholm was extremely concerned.

"I'm being held by Sven Longe! I was abducted from my place an hour ago by Longe and a Chinese guy who bundled me into a car, blindfolded. They've driven me towards Skagen or nearby, I think. They took my blindfold off as we entered a large building and I'm tied up." Longe was holding the mobile phone to Merete's ear. Before Jorgsholm could reply, the phone was snatched away from the hostage. Sven Longe spoke into the phone.

"Hello, Carl. How are you? Long time no see. Isn't it time you retired? You're getting too old for all this running around, aren't you?" Longe's voice was the essence of calmness and serenity. Jorgsholm knew he was being teased.

"Listen here, Longe, I'm only going to ask you this once. Release my detective unharmed or else!" Knutson had stopped the VW on the roadside and the three armed police pulled up behind them.

"Or else what, Chief Superintendent?" His voice became surly, he remained positive. "You're not calling the shots any more, Carl. Sorry, no pun intended. Ha ha! You've failed miserably to catch me and now you think you can tell me what to do. We have Glym and she means nothing to us, but you wouldn't want to lose her would you? Life is cheap." Carl Jorgsholm's blood pressure quickly rose to a level too high for his health, his brain neurons were sparking at the speed of light. What was the best plan of action right now? Leadership, detective and negotiation skills were being tested to the ultimate. Jorgsholm had to buy time.

"Listen, Longe. Maybe we can reach an agreement? Tell me what you want?" Jorgsholm's pulse rate was way above the normal 72 beats a minute. Knutson looked very concerned as he watched his boss.

"We want you to call off the search for twenty four hours. If you don't, if you attempt to rescue Glym, she's dead. We have plans." Of course they had plans! Leave the country, kill somebody else, tattoo someone who'd been indoctrinated.

"I'll call you back on this phone in five minutes!" Jorgsholm took an intake of fresh air as he put the passenger window down. 'Blast!' he thought to himself. Knutson quickly suggested contacting the mobile phone service provider to see if they could put a 'search' on the phone. Jorgsholm knew the mobile service was *'Orange'*. Carl Jorgsholm asked Knutson to handle it while he thought about a few things. Getting onto a colleague at police HQ, Knutson gave Glym's mobile number and the time of the call, stressing how urgent it was. In under two minutes Knutson's colleague called back with the details. The mobile phone had been used at a location about 20 kilometres from where they were parked. 57 degrees and 10 minutes north, 11 degrees and 34 minutes west. Knutson entered the data into the VW's on-board computer. Knutson's brain was working overtime, he was ahead of the game.

"Sir, it's the same location as the one we're using for the 'red dot!'

"What! Are you sure?" Jorgsholm sounded incredulous. "Double check!" Knutson looked again at the co-ordinates given by Billy to Harry, and at those from *'Orange'*. Bingo! They were identical. "Let's go!" Jorgsholm gave a cry that sounded like an eskimo shouting at his huskies pulling a sled. The VW screeched away from the roadside, followed by the Mondeo police car. Jorgsholm got onto the car radio to speak to the police officers behind and told them of the plan.

He hadn't forgotten to call Longe back – he just thought he'd make him sweat a bit.

Chapter 70

As they slowly approached their destination, Jorgsholm could see a building in the distance. Pointing to it he said,

"That must be it!" He glanced at Knutson, almost whispering although he didn't need to. Jorgsholm had phoned Longe back and told him that he wanted to know where Glym was being held hostage, feigning complete ignorance on the matter. Longe refused to tell him until Jorgsholm agreed to their demand. Only then would they release Merete Glym and tell the Chief Superintendent where she was. Jorgsholm had agreed to the demands, and Longe was to ring Jorgsholm back with the location of where she would be dumped. Little did Longe know that Jorgsholm was only minutes away from finding Glym and releasing her. A blue Volvo 240, registration number AKW 152, was parked almost out of sight beneath a tree.

Jorgsholm and his detective sergeant walked stealthily along the side of the building, hand guns drawn. Their agreed strategy was to rush the kidnappers, leaving the three armed officers in reserve and hidden outside. It was unlikely that Longe and his small gang would offer much resistance, especially as they would be taken by surprise. All they had to do was rush in, guns held in front of them and shout out the well practised 'Don't move. Police!' Longe and his thugs might be armed but they wouldn't have time to react, and the two detectives would release Merete after they'd arrested and handcuffed the members of Frihed.

Jorgsholm was rehearsing this in his head as he slowly slid the door open a few centimetres before the rush. His adrenalin was high, like an actor about to go on stage to a packed theatre on first night. He nodded at Knutson as if to say 'ready?' Knutson looked at Jorgsholm and gave a slight nod, his handgun held near his right shoulder with his index finger on the trigger. He was poised and ready. They both were.

Jorgsholm dragged the door open far enough and they rushed in.

"Don't move. Police!"

"Hello, Carl, I've been expecting you," said a familiar voice.

Chapter 71

Jorgsholm adjusted his eyes to the dimness inside. He knew that voice. Merete Glym was sitting on a chair at the end of the building holding a mug of coffee and dressed casually in a light blue vest and cargo pants, sandals on her feet. Calm and relaxed, toying with her necklace, she smiled at the Chief Superintendent. A knowing smile, enigmatic, lips slightly turned up at the edges.

"Merete, what the hell is going on, I thought you were being held . . . "Jorgsholm couldn't finish his sentence.

"Drop those guns now!" a voice shouted from behind the two detectives. Glancing at each other, Jorgsholm and Knutson had no option. They held the guns for a few seconds more. "Now, I said!" The two handguns clattered to the concrete floor. "Get your hands up and keep them there!" Sven Longe walked up behind Jorgsholm and his detective sergeant and kicked the guns well away.

"What the hell . . .?" Jorgsholm was cut off in mid flow.

"Shut your filthy mouth, you police pig!" Longe shouted at him. The Tu Ying brothers walked across the floor towards the policemen. Jorgsholm looked around. He would not have recognised Longe. He had been searching for a man with the 'Hawaii Five - O' look. There was Sven Longe – blonde hair and spectacles, looking as if he could have been a university lecturer. Jorgsholm immediately realised the disguise, but didn't know what Mao and Hokey looked like. They could have been twins.

In the building were a number of caravans, and some looked as though they were occupied. Jorgsholm's observation powers were working rapidly, taking in a load of minute detail. What was going on in here? However, his brain was absorbing confusing data, very confusing. Taking deep breaths, Jorgsholm tried again seconds later.

"Merete, what the heck are you doing here? We've come to rescue you!" He knew that he was wasting his breath. She wasn't in any danger at all.

Longe, Mao and Hokey Tu Ying walked up to Glym and stood beside her. It looked as though they were posing for a quartet photograph. They all began to laugh, gently at first and then more loudly. Jorgsholm and Knutson still had their hands up. Merete cleared her throat.

"Carl, meet my friends. Hokum, Mao and Sven. You know Carl," Glym stared at her boss and continued, "I've always despised you. You've always taken the glory and the credit while I did all the hard work in the background. You were promoted recently, while I was overlooked. I didn't get a salary increase last year." She paused, looking Jorgsholm in the eyes. "How do you think Wang Xian knew where we were staying? I left the folders in my hotel room for him to take. And there was one Vredestein car tyre supplier in Denmark, but I didn't want to tell you that." Jorgsholm recalled a few other minor issues where he'd questioned Glym's commitment and loyalty. "I'm afraid to tell you, Carl, that you won't be enjoying your retirement. Neither will you Knutson, you goody-goody." She smirked at the detective sergeant. Glym's light blue vest strap had slipped off her right shoulder, and Jorgsholm saw a rat tattoo - the sign of Frihed! "Sven has been looking for more nice girls to bring here to work. Sven, go ahead, you know what you want to do. Goodbye, Carl, it was nice working with you". Longe and the Tu Ying brothers each had a Smith and Wesson handgun, two pointed at the Chief Superintendent, the other at Knutson. Jorgsholm tensed, nipping his bladder and rectal sphincter muscles tightly.

"Merete, wait, don't be a fool! You're mistaken. We've worked together well over the years. You were never overlooked for promotion. Decisions on issues like that are made far above my head. In fact I was going to recommend your promotion to Inspector after we'd solved this case. I've always believed you were a good policewoman." Jorgsholm was buying time. He looked from Glym to Longe and back to the police sergeant. Knutson moved uneasily, hopping from one foot to the other, trying to decide what might happen next.

"Keep still!" barked Longe at Knutson, "you piece of dog dirt." He stood rigid, keeping his head fixed but searching the area with his eyes. The Tu Ying brothers had slowly walked around behind the two police officers, Knutson's pulse rate was high; Jorgsholm seemed calm. However, the Chief Superintendent felt as though his heart was about to burst through his chest wall.

"Merete, if you call all this off and hand yourself in you could get a reduced sentence – I'd see what I could do for you. After all you've given good service to the force." Glym did not reply but nodded to Longe. Very slowly, Sven Longe took off his wig and spectacles. Carl Jorgsholm looked at him and his memory bank went into replay. This was the Longe that he'd remembered. A sadistic killer who should have been put away for a long time years ago. The 'Hawaii Five - O' look was still there, eyes as dark as the menace and evil in his soul.

Longe was now standing behind the senior police officer as silence fell. The atmosphere was palpable, Jorgsholm hearing his heartbeat in his ears, ker-pumph, ker-pumph, ker-pumph. Suddenly he felt the end of a steel gun barrel touching the back of his head, just in that small channel above the top of the neck. The click of a Smith and Wesson trigger . . . Jorgsholm thought his brains were about to decorate the floor, but then he would never see that happening. He prayed, eyes tightly closed, 'dear Heavenly Father . . . '

Chapter 72

A Suzuki was making its way to the western port of Esbjerg carrying its two occupants. As far as Harry and Anthea were concerned there were no significant developments and they were booked on the ferry to Newcastle later that afternoon. Jorgsholm had promised them that he'd be in touch if there was any news. Her fully charged mobile phone had been silent – no calls or messages. Anthea had almost resigned herself to the fact that the Lunar caravan would be found, along with others, thanks to Billy's red dot. But so what? It was just another caravan that had been taken to Denmark by Hokey. Would he make a profit on it? Being bothered about that just wasn't in her head.

Deep inside she had a strange feeling, one of optimism mixed with sadness. In most of the paperback books she'd read there was a happy ending after all the heartache; boy meets girl and falls in love, the lost wedding ring found in a rubbish skip, cowboys riding off into the sunset after catching the baddies. But not this time. Although she wanted to be positive, a part of her was beginning to crumble like the sea cliffs at Crimdon Dene on the north east coast back home.

Harry focused on the driving, his eyes taking in the lovely countryside – low lying hills, copses dotted around, a river here and there, and a blue sky dotted with white cumulus clouds. He said nothing for a while, glancing at his wife from time to time and occasionally placing his left hand on her right knee and giving it three gentle taps – his way of saying 'I'm here and I love you.'

They passed a sign for Esbjerg that showed 35 km to the ferry terminal. Asking Anthea if she wanted to stop for coffee, she nodded and gave him a faint smile. Harry noticed her eyes were misted – she was either tired or upset, or both.

An hour later they joined the queue for the ferry, cars and vans to the left, lorries to the right. The blue sky had changed as dark grey clouds approached from the north.

Bad weather was coming, but it was already raining in Anthea's heart.

Chapter 73

"Look, wait," shouted Knutson, "this is crazy! We've got armed police outside, there's no way you can escape from here. Give yourselves up now!"

"Shut up, pig, you're both going to die. You came here on your own so don't give me that clap-trap about support from more pigs!" Longe continued to hold the pistol pointing above the first cervical vertebra of the Chief Superintendent. "But wait," his tone changed, "wouldn't it be a waste if we shot you now when we might be able to get a ransom for two porkers?" Seconds of quiet followed, not a sound. "What are you two worth, I wonder? Merete, any ideas?"

"What do you pay for a tin of dog food these days?" Glym joked as the others laughed.

"What about ten million euros? Is that a fair price, Hokey? That would buy some caravans for you!" Longe cackled as he laughed at his own comment.

"Too complicated," Glym had now stood up and was walking towards Carl Jorgsholm, "far too complex," she reiterated. "Better to kill them here and dump the bodies in the sea. Hokey could use his boat. Wrap them up in sailcloth with a couple of large stones for company. Over the side, a good splash and down they'd go – lobster food!" They all chortled again, Longe relishing the thought of the two policemen going to a watery grave.

"Enough of this, let's get it over with," Mao chipped in. He wasn't used to this kind of scenario and wanted out. He seemed irritable, tiring of the idle banter. "I've got a gun, I'll do it," he said.

"Sorry, bro, but you're not cut out for this type of thing. You're just faking the bravery so keep quiet," Hokey stated firmly, glaring at his younger brother.

"Don't talk to me like that!" Mao was agitated. He been taken down a peg or two with a cheap comment in front of the others. That wasn't on, not for him. He held the handgun but waived it about, smiling as he did so. "You've always bullied me but now it's going to stop."

Glym looked at Sven Longe, her eyes showing a quizzical look. She realised that there was some kind of rift between Hokey and Mao, and now wasn't the time for it to be raising its ugly head! But it was too late, Mao now had his gun pointed at Hokey. Jorgsholm had no idea what to do as he glared at Hokey. The focus had changed from him and Knutson to this internal wrangle between the two Chinese brothers. A shot rang out and Hokum Tu Ying flew back smacking into the wall with a thud, his head making a sound like a walnut in a pair of nutcrackers as blood darkened the centre of his white shirt. He slumped to the floor, seemingly in slow motion as his legs buckled under him, leaving a trail of blood down the whitewashed wall. His eyes were open, staring blindly at the neon light strips hanging high above him.

"Oh, my God!" screamed Glym, holding her hands to her mouth. Jorgsholm lowered his hands but Longe shouted at him to keep his hands high, where he could see them. He obeyed. Longe moved away from Carl Jorgsholm and stood next to Glym, Mao a couple of metres away. Behind the two police officers the wide door was slightly open, a ten centimetre gap allowing some air into the building. The armed police marksmen outside had stealthily made their way towards the entrance, moving silently. Through a narrow slit in the other side of the door they observed the scene. Glym

274

with Longe and Mao standing in front of and to the left of Jorgsholm and Knutson.

"What the hell do we do now?" Glym had calmed down but was breathing quicker than normal. Blood, the colour of 'past its sell by date' tomato ketchup, continued to seep out from Hokey's lifeless body, a long trickle following the very gradual incline of the concrete floor.

"We came here to do a job so let's do it!" Longe sounded adamant. Glym turned to look at him and noticed Longe smiling – a wicked smile, the grin of the devil.

"Here we go then," Sven Longe, the cruel ruthless killer and kidnapper, raised his handgun, straightened his arm, and pointed it straight at DCS Jorgsholm.

'This is the end', Carl thought to himself, 'where is God when you most need Him?'

Chapter 74

Carl Jorgsholm had very carefully parted his first and second finger on both hands, it was hardly noticeable. A pre-rehearsed signal to shoot to kill, within less than a second two G36 high powered assault rifles were fired, sounding as one. The two men flew back like puppets in a Punch and Judy show, necks jerking as though they had been snapped, a neat round hole in the middle of the forehead of each of them. The two bullets had passed straight through their skulls. It was over very quickly. The blood oozed across their foreheads and out of the back of their heads, down through their hair, and began spreading across the floor to meet up with Hokey's rivulet. Three pools merged into one as Glym stood there, transfixed. Carl picked up his handgun from the floor and then walked across to her, Knutson firmly clamping handcuffs on her wrists as the Chief Superintendent looked into her eyes. There was hatred as well as sadness in Glym's eyes. Jorgsholm looked into her dark pupils from a few centimetres away.

"What on earth have you done, Merete? What on earth have you done?"

"You bastard!" she cried as she spit in his face. Jorgsholm wiped the saliva away as one of the armed officers took hold of Glym, marching her outside. It was quiet again, but Jorgsholm thought he could hear a sound, like whimpering, coming from one of the caravans. He nodded to Knutson to take a look. The sergeant opened the door of the 'van and saw two blonde girls cowering as noises started to come from several other caravans. Knutson went into one of the caravans, the stale smell of cigarette smoke and beer hitting him as two girls crouched against the headboards of the two single beds on either side of the lounge. They looked afraid, wearing only a T-shirt and pair of pants; wide eyed as though drugged. He spoke to them in Danish, and then in English. One of the girls pointed to the other 'vans. Knutson gave them a reassuring smile and used his left hand, palm downward, as though to say 'wait here'.

He came out and had a word with Jorgsholm who'd been on his mobile phone talking to the most senior police officer in the local police district. Knutson walked over to a Bailey caravan and opened the door, two more girls were inside that one, too. All of the caravans contained either one or two young girls, most with thin yet strong padlocked chains around their ankles. Each girl had their initials tattooed on the inside of their left wrist. The first girl that he spoke to was called Amanda Parker, AP clearly tattooed on her white skin. Knutson looked closely at the pair of girls, both blonde, and saw that they also had chains on their ankles.

"What are you doing here?" He sat next to Amanda and she pulled away from him, until he reassured her that it was all right and that he was a policeman. She hesitated for a while before speaking in hushed tones.

"There are several of us, we're all kept here to please the businessmen who can afford to visit this place. Every night. We are all so tired, and there is no way of escape. I hate men." She seemed a little more relieved. Looking around some of the other caravans, Knutson became aware of the poor conditions in which these girls had been kept. They had their own clothes in each 'van, including those that were 'special' to wear when they had 'visitors', and were able to use the bathroom facilities. However, it was cramped, especially in those that had double occupancy. One of Hokum's assistants, Benny, was responsible for keeping any eye on things – cleaning the vans and keeping them smelling nice. The girls were allowed some exercise each day when the main doors were locked, but then only two at a time. They were literally prisoners and Knutson felt that some of them seemed to have almost lost the will to live. Benny, who had turned out to be gay, had disappeared - probably out of a back door when the police had entered.

Moving over to a girl cowering in another caravan, but reassuring her of his intentions, Knutson looked at her wrist; the letters P J were tattooed. He started to search for Juliette believing she was somewhere here, but couldn't find her. Carl Jorgsholm had already briefed his detective sergeant about the missing girl from northern England before they'd met Anthea, about her appearance and especially her long blond hair. Knutson wasn't giving up yet. He'd entered seven of the caravans before going into the last one. Inside there was a girl, aged about 24, with the initials J W on her skin. Telling her to stay where she was, he went to find his boss.

The Chief Superintendent went into the caravan and stared into the dull, opaque eyes of Juliette Watkinson for the first time in almost ten years.

She looked different but he recognised her, a face aged beyond her years, with hair untidy and cut short, but still blonde. Her teeth were as white and perfect as he'd remembered. She was alive . . . thank God! Holding her hand carefully as tears slowly welled up in his eyes, Juliette began to sob. She hadn't cried with such emotion for a long time - a very long time. She recognised him!

"Juliette, it's me, Carl Jorgsholm," he said very gently and softly. "You're safe now. Quite safe." He paused for a minute as he gave her a gentle hug. "Wait here. I'll be back very soon, I promise." He went outside into the sunlight and made a call. A mobile phone rang in Esbjerg, in a queue of cars at the ferry terminal.

"Hello, Anthea, it's Carl here. I'm not sure where you are right now, but I've got someone with me that you may be interested to see." He composed himself. "We've found Juliette and she's fine, but you will have to prepare yourself."

The bodies of Hokey, Mao and Sven Longe were loaded into body-bags and carried to a police van ready for the morgue. Glym was half hauled and half pushed into another police van with bars on the windows. Further support had arrived, including four female police officers who had special training in counselling. They were to be responsible for ensuring that all of the girls in the caravans were taken to a care centre where they were to be looked after, re-clothed and reunited with parents or guardians.

Outside, and breathing in the clean, sweet air, Carl Jorgsholm looked at Knutson. With a sense of complete relief, and speaking quietly, he said,

"Come on, Knutson, there are two people we've got to go and talk to."

They walked slowly back to their car, Knutson opening the door for his boss. Suddenly, the sun shone through a break in the clouds as Carl Jorgsholm put on his sunglasses and slipped into the passenger seat, leaning back on the headrest. The detective sergeant switched on the car engine, allowing it to idle for a few seconds.

"You know what Knutson?"

"What, sir?"

"It's not often that you get a great big high and a really deep low in the same day. But today is one of those days!" Slapping the top of the dashboard he shouted, "Let's go!"

Carl closed his eyes. Leaning back on the seat he told himself that life didn't seem too bad after all, although his body ached all over. He discovered muscles that he'd forgotten he had.

'Why did I become a policeman? he asked himself, 'I could have been a baker like my father!'

The day was getting brighter as Knutson drove away

. . . and Carl wondered if pork meatballs and dumplings would be on the table later?

Epilogue

Human and sex trafficking has been going on for thousands of years throughout the world. Juliette was in the wrong place at the wrong time. A gang involved in kidnapping young girls from a number of European countries for the ruthless pleasure of frustrated, maladjusted men had been caught. The gang had no morals, no scruples. Life did not mean much – the 'afterlife' promised more. The Tu Ying brothers, despite a long running family feud, had organised the transport of caravans to Denmark for a number of years. The one belonging to Harry and Anthea was just another one for them to use for their 'trade'. Sven Longe was committed to the objectives of the CLB and had 'dove-tailed' with the Tu Ying brothers on a trip to north east England years ago. They had kept up to twenty girls in a number of caravans, drugged most of the time.

Juliette was reunited with her parents the day after she was found. She was taken to a local hospital, checked over medically, and had a debriefing session with the Danish police. Trained counsellors spent two hours with Juliette prior to Anthea and Harry seeing her. She'd showered, her hair had been trimmed and washed, and she'd been given clean clothes and had some make up applied. She was their daughter and she hadn't changed. No, she hadn't changed. Her blonde hair would grow again.

She went back to Teesside and took a college course in Beauty Therapy. Juliette received long term psychiatric care and gradually got over her ordeal – at least as much as any human being could. She helped her mother develop and expand her business in Marton and eventually took over before becoming *President of the Teesside Ladies Business Women's Guild.* Juliette remained lifelong friends with Agnatha and Louisa and they exchanged visits frequently. The Jorgsholm girls attended her wedding to a fine, honest young man. They went on to have a family – one girl and one boy. They called them Carl and Anna.

Merete Glym was charged with various crimes against the national police, found guilty, and given a long prison sentence. She had known Wang Xian since she was at college in Copenhagen and had joined Frihed. That part of her background had never shown up in her pre-employment and criminal record checks. Jorgsholm had begun to wonder about her performance but had kept it to himself. He regretted it.

Carl Jorgsholm eventually retired and he and his wife, Anna, enjoyed spending time walking, writing, and water colour painting - especially landscapes. Anna did a lot of voluntary work, and became involved with a charity raising funds for deprived young children. Carl was awarded the *Conspicuous Service Medal* for dedication to the Danish police force.

Detective Sergeant Knutson went on to become a Chief Inspector of police in Kokkedal district and always acknowledged that Detective Chief Superintendent Jorgsholm had been his mentor in his police career.

Adam Tennant was released after serving half of his sentence, reduced for good behaviour. He went to live in Guernsey, changed his name, and led a comfortable life with the money he'd massaged into an offshore bank account, courtesy of Joan Bobbins.

Don Wilson, bull-strong, a sandwich short of a picnic, and star sign Scorpio, was convicted of the murder of Michael Barrett. He'd been in the pub on the night Harry blabbed. Wilson, a previous offender with a low IQ, had arrived at the waste ground half an hour before Harry delivered the caravan. His two years in the army had done him little good, leaving with a poor discharge report, some stolen sheets of paper and a bayonet that he 'conveniently' forgot to hand in.

And, by the way, there's still a red boat for sale moored in the water at Skagen and owing port fees. It's going for a song, and it needs a little 'tender loving care.'

But then, we all do sometimes, don't we?

The End

***

Also by A. K. Adams:

An Unknown Paradise

A. K. Adams spends his time between his home in North Yorkshire and the Costa Blanca in Spain.